A FURNACE SEALED

Also by Keith R.A. DeCandido
from eSpec Books

The Adventures of Bram Gold
FEAT OF CLAY (forthcoming)

The Precinct Series
DRAGON PRECINCT
UNICORN PRECINCT
GOBLIN PRECINCT
GRYPHON PRECINCT
TALES FROM DRAGON PRECINCT
MERMAID PRECINCT
PHOENIX PRECINCT
MANTICORE PRECINCT (forthcoming)
MORE TALES FROM DRAGON PRECINCT (forthcoming)

Other Titles
WITHOUT A LICENSE
TO HELL AND REGROUP (with David Sherman)
SYSTEMA PARADOXA: ALL-THE-WAY HOUSE

Anthologies
THE SIDE OF GOOD/THE SIDE OF EVIL
THE BEST OF DEFENDING THE FUTURE
THE BEST OF BAD-ASS FAERIES
FOOTPRINTS IN THE STARS
BEST LAID PLANS
DEVILISH AND DIVINE
A CRY OF HOUNDS

A FURNACE SEALED

Keith R.A. DeCandido

Pennsville, NJ

PUBLISHED BY
eSpec Books LLC
Danielle McPhail, Publisher
PO Box 242,
Pennsville, New Jersey 08070
www.especbooks.com

Copyright © 2024 Keith R.A. DeCandido

ISBN: 978-1-956463-41-5
ISBN (ebook): 978-1-956463-40-8

A previous version was published by WordFire Press in 2019.

All rights reserved. No part of the contents of this book may be reproduced or transmitted in any form or by any means without the written permission of the publisher.

All persons, places, and events in this book are fictitious and any resemblance to actual persons, places, or events is purely coincidental.

Interior Design: Danielle McPhail, McP Digital Graphics
Cover Art and Design: Mike McPhail, McP Digital Graphics

Stock art courtesy of www.shutterstock.com:
THE UNICORN IN CAPTIVITY, 1495_1505, Netherlandish, Northern Renaissance tapestry. © Everett Collection

Dedicated to the memory of Dale Mazur, 1964–2018, taken from us far too soon. He only became a Bronx resident in the last few years, but he loved it here, and the borough is a dimmer place for his loss.

Rest in peace my dear brother-in-law, my dear housemate, my dear friend.

> *The human dress is forged iron,*
> *The human form a fiery forge,*
> *The human face a furnace sealed,*
> *The human heart its hungry gorge.*

—William Blake, "A Divine Image"

> *Why will you die, O Eternals?*
> *Why live in unquenchable burnings?*

—William Blake, *The First Book of Urizen*

Acknowledgments

PRIMARY THANKS FOR THIS SERIES HAVE TO GO TO THE U.S. CENSUS Bureau, believe it or not. I first conceived this series while doing Census work in the Bronx in 2009 and 2010. I got to explore my home borough in ways I never had before, and it was eye-opening and glorious. So many books that take place in New York City (and so many perceptions of the Big Apple) only really look at Manhattan south of 125th Street. The outer boroughs (with the occasional exception of Brooklyn) and upper Manhattan are often given short shrift. This series is intended to address that lack, and I owe it all to spending so much time travelling all over the peninsula for the Census.

Secondary thanks go to the Bronx Historical Society in general and Lloyd Ultan in particular. Ultan's various Bronx history books (some cowritten with Gary Hermalyn) published by the society have been invaluable reference tools. Thanks also to John McNamara's *A History in Asphalt: The Origin of Bronx Street and Place Names*, which was a very useful tome. It is here that I should mention that Warham Mather, Ben Palmer, John Ferris, and Anne van Cortlandt are also real historical figures from the colonial period, whose histories I have adapted for fictional purposes, but much of how their lives are described (at least in the eighteenth century) are similar to what history has recorded. (Also, all of the locations in this book are real places, with the notable exception of Seward Place and Wardein Zerelli's house, which are completely fictional.)

Tertiary thanks go to my agent, Lucienne Diver, who is a goddess among agents; my in-house editors, GraceAnne Andreassi DeCandido and Wrenn Simms, who call me on my nonsense; and also Kevin J. Anderson, D.J. Butler, Michelle Corsillo, Aysha Rehm, Marie Whittaker,

Danielle Ackley-McPhail, Mike McPhail, and Greg Schauer, for general fabulousness.

In addition, gratitude to Meredith Peruzzi, Tina Randleman (who pointed out a major flaw in the earliest drafts of this book), the late great Dale Mazur, Matthew Holcombe, the Forebearance, the Godmommy, all the folks at my (Bronx-based!) karate dojo, and every single resident of the Boogie Down.

Chapter 1

I WOULD LIKE TO STATE FOR THE RECORD THAT STARTING SHABBOS WITH A crazed unicorn charging at you horn-first kinda sucks.

I stood stock still while it came at me, waiting until I could see the bloodshot whites of its eyes. Then at the last second, I bent my knees, ducked, and rolled away on my left shoulder—which I then wrenched on the sidewalk as I rolled.

The hardest part of my job was not screaming like a five-year-old when I felt pain. You'd think it would be easier, given that pain was inflicted on me pretty much daily, but still it took an effort.

I rolled to my feet, my right hand holding my left shoulder to make sure it didn't move around too much, since every time it did so, white-hot knives of agony shot up and down my left arm. My white-maned attacker skidded to a halt, its hooves scraping against the uneven concrete.

"Ohmigod, don't *hurt* him, Mr. Gold!"

"You out of your fuckin' *mind*, Leesa, that thing tried to *kill* me!"

Sparing a glance to the open black metal gate in front of the house on 180th Street, I saw Leesa and Siri, the young couple who rented the ground floor. They were both black women, but the similarities ended there. Leesa was short and stocky, wore thick, plastic-framed glasses, and had long hair painstakingly kept straight and tied into a ponytail held by a sparkly pink hair clip; she had a high squeaky voice and wore a flower-print sundress. Siri was tall, thin, had close-cropped hair, and didn't wear glasses; she stuck with a plain T-shirt and jeans.

Leesa had taken in the unicorn—from what I'd heard, far from her first stray—which had gone crazy when Siri came home, and even more deranged once I showed up.

I'd been hired to track down this particular beast and return it to where it belonged. Leesa needn't have worried, because the client wanted the psychotic little equine intact. I just had to get the damn talisman onto its two-foot-long, sharp golden horn, sparkling with the reflected light of the early evening sun on 180th, and currently pointed right at my spleen.

Yeah. Why did I take this job, again?

The unicorn snorted, nostrils flaring, and charged me again. This time I twisted out of the way to the right instead of rolling to the left and got shouldered in the rib cage.

Instinctively, I clutched my ribs with the arm that had the bad shoulder, then winced in pain. At least they weren't busted—they felt bruised, but that was it.

The unicorn stopped, turned around, and now was snarling.

I think I pissed the thing off.

Okay, third time's the charm, a cliché that has never, in my life, had any kind of practical application, but it made me feel better to think it.

I reached into my denim jacket's inner pocket and pulled out my New York Yankees lighter and the talisman. The latter was a canvas pouch filled with herbs; a long leather string looped through it.

I flicked the lighter on with my thumb. By some miracle, the thing actually lit the first time, which I chalked up to karma taking pity on me for once. I held the flickering flame under the talisman.

Two seconds later, the talisman made a popping sound and I let go of the lighter, the fire dying instantly.

I'd forgotten to hold my breath.

Okay, picture an enclosed wooden space with no air circulation where the sun's been beating down for most of a day. That space is filled floor to ceiling with animals that have been dead for almost a week. The flesh is baked and putrid and rotting, the maggots are having a field day, and it's the worst thing you've ever smelled in your life.

That was where I would've gone at that moment to get the smell of the talisman out of my nose. As I tried to breathe through my mouth and blink the tears out of my eyes, I made a mental note to have a little chat with Ahondjon, the guy who sold me the talisman, and who seriously undersold just how much the thing would reek when activated.

"What the *hell* is that?" That was Siri, and I could practically *hear* her nose wrinkling as she spoke. It was a legitimate question, mind you, but one I wasn't really in a position to answer just at the moment.

The unicorn charged again.

I dodged to the left this time — offering the beast a different set of sacrificial ribs — and tried to loop the string onto the horn.

Emphasis on "tried." It missed my ribs, thank G-d, but I missed, too. The tip of the horn hit the string and sent the talisman flying across the street, right toward a gutter.

Crap.

Trying to pretend that my shoulder and ribs didn't hurt, and failing spectacularly, I ran and dove for the talisman before it fell through the grate into the sewers, never to be seen again except by nonexistent alligators.

Using my good arm to brace the dive to the asphalt, I used my bad arm to nab the talisman's string before the pouch fell through. Once again, I failed to scream.

It's the little victories that get you through the day.

Struggling slowly to my feet, I heard someone else scream.

Apparently, being across the street from it got me off the unicorn's radar, and it was back to what it was doing before I showed up: trying to kill Siri.

Leesa was standing between Siri and the unicorn, her right hand out. "Take it easy, Snowball! It's just Siri! She's okay!"

Of *course*, she named the unicorn, and of *course*, she gave it a sweet nickname.

The unicorn snarled and tapped its front right hoof on the sidewalk a few times. Leesa looked devastated, like finding out that your golden retriever was a rabid hellhound on crack — a pretty good analogy, all things considered — and Siri had the wide-eyed, kidney-constricting look of terror that most people get when wild animals are about to gut them.

But the unicorn's ass was facing me, and it was focused, so I thought *maybe* I might have another shot at this.

You ever try to run fast with bruised ribs? As much as you think it hurts, that's nothing compared to how much it *actually* hurts.

I did it, though, and got inside the unicorn's smell range before it had a chance to react to my scent. This time I looped the string right around the horn.

Just like that, it stopped snarling, stopped being agitated, and just stood there, docilely. Ahondjon's talisman may've stunk like week-old gefilte fish, but it worked.

Leesa broke into a huge grin. "*That's* my Snowball!"

Siri just stared at her girlfriend like she was insane. "*That* stinks like a moose fuckin' a dead octopus."

I blinked, making a mental note to use *that* simile instead of the gefilte fish one when I had my chat with Ahondjon.

After shooting her girlfriend an annoyed look, Leesa looked at me. "I can take him back now that he's calmed down, right, Mr. Gold?"

"Not hardly," I said. "I need to return it to its rightful owner. They're the ones who hired me."

"Oh." Leesa deflated, her shoulders slumping.

"Besides, it'll only stay calm as long as the stinky thing on its horn lasts—which won't be more than an hour or two. I gotta get him back."

"I don't get it." Leesa was almost whining now. "Snowball was just fine with me for a week!"

"Yeah," Siri added, "then when I got back home from school today, he was all up in my face. What's that about?"

I let out a long breath. "Unicorns are obsessed with women who are…" I trailed off, trying to figure out the best way to put it.

Siri laughed. "What, that shit about virgins? Ain't neither of *us* virgins, mister."

"Not exactly, though virgins qualify. See, unicorns tend to gravitate toward women who don't have the smell of men on them. Man-funk drives 'em nuts, whether it's on a man or on a woman who slept with a man any time in the last week or two. So virgins are usually okay—but so're lesbians. And nuns. Worst unicorn infestation ever was in a convent in France back around 1500. In fact—"

"What the *hell*, Siri?"

Leesa had cut off my colloquy on unicorns to give her girlfriend a look so nasty it made me nostalgic for a charging unicorn. She'd gone from whiny to furious in about half a second, made more interesting by Siri's look of pure guilt.

That's when I put it together.

"Look," Siri said, "I was drunk, a'ight? There was a party in the dorm, and—it's *college*, Leesa, I was experimentin', and shit!"

Domestic disputes were *not* part of my job description, and besides, I needed to get a move on. "Hope you two can work this out," I said with very little conviction as I put my hand on the unicorn's neck and guided it toward the twenty-six-foot truck I had parked across the street. It was blocking a driveway and a fire hydrant, but I'd left the back open with the ramp down. That's universal sign language for "I'm in the middle of moving," so chances were good that the cops wouldn't give it a ticket. Of course, even if they did, I'd just put it on my bill.

I led the unicorn up the ramp. Some of Leesa and Siri's neighbors were standing in their doorways or by their front gates looking annoyed or confused or curious, but I just ignored them. They'd have something fun to talk about over Friday dinner, that was for sure.

Once the unicorn was fully in the truck's cargo box, I slid the ramp back under the truck, then pulled the door shut, both actions making metallic rattles that echoed through the street. As long as the talisman lasted, the unicorn wouldn't move unless I physically guided it.

If the talisman had fallen down the gutter, the plan was to lure the thing into the truck and shut the door real fast, then hope that the beast didn't totally destroy the vehicle from the inside before I could deliver it. Of course, that was why I got the insurance rider. As for the deductible, well, *that'd* go on my bill, too...

Because I'm not a complete idiot, I always kept some ibuprofen in my denim jacket's pocket, and I'd filled a metal thermos with some nice cold tap water before I left. That was in the truck's cup holder. All things being equal, I'd have waited until the three pills I washed down with the water kicked in before driving, but the talisman had a clock.

Before starting the truck up, I called the client on my cell and said I was on my way. It took forever to navigate a gigunda truck through the one-way streets of the University Heights neighborhood of the Bronx before I finally turned left on Fordham Road. There, it was a straight—if slow, since I was driving west and the sun was setting right in my face—shot across the 207th Street Bridge. Then I went through Inwood, the northernmost part of Manhattan, navigating around more than one double-parked car to Fort Tryon Park and my destination: the Cloisters.

Tourists often thought the Cloisters, a branch of the Metropolitan Museum of Art, was an old abbey that was brought over from Europe, but no. Instead, it was a hodgepodge of different structures from medieval Europe—chapels, gardens, tombs, reliquaries—all kitbashed into one stone building. The place used to freak me out as a kid when my parents took me here—this nice Jewish boy found the overwhelming Christianity to be a little daunting—but they've got some gorgeous stuff.

Besides, I've gotten more tolerant of other beliefs in my adulthood...

A volunteer was waiting for my truck at the front entrance, and she told me to go up the inclined cobblestone driveway. I'd been up this driveway once before, but that was in a sedan—it was a lot more nerve-wracking to go up the tightly curved hill in a truck. But I got to the top, where the handicapped entrance was. The guy who hired me was waiting semi-patiently for me there: Joseph Rodzinski, one of the muckety-mucks for the Met.

A short, pudgy specimen, Rodzinski was wearing a gray blazer, a blue polo shirt, and khakis. Perspiration drenched his forehead under his receding hairline, even though it was a nice 50-degree Friday evening. Then again, if I was responsible for letting a lunatic mythical beast loose on the city, I might be shvitzing, too.

Wiping sweat off his high forehead with the back of his wrist, Rodzinski looked at the truck as I jumped down from the driver's seat of the cab.

"A twenty-six-footer? Why'd you get something so big? I only intend to pay for a thirteen-footer."

I stared at him. "Seriously? I risk life and limb, bruise my ribs and wrench my shoulder to get your unicorn, and you're gonna nickel-and-dime me over the *truck*?"

Waving his arm, he said, "Whatever. It's in the back?"

"No, I thought I'd let it ride shotgun." Rolling my eyes, I went to open the rear door.

It slid upward, revealing the unicorn in virtually the exact same position I left it in. Yanking the ramp down, I started to guide it out.

Rodzinski's face scrunched up. "Jesus, what is that *smell*?"

"The only thing stopping the unicorn from shoving its horn up your ass." I'd meant that as a joke, but it came out kinda nasty, so I smiled broadly and added: "And don't call me Jesus." I figure the harshness of my tone was due to either my pain or his attitude. Or both. Probably both.

"Whatever, let's just bring it inside and get this over with."

We ambled on the cobblestone walkway to the handicapped entrance, and through the big wooden door into the main part of the Cloisters itself.

It was already past closing, so there wasn't anyone around, and I was struck by how peaceful the place was. 'Course, even when it was crowded it was like that, but I'd never been here when it was this empty. With all the stonework and the high ceilings, and the near-total lack of people, it was one of those loud quiets.

Or, at least, it would've been, except for a unicorn clopping on the floor, the sound echoing off the stone walls.

We passed through a bunch of different rooms that were filled with Christian iconography, finally reaching a room with a huge golden altar with three painted saints' heads on it. Medieval Christians really knew how to party...

Across from that really gaudy altar was a doorway that was currently blocked by a large piece of wood with a sign on it saying, "Closed for Renovation." That barricade and sign, which had both been up for eight days, were both a lie and the wellspring of Rodzinski's copious amounts of sweat.

That was the doorway that led to the unicorn tapestries. It was a big room, with more than half a dozen different tapestries with a unicorn theme. No one was entirely sure who made them, but most seemed to be part of a sequence that was about a bunch of guys hunting a unicorn down.

One that definitely wasn't part of the sequence was probably the most popular piece in the Cloisters: *The Unicorn in Captivity*. A beautiful work, probably the most commonly reproduced tapestry in the world—in the gift shop at the Cloisters alone you could get it as a print, a photo, a postcard, a book cover, a brooch, a throw pillow, or a blanket. It was the centerpiece of the Cloisters.

It was also not just an ordinary tapestry. Remember that unicorn infestation in a French convent I mentioned? There were three of them—two were killed, to the chagrin of the nuns, so rather than see a third beast slaughtered, the nuns magicked the last unicorn into a tapestry. Mind you, they had to do *something*—if they hadn't, it would've killed half the priests and monks in France.

The unicorn was trapped with a helluva binding spell. And all those souvenirs I mentioned? They reinforced the spell.

Which begged the question as to how it got out, but again, that wasn't my problem.

Rodzinski slid the barricade aside, and I guided the unicorn through the doorway.

The room looked almost like usual: big fireplace (which matched the patchwork nature of the Cloisters, since the different parts that made up the fireplace were from five different countries) and tapestries covering each wall from floor to ceiling.

On one of those walls—the first place your eye fell when you walked into the room on the immediate right, which was why they put it there—was what right now looked like a big green tapestry showing an empty gazebo.

Normally, there was a unicorn chained to the gazebo.

"All right, Gold," Rodzinski said as I walked the unicorn toward the work of art that had been its home for five hundred years, "put the unicorn back in the tapestry."

I stopped dead in my tracks. "*Excuse* me?"

Rodzinski pointed at the unicorn with a chubby finger. "Put it back in the tapestry! What do you think I'm *paying* you for?"

"To track down a dangerous animal that *you* let loose and bring it back."

"Right, you handle all this supernatural"—he waved an arm back and forth— "y'know, *stuff*."

I couldn't believe I was hearing this. "Did you even *read* my contract before you signed it? I don't cast spells. I deal with supernatural phenomena, yeah, but I haven't the first clue how to restore a binding spell. You need a specialist for that."

"How'd you get the unicorn to be docile?"

"With a talisman I bought from a dealer."

Rodzinski's nostrils were flaring in a manner depressingly similar to that of the unicorn when it had been about to play bull to my bullfighter on 180th Street. "You mean I could've just bought that smelly necklace and done this myself?"

Somehow I managed not to laugh in Rodzinski's face. "Assuming you could've found the unicorn and gotten close enough to the unicorn to put the talisman on without being shish-kebabbed—no, you still couldn't have. Because my dealer wouldn't sell to someone unlicensed."

Making a noise like a steam pipe bursting, Rodzinski turned away from me. "This is ridiculous. I need this unicorn back in the tapestry where it belongs. It's our biggest attraction! Without it…"

He trailed off. I didn't finish his sentence the way I wanted to: "… lots of people will die." That didn't seem to be his concern so much as the bottom line of his museum. In his defense, that was his job, and besides, they probably didn't teach "Binding Spells and How They Can

Screw Up Your Day When They Go Bad" in administrator school, so I didn't blame him for the compassion-ectomy.

Sighing, I said, "Let me see if I can find one of those specialists I mentioned." I looked at my bare wrist for a full second before I remembered that my watch was eaten by a dragon last week. Then I took out my cell phone, which I needed anyhow. Based on the time on the phone's display, it had been forty minutes since I dropped the talisman on the horn. At worst, we had twenty minutes. Ahondjon was kinda vague on the exact time frame of the thing's effectiveness, something I intended to take up with him right after we discussed the odor.

"Whatever." Rodzinski took out his own phone and started stabbing angrily at it. "But this is coming out of your fee."

"Like hell," I said as I called up my phone's address book. "Read the contract again."

"You really think a contract for something like *this* is binding in a court of law?" Rodzinski asked in a dismissive tone that made me wonder if he had ever intended to pay me at all.

"Doesn't need to be." I didn't even look up at him. "The Wardein of Manhattan's already gonna be paying you a visit after this, and if you violate a single dot on a single 'i' of my contract, he'll pay you another visit. Trust me, you don't wanna piss him off twice."

Rodzinski frowned. "Who the hell is the war-deen of Manhattan?"

"From the moment this unicorn got loose? Your worst nightmare."

Wardeins were in charge of all magickal activity within their demesne. The island of Manhattan was a single demesne, and for all of my life to date, its wardein had been an old bastard named Damien van Owen, and he would probably whittle Rodzinski down to size in six-and-a-half seconds. If I could've, I'd've sold tickets.

But right now, I had bigger problems. I didn't deal with van Owen that often because I usually stuck to the Bronx, which had a different wardein. Most of the spellcasters I knew were in the Boogie Down, also, which luckily wasn't all that far from Fort Tryon Park.

I started scrolling through the cell's alphabetically sorted address book. Atkins was out of town. Fofanah still wasn't talking to me after that incident with the bajloz on Pelham Parkway. Hwang and Kanchibhotla were both on vacation—together, if the rumors were true, but I was pretty sure that Hwang only had eyes for McGillicuddy. Saravia lived too far away and didn't have a car. Solano had her son this weekend, so she wouldn't be doing anything. Teitelbaum was Orthodox, so he probably wouldn't even answer the phone on a Friday night this close to sunset.

Which led me to my only option: Velez.

I sighed. I really didn't want to deal with Velez.

On the other hand, Rodzinski probably didn't want to deal with him, either, and watching him be forced to would be highly entertaining.

So I called him, praying to a deity I didn't believe in nearly as often as I should that it didn't go to voicemail.

As it rang, Rodzinski looked up from his phone and pointed a chubby finger at me. "This friend of yours better put the unicorn back, because if he doesn't, I will *sue* you for breach of contract, you understand me?"

I grinned. "You really think a contract for something like *this* is binding in a court of law?"

Chapter 2

MY NAME IS BRAM GOLD, AND I'M A COURSER.

Coursers are folks from all across the globe who get hired to hunt the peculiar, police the strange, and so on—whether we're talking ordinary folks who used the supernatural to do bad things, or actual paranormal creatures who didn't play by the rules. There were a lot fewer of the second kind than people think. Most of them just minded their own business and lived their lives like anybody else. Best Hanukkah present I ever got was from a domovoy, just as a for-instance. And some of those paranormal creatures were like the unicorn: victims of their nature.

The name always threw people. Coursers were people who hunted with dogs—it came from Europe in the Middle Ages, I think. Had to do with big-game hunts and that sort of nonsense. I don't know, I didn't come up with this crap. All I know is we used to be called Slayers. Then *Buffy the Vampire Slayer* got popular on TV, and people stopped taking us seriously, and figured we were just role-playing or something. So fine, no problem, we went ahead and changed our name to Hunters—which was more accurate, anyhow, since we weren't just about the killing—but then *Supernatural* got popular, and the whole nonsense started all over.

Now we're called Coursers, mainly because we figure nobody in Hollywood knows what that is.

So—that's what I do.

As for my name, I wasn't actually born Bram Gold. And thank G-d for that, honestly. No, Rachel and Mordechai Goldblume named their bouncing baby boy "Abraham." They probably already had my shingle out when Mom got pregnant, figuring I would just join their practice—

they were both doctors, and I was always groomed for the family business.

That lasted right up until my parents were killed by a golem run amuck.

So instead of seeing old farts bitching about their latest ailment, I became somebody people hired to kill demons or hunt nixies or slay dragons or what-the-hell-ever. And if that was what you were looking for, you weren't about to hire some schmuck named Abe Goldblume, right?

Bram Gold, though, he sounded like the kind of guy who got things done. So that was the name on the big piece of metal outside my office on West 230th Street just off Broadway in the Bronx.

Of course, my nametag for Montefiore Hospital's ER says DR. ABRAHAM GOLDBLUME. I put in two days a week there. It's been good to stay in the medical game, especially since the other Coursers sometimes made use of my services. Most other ER docs tended to call for psych consults when patients explained that they've been, say, gored by a unicorn.

Luckily, this particular unicorn wouldn't be a problem anymore. José Velez answered on the third ring, and he said he could be there in ten minutes, which he was. He only gave me a hard time about it for a few seconds before I conveyed the rush nature of the job. That just meant he'd be back to giving me crap afterward.

But he cast the spell, the unicorn popped back into the tapestry, he and Rodzinski argued for a while about the price, eventually agreeing to an amount and having me add it to my overall fee and I'd then pay Velez. Just as Rodzinski and Velez shook hands—Rodzinski looking like he wanted to be anywhere else just then—the talisman made another popping sound and crumbled to dust, leaving me holding a leather string and staring at a pile of dust on the floor.

I wondered if Rodzinski would dock the floor sweeping off my fee.

When we got out to the driveway, I saw Velez's bright red 3000GT parked right behind my rental truck. I had no idea how Velez squeezed his three-hundred-and-fifty-pound frame into the two-seater, but he managed it.

"Thanks again for coming," I told him. "You were the first guy I thought of."

"That's some *bull*shit. First person your ass thought of was Vanessa Fofanah," he said with a laugh, "but she is *pissed* at you."

I gave that the response it deserved, which was silence.

Velez shrugged. "Whatever, yo—look, I was already on my way down the Deegan."

I chuckled, realizing the most likely place Velez could be headed via the Major Deegan Expressway on a Friday night when he could drop what he was doing and come help me. "You were going to see Katrina again, weren't you?"

"*Fuck* you, Gold, you don't know shit, okay?"

"I'll take that as a yes." Indicating the Cloisters with my head, I added, "By the way, when'd you start adding basil to the binding spell?"

Velez had no discernible neck—he went straight from his chin to his broad shoulders—so he looked very silly when he shrugged. "A few months back. Clients like it if the spells don't stink. You should try that."

I held up both hands. "Don't look at me, I bought that talisman."

"Lemme guess—Ahondjon? That fool's always bringin' it old school up in here. Someone oughtta tell his ass that it don't gotta smell like shit to work right." He reached for his car keys. "You wanna get a beer?"

"Really?" I gave him another grin. "Katrina might still be up."

This time *he* ignored *my* dig. "I seriously need me some alcohol, yo. Putting *El Blanco* back in the rug took a *shit*load outta me."

That got my attention. "Seriously? What happened?"

"Hell if I know." Velez shook his head, running his hand over his close-cropped hair. "Whatever undid that motherfucker was *harsh*. Took *way* more mojo to put that bad boy back than it shoulda."

"Weird."

Holding out his arms in a "well?" gesture, Velez asked, "So, beer?"

I jerked a thumb at the truck. "Nah, I gotta get this monster to the parking lot before it gets too late." There was a big outdoor parking lot near where I kept my office, right off the Deegan. If I didn't get there before midnight, though, all the truck-sized spots would be taken up by tractor-trailers settling in for the night before getting back on the road in the morning. You ever try parking a twenty-six-foot truck on the street?

"So bring your sorry ass by afterward."

"Where?"

"Freddie's."

That settled that. No way I was going to *that* dump again. "Lemme see how I feel. I gotta check in with van Owen, and I got some other crap I need to take care of." That was almost true.

"A'ight. Thanks for throwin' me the work." He held up his hand. I grabbed it and we did the man-hug one-pat-on-the-back thing.

"Hey, it was that or let the unicorn disembowel me."

Velez chuckled. "Peace." He squeezed into the GT while I climbed into the truck, and we headed out into the night.

I was able to park in the lot I mentioned without any hassle, which was a huge relief. Seriously, all the other parking lots around were indoor ones in which the truck wouldn't even fit. It was hard enough finding street parking for a normal-sized car, much less this monstrosity. My driveway was too small to accommodate it—it would stick out onto the sidewalk, and I'd get a ticket. I mean, yeah, I could've added that to Rodzinski's bill, but why risk it? I was already pretty sure he wouldn't accept the parking fee.

But it was all good, and I walked to Broadway, standing under the elevated train, waiting for the bus that would take me to Riverdale and my home. I called van Owen while I waited and left a message on his voicemail, telling him how it went down with the unicorn, including what Velez said about how hard it was to restore the binding spell. Between that and a binding that strong coming unraveled in the first place, something funny was going on, and he needed to know about it.

As soon as I hung up with van Owen's voicemail, the cell phone rang with the opening bars of "Daytripper" by the Beatles, which startled the crap out of me. That ringtone meant that it was Miriam Zerelli calling.

Remember when I said that the Bronx had a different wardein than van Owen? That was Miriam. Her demesne included not only the Bronx, but also some parts of Westchester and western Connecticut—the boundaries for these things were geographic, not political.

Miriam and I've actually been friends since childhood. Her dad—the previous Wardein of the Bronx—was good friends with Esther Lieberman, who was both my aunt and my family's rabbi. Miriam and I, we've been through some stuff together.

"Hey there, Mimi."

"Where the hell are you?"

I blinked. "I'm on Broadway waiting for the bus up the hill. I had to park a truck in the lot down by 230th. Why, I—"

"Oh, good, so you're on your way."

"Uh..." As soon as I heard the tone in Miriam's voice, I knew there was *something* going on that I had forgotten, but I couldn't for the life of me remember what the heck it was.

Correctly reading my hesitation as cluelessness, Miriam spoke very slowly, as if to a not-too-bright four-year-old. "Because if you don't get here when the *full moon* rises—"

I snapped my fingers, suddenly very grateful I hadn't accepted Velez's offer of a post-unicorn beer. "Right! The werewolves! It's my turn to babysit!"

Miriam said in a very tight voice, "Yes. And you forgot. Again."

The bus came, and I hopped onto it, dropping my MetroCard into the slot. It beeped and informed me that my remaining balance was a buck-seventy-five, which meant I'd need to refill it before I could use it again. I'd probably remember that with the same attention that I remembered my plans for tonight.

"I'm sorry, Miriam."

"Yes, you are. You *really* should hire an assistant to deal with your forgetfulness."

"I know, but I keep forgetting."

I could practically hear her rolling her eyes as I took a seat near the back of the bus across from two white teenagers sharing earbuds and next to a Latino guy in a doorman's uniform.

"Don't worry, Miriam, I'm headed there right now."

"You'd better be, boychik."

I winced. "Mimi, bubbe, please—don't bring the Yiddish."

"Then stop calling me 'Mimi.' See you soon."

She ended the call and I let out a long sigh that twinged my aching ribs. I briefly toyed with the notion of once again going through my cell's address book, this time to find a replacement werewolf minder, but the full moon would be up in half an hour.

Besides, Miriam *did* pay me for doing this. So what if my bed was calling to me like the sirens to Odysseus?

I got off the bus and went, not toward my townhouse on Johnson Avenue, but in the direction of a beautiful old house on Seward Place just off Netherland Avenue. And when I say old, I mean *old*—it was built in 1841 by William H. Seward, who was the New York State governor at the time. He never actually *lived* there, though. Later on, Seward became a senator, then President Lincoln's Secretary of State—even helped write the Emancipation Proclamation. He was killed the same night as Lincoln in 1865, and sometime after that, the teeny cul-de-sac off Netherland Avenue got named after him.

Nowadays, Seward Place was just a glorified alleyway, really: a small strip of pavement, the sole purpose of which was to lead to Miriam's front door. Well, actually to the two ten-foot stone posts just wide enough to fit a car. Each post had a square near the top engraved with an ornate pattern. Those were wards that kept anyone Miriam didn't want out of the house.

For about half a second, I thought she was pissed off enough at me to keep me out, so I breathed a sigh of relief when I made it through the posts okay.

I walked past the empty driveway—Miriam hadn't owned a car since the accident—to the front porch, on which stood one of the four werewolves I'd be taking care of tonight, Anna Maria Weintraub, smoking a cigarette. Half-Italian, half-Jewish, and all attitude, Anna Maria glared at me through a cloud of smoke.

"About time you showed up, honey. Miriam's ripshit. Where you been, anyhow?"

"Trying not to get killed by a unicorn."

Anna Maria regarded me with a raised eyebrow. "Seriously? Unicorns are *real*?"

I held out my hands. "You're half an hour from turning into a hairy mutt, but about this, you're skeptical?"

She shrugged. "Well, yeah, I guess, but—*unicorns*? Anyhow, you missed the cannolis." Anna Maria lived in Belmont, the Little Italy section of the Bronx, home to some of the finest bakeries in town, and she often brought pastries of some kind. Naturally, I was too late to get any. Story of my night...

My ribs were throbbing to the point where I really wished I'd had the time to stop at home and grab my prescription painkillers, as the ibuprofen wasn't really doing the trick. I felt my chest again to reassure myself that they weren't broken, then followed Anna Maria—who dropped her cigarette and stepped on it—inside.

Miriam glared up at me from her wheelchair in the house's foyer. She was thirty, the same age as me, but had gone prematurely gray in her mid-twenties. Since the accident, she'd kept her hair short—she used to have it down to her waist, and it had been lovely. But with the chair, it just got in the way. Her porcelain skin had gotten a little blotchy the last couple of years, which, in my medical opinion, was due to stress.

As I walked in, Miriam was flanked by the other three werewolves: Mark McAvoy, a nebbishy white guy; Tyrone Morris, a burly black guy; and Katie Gonzalez, a petite Latina woman. Tyrone was holding a big, empty backpack.

Katie smiled and gave a small wave. "Hiya, Bram."

Miriam was not smiling. "Nice of you to turn up."

Holding up my hands, I said, "Look, I'm sorry, I forgot. The Cloisters hired me to wrangle a unicorn."

Now Miriam's hazel eyes went wide. "It got out of the tapestry?"

I nodded.

"How the hell did *that* happen?"

"I dunno, but Velez had a bitch of a time getting it back in there."

That turned the wide eyes into a dubious squint. "They hired *Velez*?"

"Schmuck-nose at the Cloisters didn't realize that Coursers don't do spells, so I needed someone last minute." I grinned. "'Sides, he was just gonna try to see Katrina again, so I saved him from that."

"And the public is grateful." Miriam sighed as she reached into a pouch in her wheelchair, took out a stone disc, and handed it to me. "You know the drill. Put the ward on the fence, keep an eye on them, don't let them eat anything they shouldn't"—that part was given with a glare at Anna Maria—"and don't forget to bring the ward *back*. See you at sunrise."

Dropping the disc—which was a ward that would keep anyone who wasn't me or a werewolf out of the dog run—into the inner pocket of my denim jacket, I said, "No worries, Mimi, I'll take care of them."

The five of us walked out the door, Katie calling behind her, "Thanks again for dinner, Miriam!"

Smiling for the first time since I walked in, Miriam said, "My pleasure, Katie. Be safe." Miriam always made a nice dinner for the werewolves before they had to go out on their run.

Lighting up another cigarette as soon as her open-toed sandals hit the porch, Anna Maria muttered, "Don't know why she was looking at *me* when she talked about eating shit."

Tyrone shot her a dubious look. "You serious? Girl, have you forgotten what happened last June?"

"Look, I *paid* for the woman's entire flowerbed to be replanted, didn't I? And it was almost a year ago, can't we just let it go?"

I grinned. "Apparently not."

"You know," Mark said in his usual subdued tone, "you really don't have to stay all night. I mean, okay, put the ward in, but we can take care of ourselves."

"That's not what I'm getting paid for. Besides, what if one of you jumps the fence?"

Anna Maria snorted. "Not with these knees."

I looked at her. "You taking glucosamine like I told you to?" I know, I know, but once a doctor…

She puffed on her cigarette as the three of us turned onto 232nd Street. "Yeah, and now they just hurt like hell instead of hurting like fuck."

"Seriously, though," Mark said, "I don't think we need to be watched the whole night. I mean, I've been doing this for two years now, and I'm the newbie. I think we're capable of staying in the dog run. We can take care of ourselves," he repeated.

I didn't really have anything to say to that, so I just kept walking, about a step or two ahead of the others, trying not to think about the pain in my shoulder and ribs and doing a pretty crummy job of it, all told.

Mark sighed. "I bet the last wardein was a lot nicer."

I heard Katie inhale quickly. She'd been looking right at me, so while it was possible that she was reacting to what Mark said, it was more likely that she was reacting to the way I reacted to what Mark said.

Which, for the record, wasn't pretty.

I stopped, turned, and faced Mark, who swallowed as I pointed a finger at his chest. "First of all, the last wardein also used to hire Coursers to deal with werewolves, except he hired us to shoot them down like dogs instead of letting them run around a park. Secondly, the reason why he's the last wardein instead of the current one is because he was killed by a drunk driver, which is also why the current wardein, his daughter, is in a wheelchair, seeing as how she was in the passenger seat. And thirdly, I'm minding you for the whole night because Miriam said so, and when it comes to stuff like this, what the wardein says, goes. Are we clear?"

Mark just nodded quickly, audibly swallowing a second time.

"Good. Let's move."

I probably shouldn't have mouthed off like that, but I was very protective of Miriam. A lot of folks thought she was too young to be wardein. It's an inherited job—most didn't even start until they were in their fifties. Not that it was her fault...

After about ten seconds of awkward silence, Katie walked up alongside me and said, "You missed a really good dinner."

I grinned. Miriam was an excellent cook. "I'll bet. What'd she make?"

The rest of the walk went by quickly as Katie regaled me with tales of Miriam's tomato-and-mozzarella salad, vegetable soup, and rigatoni with vodka sauce, followed by Anna Maria's cannolis.

Katie was just about to describe the Moscato d'Asti, the sweet dessert wine they'd had with the cannolis, when we arrived at Ewen Park. Built into a hill that used to be the estate of a Civil War general, right in the park's center was a dog run.

Proving that my luck might well have been improving, the run was empty. I stuck the ward in between two links of the fence while the other four walked through the gate and quickly stripped naked.

Moments later, the full moon started to appear in the sky and they started gyrating and contorting. I *hated* watching this part, so I pointedly didn't look as I gathered their clothes up into the backpack Tyrone had been holding.

Once I heard snarling and howling, I turned to look, and four naked humans had been replaced by four wolves, running around the fenced area. Honestly, they looked more like a bunch of really big huskies or keeshonds or one of the Scandinavian breeds. This was handy. While the ward kept people away, the run was still visible from other parts of the park, including a fairly popular paved walkway.

Only after the quartet settled into their galumphing did I realize just what a nightmare I had let myself in for. I had ibuprofen left, but nothing to wash it down with. I hadn't had time to grab anything (like a cup of coffee, which would've been *very* welcome right now), and I just remembered that I left my water bottle in the truck in the parking lot. My ribs were doing a rhumba in my chest, my shoulder still ached, and somehow I had to stay awake without any caffeine until sunrise.

At least the werewolves were pretty well-behaved. Honestly, Mark was right. I could probably have let them go for a bit while I ran to take a nap. Or at least grabbed a cup of coffee.

But I didn't trust my luck enough to do that. The microsecond I walked over to the deli on 231st, Tyrone would jump the fence or Anna Maria would pick a fight with Mark, or some damn thing. Wasn't worth the risk.

After the sun went down, the temperature plummeted, and the wind kicked up, plowing through my denim jacket and black T-shirt like they were made of toilet paper. The cold just made the shoulder and ribs throb more even through the ibuprofen that I'd dry swallowed. I started pacing and walking around the periphery of the run just to keep my circulation going.

After my fifth turn around the run I decided to expand the perimeter of my perambulations. The wolves were barely moving — Tyrone was ambling around a bit, but Katie was asleep, and both Anna Maria and Mark were grooming themselves. Knowing that he was spending some serious quality time licking his testicles ameliorated my annoyance with Mark considerably.

Wandering up the hill toward a giant oak tree that was a couple hundred feet from the edge of the dog run, I noticed a bunch of flies flitting about. That was odd in and of itself, since it was a little cold for that number of insects, but then I caught a whiff.

As a doctor and a Courser, I knew the smell of dead body anywhere.

Chapter 3

THE CORPSE WAS ON THE OTHER SIDE OF THE TREE FROM THE ONE FACING the dog run.

My first thought was that I did *not* need the aggravation. Dead bodies meant cops, and cops took *forever* at a crime scene. It was only midnight, but there was no guarantee they'd be done in six hours, and no way was I gonna be able to explain four "dogs" turning into naked people at dawn to a bunch of city cops.

My second was that I now had a pounding headache to go with the achy shoulder and the bruised ribs, and my expert medical opinion was that this damn corpse brought it on.

My third was identifying the body in question. Once I placed it, I realized that having cops around was gonna be the absolute *least* of my problems.

What got me to recognize the corpse was the awful smell. Not so much the dead-body smell, but the extra stench of sweat and dirt, which meant a homeless guy, mixed with single malt Scotch, which meant a homeless guy I knew: Warren.

People around the neighborhood knew Warren as one of the locals. He'd hang out at various spots around Riverdale and Kingsbridge, always with a large cardboard coffee cup that he'd rattle back and forth in one hand and a bottle of Glenlivet or Laphroaig or Macallan in the other. He was the only homeless guy in the history of the universe who drank single malt. Most people didn't get how he could afford it.

I did, though, because I knew that Warren was really Warham Mather. He first moved to the Bronx when he was assigned to be the minister of Lower Yonkers around 1700.

Mather was immortal. That was why he could afford single malt on a panhandler's salary—he didn't have the same need to eat that the rest of us do. Killing an immortal was only possible through magickal means, which meant it fell more into my bailiwick than the cops'.

Once I recognized Mather, I knew my first step was still to call the cops—or, rather, one cop in particular. As a general rule, Coursers didn't get along with the police, but there were exceptions, and one of them worked this neighborhood. I didn't have any means of disposing of the body (werewolves, for the record, *don't* eat dead human flesh—hell, Mark was a vegetarian, that was why Miriam's meal had no meat). Besides, this was what the NYPD did, and for a skell like this, they wouldn't be wasting too much of the taxpayers' money on investigating.

After two rings, Detective Lydia Toscano of the 50th Precinct answered my cell phone call with her thick Bronx accent made scratchy by years of cigarette smoke. "This is Toscano—what kinda spook shit you dumpin' on me this time, Brammy?"

I winced. Someday I hoped to get Toscano to stop calling me "Brammy." It'd probably happen the same day I stopped calling Miriam "Mimi." "Sorry to bother you so late, Lyd," I said, meaning it.

"Can it, kid. I know you wouldn't call without a reason, and if it'd been anyone but you, I wouldn't'a even answered."

"I've got a body in Ewen Park in the dog run—it's a homeless guy, but he's from my end of things."

Toscano grunted. She had also been friends with Mike Zerelli—rumor had it that they'd been more than friends, but I never pried—when he was wardein, and knew the drill. Didn't *like* it a whole helluva lot, but she also knew better than to complain. Unlike most cops, she'd seen our world, and she was just as happy to keep it out of *her* world as much as humanly possible.

I added, "If you can get your people here about five minutes after sunup, that'd be perfect."

"Five minutes after—no, forget it, I don't even wanna know. But if it's one'a yours, whaddaya need *my* people for?"

"Because I don't have a morgue. Look, it's Warren."

"That's the panhandler who drinks Glenlivet, right?"

"Yeah."

"Christ, he's a fixture. How'd he die?"

"The makings to do a full autopsy here in the dog run, I don't have, Lyd. That's why I need your morgue."

She snorted, followed quickly by a ragged cough. "Oh, so you want us to do the work on our pitiful budget for nothin'?"

"Look, he's a homeless drunk. He'll just fall into the system like everyone else and be buried in Potter's Field. It won't interfere with your life at all, I promise."

"Last time you promised me that, Brammy, I had a case I couldn't close, with two mountains'a paperwork. Sergeant *still* gives me shit about that, y'know."

I winced. That was the time that nixie started making trouble on City Island. I had been hired to take care of it by the family she was bothering, but when I stuck my oversized nose in, she showed up on Wave Hill. It was a big mess on my end, too, but I managed to banish the little monster, which meant there was nobody for Toscano to arrest in the end. Didn't exactly goose her career along.

Trying to sound reassuring, I said, "Look, Lyd, I'll try my best, okay? But this—"

"Is one'a yours, right." Toscano let out a very long, raspy breath that sounded like a car running over glass. "There'll be two unis there five minutes past sunrise. Talk to you later, and I hope you catch the fucker."

"Thanks, Lyd."

She hung up. I knew Toscano would keep the NYPD's touch on this light—not that it'd be that hard. From their POV, it really was just what I said: a nobody who'd be buried in Potter's Field with all the John and Jane Does and the other people with no fixed address and no next of kin.

From *my* POV, though, I still needed to know how someone killed an immortal.

I knelt down to look at Mather, causing my ribs to do the rhumba a few more times. The hill the park was built on separated the neighborhoods of Kingsbridge and Riverdale. General John Ewen used to live on that property, and later on it became a city park named after him. The dog run was on one of the park's plateaus.

Because of the dog run—not to mention the paved footpath nearby—this part of the park was pretty well lit by streetlamps, plus, of course, it was a full moon. So I got a good look at Mather's corpse, even though the tree blocked some of the light.

The two main things I noticed were that he was *incredibly* pale, even by dead-body standards, and he had two puncture wounds in his neck.

Okay, more explaining. Everything you think you know about vampires is totally wrong. Not that that should be much of a surprise, since half of what you know about vampires probably contradicts the other half. It ain't Bram Stoker, it ain't Anne Rice, it ain't Joss Whedon, and it ain't Stephenie Meyer.

Reality, though, made for lousy fiction, which was why the fiction was all wrong. Vampires lived a lot longer than normal humans, yeah, and they were pale, allergic to garlic, and fed on blood. But mostly they were sickly and weak, they hated sunlight (though they didn't burn when exposed to it; that was all F.W. Murnau in *Nosferatu*), and didn't like to associate with people much. They almost *never* fed on humans, because — well, honestly, it's way too much hassle. Most butchers'll sell animal blood no problem — I knew a few down in Morrisania and Mott Haven that gave it away for free to the vamps who couldn't really afford it. For that matter, Aunt Esther, aka Rabbi Lieberman, had a line on some blood that's as close to kosher as possible for the Chosen People among the undead. (Basically, for meat to be kosher, the blood had to be drained a certain way, and that drained blood was what the Jewish vamps drank. The Reform ones, anyhow. The Orthodox vamps just starved to death; we generally treated turning one of them as a homicide.)

Okay, sure, every once in a while, you got some nutjob with delusions of Dracula-dom, but if the intended victim was able-bodied, he or she could probably take the vamp in a fight. These guys were total wusses. And while bullets couldn't kill them, they still hurt a lot and the wounds took forever to heal.

I may've had one or more of those nutjobs on my hands here. I may've had something else. There wasn't much blood pooled under the body or at the wounds, and the carotid artery bleeds like crazy when it's ripped open like this. But then, a vampire would've gulped down whatever gushed out, so there wouldn't be much anyhow.

Whatever it was, though, I had a feeling I wasn't gonna like it.

The next six hours were spent wandering gingerly around the dog run, keeping an eye on four gallivanting werewolves, pretending my entire body hadn't turned into a giant bruise, and wondering why the heck a vampire would kill an immortal.

Just as the sun was starting to brighten the sky, all four werewolves began rolling around on the grass, making weird mewling noises. Except Anna Maria — she just gurgled. Their hind legs straightened, their forelegs shortened, their snouts and wolf ears receded even as their noses and human ears grew out.

The really hilarious part—and why I could watch them change back, as opposed to being grossed out by the first change—was that all their fur just fell off. It was like watching a Maine Coon cat shed at high speed. Funniest thing ever, though I wasn't so rude as to laugh. Besides, laughing hurt right now. Hell, breathing hurt right now.

I reached over the fence for the backpack. That hurt, too.

"Hurry up, hurry up," Mark was saying anxiously like he always did, both his arms crossed over his crotch. One of his fingers would've been more than enough to cover up what was down there, if you know what I mean.

"Jesus Christ, Mark, get over your big self, willya?" Anna Maria was totally unselfconscious in her nudity, despite a figure that could generously be called Rubenesque. In fact, the first time I met her, I'd used that word, and she had just laughed and said, "It's okay, honey—I'm fat. I could be skinny, but then I can't eat latkes anymore. Small price to pay."

The mere thought of latkes reminded me (again) that I hadn't eaten since before my dustup with the unicorn. But of course, I couldn't go eat yet—I had to wait for the cops...

Just to piss off Mark, I gave Anna Maria her clothes first, and Mark his last. "You guys gotta get a move on," I said, indicating Mather's corpse. "The cops'll be here any minute."

"Shit," said Tyrone, who always made that word about three or four syllables, depending on his mood. "I always liked that crazy white dude, too."

Mark's eyes went wide as he climbed into his pants. Everyone else wore pullovers, and both Anna Maria and Katie wore skirts, while Tyrone wore sweats. Mark kept insisting on button-down shirts and slacks instead of something quick to get in and out of. "We didn't do that, did we?" he asked, aghast.

"No," I said firmly.

"I would've remembered something like that," Anna Maria said, "but all I got is rolling around in the dirt."

Mark was now fumbling with his shirt buttons. "I'll take your word for it." How much werewolves remembered from when they changed varied from person to person—usually, if someone remembered their dreams, then they remembered most of their wolfen antics. Anna Maria always remembered everything — which was why she couldn't deny being the culprit in the flower-bed-eating incident — but Mark never recalled a damn thing. Tyrone and Katie just recalled bits and pieces.

"I'm out," Tyrone said. "Gotta take the kid to school." He dashed off before he had finished tying the drawstring on his sweats, heading down the pathway to the bus that would get him to his ex-wife's place. Ever since the divorce — she couldn't handle the werewolf thing, apparently — he'd made sure to always make as much time for his daughter as he could.

Mark finished buttoning his shirt and went up the hill toward where he'd parked his car on Johnson Avenue without saying goodbye. Guess giving him his clothes last really *did* piss him off. I lived with the disappointment.

Anna Maria and Katie both took the time to say goodbye. Katie added, "You know, I'd love to thank you some time. Maybe get together for coffee? There's a great new café that opened up over on Riverdale Avenue."

I blinked. I hadn't expected that at all. Then again, I've apparently been flirted with half a dozen times and totally missed it. If it wasn't for Miriam or Velez or one of my fellow Coursers telling me after the fact, I never would have known. So her asking me out kinda had me gobsmacked.

My initial thought was that Katie was too sweet a person to get introduced to my crazy life of hunting the monsters of the world. My second thought was that, to most folks, *she* was one of the monsters of the world. And a sweet person in my life would be kinda nice.

However, now wasn't the time to check our metaphorical calendars. "Look, the cops really will be here any second, you guys need to get a move on. Give me a call and we'll figure out a time, okay?" I knew she had my number, as Miriam had made sure we all had each other's cell numbers just in case.

That got me a big, bright smile from Katie that I had to admit was *really* appealing. I'd gladly sit across a table from that smile over coffee at the very least. "Great! Talk to you soon!"

"Take care, honey," Anna Maria added. "And next month, I'll make sure to bring more cannolis." Then she leaned in close and whispered, "Thanks for saying yes."

Before I could respond to that, she jogged to catch up with Katie and elbowed her playfully in the ribs. "*Toldja* to just ask."

I really am oblivious. Shaking my head, I went to remove the ward from the fence.

Two uniforms from the five-oh showed up two or three minutes later. The short one with the flat nose and the nameplate that read RODRIGUEZ came up to me while the taller one went to look at the corpse.

"You found the body?"

I nodded. "Abe Goldblume."

"Jesus," came the voice of Rodriguez's partner from by the tree. "It's Warren."

"Who?" Rodriguez had a blank look on his face.

His partner looked up. He had a pockmarked face and a thick mustache. "Y'know, the panhandler. Always drinkin' the good shit?"

Rodriguez shrugged. "I don't pay attention to those guys." He looked at me. "Can I have your address and phone number, please?"

I gave them that, told them I worked as an ER doctor at Montefiore (telling them my other occupation would just complicate things, which was also why I went with the name on my birth certificate), then I told them that I found the body when I was taking a pre-sunrise walk through the park.

Rodriguez wrote all this down in his pad, then asked me a few more questions, before finally saying, "Okay, Dr. Goldblume, I don't think we need anything else. If we do, someone'll call you."

The one with the pockmarked face had walked toward us while Rodriguez questioned me. Now I could see his nameplate, which told me he was Officer Samuels. "That ain't likely. I mean, Warren was a decent guy for a skell, but he was still a skell. Basically, this means we get to sit on our thumbs for three hours while we wait for the ME to show up, then we fill out paperwork, then we go home."

"My kinda shift," Rodriguez said.

I smiled. "Well, then, I'll let you guys sit on your thumbs in peace."

As I started to walk off, Samuels put a hand on my shoulder. "Hey, Doc, you okay?"

"Uh, yeah, why?" I was kinda surprised that they'd ask me that—then I remembered who I was talking to. Guys who got shot at while wearing Kevlar vests probably knew exactly what someone walking with bruised ribs looked like. "Oh, right. Yeah, my dog crashed into me—golden retriever, doesn't know his own strength. Don't worry, though, they're just bruised."

"Well, you oughtta know," Samuels said. "Take it easy, though, those things take for-fuckin'-ever to heal."

"Thanks!"

I gave the cops a little wave, and then headed up the incline of the park. More than anything else in the universe, I wanted to go home to my hot shower, my prescription drugs, and my bed.

That wasn't an option, however. Miriam needed to know about Warham Mather, and she needed to make a decision on what to do about his murder.

But I was for damn sure stopping at the bagel place for some coffee first...

Chapter 4

AFTER GETTING COFFEE AND BAGELS—POPPY SEED FOR ME, AN EVERYTHING bagel with cream cheese and lox for Miriam—I went to Seward Place and filled the wardein in. She was still pissed with me for about half a second before she saw how bad I looked. Not sure how bad I actually *did* look, but if it was even the tiniest fraction of how bad I *felt*, Mather's corpse probably seemed the picture of health by comparison.

I gave her the high points and promised a more detailed report after I'd slept for a year. She thanked me for the bagel and shooed me out so I could go home and collapse.

My house was a nice little three-story brick place that looked like eighty gajillion other three-story brick places all over the Bronx: a one-car garage and a small apartment on the ground floor, larger (and identical) apartments on the second and third.

Miriam's place was only about a seven-minute hike from me, though that morning I did it shuffling like a zombie. I shambled in the front door just as my cousin Rebekah was running out, a small white box from the drug store with the copy machine under her arm. Those were probably flyers for whatever talk, rally, or march she was currently involved with.

"Oh, hey, Bram." Rebekah shoved her large plastic-framed glasses up her button nose. Her dark hair was flying in several directions at once, and there was an ink smudge on her cheek. She'd put on her sweater inside out—once upon a time, before Rebekah was born, that was fashionable, but she just hadn't noticed it was on wrong. At least her socks matched, which usually only happened once a month or so.

My cousin, I loved her. But she tended to get caught up in causes. If she'd stayed under the same roof as her parents (my uncle Isaac's philosophy had always been, "Let things work out on their own, why don't you?"), there'd have been a homicide, so I let Rebekah have the ground-floor apartment in my townhouse to keep peace in the family. It was a nice little one-bedroom, it was close to where she went to school at Manhattan College, it got her and Isaac and Judy out of each other's hair, and, as an added bonus, I got a free housecleaner. Twice a week, Rebekah would come upstairs and vacuum and dust and deal with my inevitable clutter.

Okay, it wasn't really *free*, since I could've rented the place for at least a thousand a month, but at least she knew about what I did for a living, which wasn't something I wanted to have to explain to a renter. Or, for that matter, to a housecleaner, especially for the third-floor apartment, which I used as a workshop, workout space, examination room, and armory.

"Hey, kid. How're your mom and dad?" I asked. Rebekah was still a good daughter, and usually went by Isaac and Judy's place for Shabbos dinner, and I just assumed she was there last night.

Rebekah tended to look down when she talked. Judy always used to say that she liked talking to the floor. "I didn't go to Mom and Dad's."

How Judy reacted to *that* didn't bear thinking about. My aunt was convinced that Rebekah never ate unless Judy was a witness to it. Based on what I'd seen, she wasn't that far off—Rebekah kept forgetting to eat...

She added, "I finished that book on the Algonquins you lent me— I left it on your couch. Thanks!"

I smiled. "No problem." Rebekah loved to read, and I had amassed a huge library over the years. The book she was talking about was a hardcover illustrated history of the Algonquin peoples of New York City that I'd picked up at an estate sale a few years back.

"Oh," she said, looking at the box under her arm so suddenly that her glasses fell back down her nose, "I've got some flyers here. Can you hang some up for me? It's for Dr. Grofsky."

As she opened the box and yanked out several eight-and-a-half-by-eleven sheets of paper, I asked, "Why do I know that name?"

"He's a doctor at an abortion clinic in Yonkers—he got shot at last week."

Then I remembered. A couple of the other ER doctors at Montefiore were talking about it in pretty disgusted tones. "One of these decades, I'll catch up on the news." I took the flyers from her, making a mental note that I was sure to forget to put them in the car. "I only just found out that Dewey defeated Truman."

Rebekah actually looked up for that. "Huh?"

I sighed. "*Chicago Tribune*, 1948? They called the election for Governor Dewey even though Truman actually won reelection?"

"Okay." Rebekah looked back down and said to the floor, "I can't believe anybody would do something like that."

"Like what, try to kill someone?"

"Try to kill someone who helps people, who does good in the world. He's a *doctor*."

I shrugged. "It's all relative. Far as they're concerned, they're righteous—shooting at doctors who, to their mind, commit murder."

"They shouldn't have the right to do that, to just kill good people. That's why we're protesting." She looked up at me for a second then said, "Gotta go. Seeya!" She dashed out past me.

Shaking my head, I took the flyers upstairs with me to my second-floor apartment, my ribs barking in pain as I did so.

Mittens, my twenty-pound gray-and-white Maine Coon, was waiting for me at the door, expecting scritches on his head. I obliged, even though bending over hurt like a sonofabitch. I checked his food and water bowls in the kitchen; both were empty. Looking down at the oversized moggy, who'd waddled into the kitchen behind me, I said, "I just filled those yesterday afternoon! You swallowed a tapeworm, didn't you?" I shook my head. "Maybe I will need to rent out downstairs, just to pay for your food, you little freser."

"*Mrow*," was all he'd say in response.

After dumping enough dry food to last a normal cat for two days—which meant Mittens would devour it in an hour or two—in one bowl and refilling the other with tap water, I dropped the flyers and my denim jacket on the living room couch right next to the Algonquin book. Rebekah had cleaned Friday morning, and the place was spotless, with only a bit of gray cat fur on the big blue chair that Mittens usually spent half his day on—it got the best sunbeam. Otherwise, it was swept, vacuumed, and dusted. Almost gleaming.

Okay, probably not worth a thousand a month, but still pretty damned nice.

Stopping in the bathroom to pop some painkillers—it's handy working in a hospital, prescriptions get filled so easily—I stumbled toward the bedroom and fell right to sleep without even bothering to undress.

In the dream, my parents were still alive.

They were practicing medicine in their offices on the ground floor of the building we lived in on Henry Hudson Parkway. I was there, not as a fellow doctor, but as a patient, my ribs having been bruised by a unicorn. Mom said, "I *warned* you this would happen if you spent all your time roughhousing, Abe." Dad shook his head and said, "Stop *fussing* over the boy, Rachel!" Mom tut-tutted. "I'm his mother *and* his doctor. What else should I do *but* fuss?"

But Mom wasn't speaking in her own voice, it was Miriam's. And Dad sounded like Velez.

Then the unicorn came crashing through the office window and stabbed Mom and Dad right in the chest with its horn, despite their being on opposite sides of the room.

I woke up in a cold sweat, bedclothes tangled around my legs. I didn't scream, though—this wouldn't even have cracked the top one hundred of worst nightmares I'd had since becoming a Courser.

Looking over at my nightstand, the numbers 4:27 glowed at me in green. I'd slept most of the afternoon away, which was actually what I was hoping for. Just wished it hadn't ended quite like that.

Slowly, I untangled myself from the sheets and climbed out of bed—the painkillers I'd popped before collapsing had long since worn off—and gingerly removed my now-very-wrinkled clothes, tossing them into the hamper. As I stumbled to the bathroom, Mittens just looked up from the blue chair long enough to give me a desultory "*mrow*" before falling back asleep.

First I popped some more pills, then started the shower going on hot. I figured that between the pelting hot water on my shoulder and the pharmaceuticals, I'd be almost lifelike.

Staring at myself in the mirror, I saw a tall, lanky Jew with short brown hair that probably should've been styled in a manner other than "comb it once and hope for the best," a thin beard that was an attempt to deal with my being too lazy to shave, and a very un-macho thatch of chest hair. I also saw red and purple splotches on my abdomen where the unicorn bashed into me last night.

It had been a while since I'd dreamt about Mom and Dad. Not sure what prompted it this time, honestly. Probably the painkillers wearing off while I slept.

We really did live in a co-op apartment on the tenth floor of a big building on the service road for the Henry Hudson Parkway, with Mom and Dad's medical practice one of many that took up the ground-floor spaces. "Easiest commute you could ask for," Mom always said.

When I was a little kid, Dad had carried on about how he wanted a house with a back yard so he could have a garden. Mom would just look at him and say, "What're you gonna do with a garden besides kill it?"

Dad was stubborn, and Mom always believed in letting people make their own stupid mistakes, as long as she got to say "I told you so" afterward. So Dad bought the house, the garden was a total disaster filled with weeds, overgrown grass, and dead flowers after two years, Mom said, "I told you so," and then they sold it and bought the co-op in the same place that already had their practice.

I always knew about what Toscano had called "spook shit" from when I was a kid. It was always part of the world for me. I first met Miriam when our synagogue held a cookout on Labor Day weekend. Mike Zerelli—who had been friends with Aunt Esther for ages— showed up with his daughter, and we started talking. Miriam was shy and was scared of all the grown-ups, and I was fearless and would talk to anyone, so we hit it off pretty quick. She only spit on me once, which for a ten-year-old girl is practically a declaration of eternal friendship to a ten-year-old boy.

The position of wardein was inherited, and Miriam had been trained from birth to take on the mantle when her father died. After that Labor Day cookout, Miriam and I became playmates, and I'd actually studied a bit alongside her from time to time. I'd found it fascinating. In fact, when we were teenagers, we'd seriously discussed talking with the Curia—the one-hundred-person council that supervised the wardeins— about making an exception, letting me take over as wardein instead of Miriam, allowing her to become an English teacher like she'd always wanted.

But the Curia said no, the wardeins *had* to be a hereditary line, and ultimately, *my* parents' desires trumped everything anyhow, and I was soon off to Harvard as a premed student.

It was during my first semester that some jackass animated a golem, which went on a rampage, killing, among others, Rachel and Mordechai Goldblume.

Yeah.

I was a complete mess after that. Aunt Esther hired a Courser named Hugues Baptiste to stop the golem. Hugues was short, stocky, always smiling, and absolutely merciless in a fight. Took him four days to track down the golem and destroy it.

All my life, I'd been told by my parents I was going to be a doctor. Now they were dead, and the last thing in the world I wanted to do was hop on Amtrak back up to Cambridge. No, I wanted to do what Hugues did. I didn't want anyone else to have to face living without their parents because nobody could stop the things that went bump in the night.

I practically begged Hugues to take me on as an apprentice. It turned out that all Coursers were required to train at least one apprentice, and Hugues had been avoiding that particular duty for years. (In fact, I was gonna need to start thinking about taking on one of my own soon.) Miriam had told me that her father was gonna have to sanction him if he didn't get up off his ass and do it, and I thought I'd be the perfect guy. I already *knew* about spells and magick and dimensional portals and all that other garbage. Who better?

After I hounded Hugues for the better part of a week, he finally made me a deal. In his thick Haitian accent, he said, "Look, child, your parents, they wanted you to go to medical school, okay?"

"Well, yeah," I replied reluctantly.

"They be payin' for it and they want you to be a doctor, okay? So here's what we'll be doin'. You return to school, achieve your MD, become an actual doctor person, and then we shall speak about my training you. That's what is best, okay?"

I didn't like it. I was eighteen, my parents had just died, and I wanted what *I* wanted, not what was best.

But I didn't have a choice—especially once I found out that the notion for that particular deal came, not from Hugues, but from Aunt Esther. Nobody busybodies quite like a Jewish aunt, except maybe a rabbi, and Esther's both. She knew my parents as well as anyone, and she also knew that if I hadn't gotten my MD, I'd have regretted it.

Of course, it was a lot easier for my thirty-year-old self to understand that now than it was for my grieving younger self twelve years ago.

But it all worked out in the end. I did the full premed-to-med-school program at Harvard, graduated near the top of my class, got my shiny degree, and put two letters after my name forevermore. *Then* Hugues started training me.

Within a year, Mike Zerelli presented me with my Courser's license, and I had found my calling.

I also sold my parents' co-op and bought the townhouse. I'd inherited enough so that I could manage until the Courser business picked up.

Being friends with Miriam and Mike helped. Honestly, I wouldn't have survived any of what had happened without Miriam there. She was my rock.

Which was handy for her, because it meant I was there to return the favor after the accident.

After showering, which made my shoulder feel almost workable again, I dried off, slid on the comfy flannel bathrobe that my aunt and uncle gave me for my last birthday, and dug into my denim jacket's pocket for my cell phone.

The battery was, of course, dead. Knew I forgot to do something last night.

After I plugged it into the charger, it activated and had three status updates: a text message from Velez and a missed call and a voicemail, both from van Owen. The latter was actually a relief—meant I didn't have to actually *talk* to the persnickety old bastard.

Velez's text message didn't bode well for what would be in the voicemail, as it read: *"The fuck, yo? van Owen just bitched me out. I don't need that shit from a paying client."*

With a due sense of anticipation and dread, I played van Owen's voicemail.

"Gold, it's van Owen. Got your message. Glad you managed to retrieve the unicorn—that would've been a damned mess. Wish you hadn't used Velez to put it back—apparently, he rubbed Rodzinski the wrong way. So did you, actually, but that's hardly surprising. I'm dealing with Rodzinski, but he's got more problems. Apparently, *another* animal got out of *another* piece of art. This time it was a crane in a painting in the Asian galleries in the Met. This one's not as much of an issue—the crane comes and goes as he pleases, apparently, but he *usually* just comes out when the museum's closed. This time, however, he wandered out unexpectedly during the middle of a Saturday morning, when there were half a dozen witnesses. I'll have a Courser look into it—but not you. Rodzinski didn't like you—advised me to take away your license, in fact—and wanted someone else. Again, hardly a surprise. I'd rather a *professional* handled this."

I stared at the phone with a look of disgust on my face. "He hired *me*, you *schmuck!*" Then I sighed and restrained myself from throwing the phone across the room. The thing was still plugged in, anyhow, so that would've been difficult. Van Owen had never thought highly of Hugues, and since Hugues trained me, that meant I had to suck, too. And it looked like he took time out of his busy schedule to share Rodzinski's complaints about him with Velez. Which was just uncalled for, if you asked me. In the same situation, Miriam would've defended whoever the Courser she hired had subcontracted, and certainly wouldn't have turned around and bitched at the subcontractor in question. She'd probably give me crap about it afterward, but that's as far as it'd go.

I was grumpy, and also starving, so I called the deli around the corner and made a delivery order of corned beef on rye (hey, I'm perfectly happy to live the cliché when it's corned beef), then poured myself a glass of tap water and sat down at my computer. I downloaded my email, which included a notification that Miriam had electronically sent me my fee for babysitting the werewolves. That reminded me that I'd promised her I'd get the word out about the possibility of a new vampire in town, so I popped onto the private, encrypted bulletin board that the Coursers used to keep in touch. I started a new topic saying that there *might* have been a new vampire in the Bronx and gave what I knew about Warren's death.

I ended with: *"Screams vampire, though the fact that it's an immortal makes me wonder if there's more."*

Within a minute, I got three chat requests. One was from Charlie Kalani, which I ignored on general principle. Charlie worked Hawai'i, and he seemed to spend *all* his time online chatting with anyone who was dumb enough to accept his chat request rather than, y'know, hunting things. Tonight, I was not that dumb. The second was from Nishanda Castro, a Courser out of Los Angeles, who was wondering if I had a line on silver-tipped crossbow bolts. I quickly told her that my supplier didn't ship across the country but put her in touch with a friend in San Francisco who might've been able to help.

The third I accepted for more than the two seconds it took to answer Nishanda's question: it was from Hugues.

We caught each other up on what we'd been doing. I told him about the unicorn and the werewolves and Warren.

Hugues typed back at me. I should mention that Hugues always capitalized to symbolize italics, and he couldn't spell worth a damn. Also he didn't believe in apostrophes or commas.

"*A couple hired me to track down a DJINN that got loose from the storage closet in the bsmt of there apt bldg. DONT ask me why they kept it in their bldgs bsmt.*"

That got my attention. "Got loose? Was it a binding spell?"

"*I think so ya. Why?*"

I told him about the unicorn and that crane that van Owen mentioned. "You should contact van Owen and Miriam and let them know. There may be some kind of weird thingie that's causing spells to unbind."

"*Wierd thingie huh? Very desscriptive.*"

"At least I spelled 'weird' right." I laughed as I typed.

"*O that reminds me I have a job for you if you want it.*"

That surprised me. Hugues very rarely passed on work—and when he did, he rarely passed it on to me. "What is it?"

"*Family in Edenwald discovered a neighbor doing a ritual to trap one of the loa in Seton Falls Park tomorrow at noon. Its the vernal equinox.*"

I started to type a question about why it had to wait until tomorrow—trying to capture any of the loa was serious business—when more text showed up: *They dont know where the spell components are so they have to be caught in the act.*"

"Why can't you do it?"

"*Jesus shit child were you dropped on your head as a baby?*" Hugues always asked me that question for some reason. "*Tomorrow is Tonis graduation!*"

I had totally forgotten that Hugues's daughter Antoinette was graduating from New York University this weekend. "Mazel tov!" I typed.

"*Thats what you said when I told you the FIRST 40 times.*"

"Yeah, yeah. Email me the details on the job, okay?"

Hugues said he would, we exchanged a few more pleasantries, and then he signed off, right when the doorbell rang with my sandwich.

As usual, the deli gave me a sandwich big enough to feed a family of five. I put half in the fridge and put the other half on a plate. I read the rest of my emails while wolfing it down. I also checked around various social media sites. While doing so, I got a notification that Katie Gonzalez was doing a live video.

Curious, I clicked on it, and Katie's face smiled out at me, standing on a sidewalk in front of a Japanese restaurant. *"Hi, everyone! So I'm finally doing it. I know I've been saying I'd eat sushi for months, but today's the day I do it. I saw something horrible early this morning, and it made me realize that I need to start living, not just existing. And that means getting over my fear of raw fish and just having it already! Wish me luck!"*

As I chewed my corned beef, I put a few things together. Based on how Anna Maria had acted, Katie had been thinking of asking me out for a while. Based on this video, seeing Warham Mather's dead body emboldened her enough to eat sushi for the first time. It probably was why she asked me out, too.

I thought about maybe not waiting for her to call me and instead going ahead and calling her—but not now. She was obviously in the middle of her big sushi experiment, and I didn't want to interrupt it.

By the time I finished the sandwich and tossed the plate into the sink, Hugues's email had finally shown up.

The client was a Haitian couple who lived on De Reimer Avenue near the park in question. Their neighbor was gloating about how she was going to subsume one of the loa—the spirits of the Vodou religion still practiced by many Haitians—to her will. Apparently, this same woman had served as a healer in the neighborhood, which made me wonder how popular I'd be if I took her away.

I called the number for the client and got a deep male voice with a thick *patois*.

"'Allo?"

"Hello, my name is Bram Gold, I'm a Courser. I was told to call this number by Hugues Baptiste. Is this Trevor Alty?"

"Yes, this is he. Mr. Baptiste told us he would be unable to accept our commission."

"It's for a personal engagement he couldn't get out of. However, Mr. Baptiste was the man who trained me, so I know everything he knows." That was a lie—Hugues was a very reluctant trainer, and I honestly think that if I hadn't already had plenty of grounding in magick from growing up alongside Miriam, I would've become the world's worst Courser under his tutelage.

Some would argue I had anyhow, of course…

"You need to get to the Seton Falls Park before noon tomorrow please, Mr. Gold. Madame Vérité will be performing the ritual at precisely noon on the equinox at the falls in the park."

"Please tell me that Madame Vérité isn't her real name."

"No. I looked her up on the Internet, and she is not even Haitian — she is Dominican!" Alty's outrage was palpable. "She is called Bonita Soriano. My wife and I, we have tried to sign a petition to get her away, but no matter how many signatures we obtain, she will not go."

Okay, so maybe the neighborhood wouldn't be so peeved. Either way, though, binding gods and spirits were near the top of the Curia's no-no list, so Miriam would come down hard on "Mrs. Truth."

Assuming I caught her.

"Mr. Alty, I have your email address — if you don't mind, I'll send you my standard contract."

That seemed to bring him up short. "Mr. Baptiste did not have a contract."

Yeah, and he and I had argued about that, y'know, a lot. "Be that as it may, I do. I've had some bad experiences, and I'm afraid I need to have the agreement in writing."

There was a very long pause before: "Very well. I do not know you, you do not know me, so we have a contract."

"I'll send it in within the next thirty minutes, all right?"

"Yes. Thank you, Mr. Gold."

"You're very welcome, Mr. Alty."

After I tailored my boilerplate contract to this job and converted the file to a PDF, I sent it off to Alty. Then I stared at the lower-right-hand corner of the screen, which told me that it was now almost six. It was too late to go to Ahondjon's to discuss the shortcomings of his talismans — he closed early on Saturdays — and I was at the computer anyhow, so I composed an email to Miriam detailing everything that happened with the werewolves and with Warren. I threw in what van Owen told me about the crane and Hugues said about the djinn.

By the time I hit SEND, I yawned for the fifth time in thirty seconds and I realized that, now that I'd caught up on Friday night's sleep, my body was crying out for tonight's sleep. I had at least three things on my agenda tomorrow — Ahondjon, calling Katie, and "Madame Vérité" — plus whatever else I had to do that I'd forgotten about, so more sleep was probably a good idea.

My throbbing ribs agreed with me very wholeheartedly.

So I gave Mittens a final scritch and crawled back into bed.

Just as my head hit the pillow, I remembered that I never got the truck out of the parking lot and back to the rental place. The latter was closed now, and was also closed on Sunday, but I made a mental note as I faded into the sandman's embrace to take care of it first thing Monday morning.

That also reminded me that I still had to pull together an invoice for Rodzinski. Somehow, I didn't think I would get away with billing him for the extra two days on the truck...

Chapter 5

LATE SUNDAY MORNING—SUE ME, I NEEDED TO RECOVER, AND THAT meant a lot of rest for my poor bruised ribs—I threw on my denim jacket and hopped into my beat-up old 2003 Toyota Corolla. Like I did every time I got into it, I imagined Dad turning over in his grave. He had a thing for high-performance cars—a Mercedes here, a Lexus there, plus an ongoing stream of sports cars. Me, I preferred a car that *worked*—beyond that, I could give a damn. I'd kept the Maxima they'd given me when I got into Harvard right up until graduation. Then, when I had come back home, I'd switched to the Corolla. More fuel-efficient, especially right after I'd gotten it, which was when gas had hit four bucks a gallon...

I was already on my third mug of coffee—the first when I got up, the second after my shower, the third in a travel mug with me in the car—when I drove over to Jerome Avenue. The 4 train ran elevated over Jerome from Bainbridge Avenue all the way down to 170th Street, and that subway meant there were tons of shops all up and down the street. The one I wanted was one of about a billion little shops that sold newspapers, magazines, candy, cigarettes, and lottery tickets, located on the corner of 193rd. Like a lot of them, it catered mostly to people coming on and off the 4 at the Kingsbridge Road station a block away, or going into or out of St. James Park across the street.

Well, okay, they also catered to another clientele, but we weren't interested in anything on or under the counter on the left as you came in the narrow shop. (That had bulletproof glass protecting the guy behind the counter, currently a Pakistani guy who nodded hi and waved me back—one of these days, I needed to get the guy's name.) We didn't want the magazines and papers that took up the entire right-hand-side wall, either. No, we went past those, and past the big rack of greeting cards that blocked the view of the back wall—including the door that led to the steep metal staircase that went down to the basement.

Downstairs was Ahondjon's magick shop. The man himself wasn't in—his nephew Medawe was, and he was talking on the cordless phone.

He waved at me as I came down the metal stairs. The place was dank, lit only by crummy fluorescent lights, since there weren't any windows.

"Nah, he ain't here," Medawe was saying. Unlike his uncle, he was born in the Bronx, so he didn't have Ahondjon's thick West African accent. "It's Sunday, he's in church... Nah, I ain't telling you what church... What, you telling me you found Jesus now? Bullshit. Just gimme the message, I'll let him know when he gets back... I don't know when, I ain't found no Jesus, neither. 'Sides, you know how he likes talking to folks. Could be hours... Yeah, well, fuck you too."

Shaking his head, Medawe pressed the END button on the phone.

"Another satisfied customer?"

Medawe snorted. "Yeah, somethin' like that. What'cha need, Gold?"

"I need to talk to Ahondjon. He really in church?"

"Hell, no. Only time his ass goes into a church is to deliver their holy water."

I blinked. "Wait, churches buy holy water from *him*?"

"They do if they want the shit that *works*."

"Well, I hope his holy water smells better than his talisman to stop a unicorn."

Medawe frowned. "What, it didn't work?"

I smiled. "It worked fine." Then I remembered how Siri described it. "When I activated it, it smelled like a moose fucking a dead octopus."

"Yeah, well, you want shit that *works*, it's gonna stink."

I thought about reminding Medawe about what Velez had said, then decided it wasn't worth it. Besides, Medawe was just the hired help—Ahondjon was the one who put the talismans together, so if I was gonna get them to not stink up the place, I'd need to talk to him.

"Still," I finally said, "I've had some complaints. The first being from my hooter." I pointed to my oversized schnozz.

Medawe chuckled. "Look, I'll pass it on, but you know my uncle."

"I do indeed." I also noticed that Medawe hadn't actually answered my question about when Ahondjon would be back, which led me to think he either didn't know or couldn't tell me.

Whatever, I had a binding spell to stop. "Hey, I wanna double check, what would the components be if you wanted to cast a binding spell on a loa?"

That got me another snort from Medawe. "A thing'a lipstick so you can kiss your ass goodbye. Who'd be stupid enough to do that?"

"Woman over in Seton Falls Park, apparently."

Shaking his head, Medawe said, "Well, there's lotsa binding spells, but if you want to bind a loa, you're gonna need an Obsidian candle, thick rope, a red ribbon, and sandalwood."

I winced. Except for the candle, that was stuff you could get over the counter anyplace. Hell, you could probably get all that at Target. "Does it have to be an Obsidian candle, or can any black candle do it?"

"Depends."

"On what?"

"If you want the binding to *work* or not."

Ask a stupid question... "Yeah, okay, thanks, Medawe. And tell your uncle—"

"Moose fuckin' a dead octopus, you got it."

I grinned. "Thanks."

I hopped back upstairs and went out through the newsstand, sliding past a stooped-over Latina woman who was buying one of every possible kind of lottery ticket, and walked out into the briskness. It was as chilly today as it had been Friday night in the dog run, and as I stepped out onto the Jerome Avenue sidewalk, a cold wind sliced through the air, and through the painkillers that were doing a mediocre job of keeping my ribs from throbbing.

At least now I knew for sure what components I needed to look for. It wouldn't be enough to just stop Madame Vérité, I needed to catch her in possession of the spell components. The Obsidian candle was the key, since those could only be used in magickal rituals—combine them with the ribbon, rope, and sandalwood, and I'd have a case for Miriam to sanction her.

If not, she'd just try again on the summer solstice...

My car was blocked in by someone who had double-parked. I sighed. It was Sunday, the parking meters on Jerome weren't active today, why did people have to double-park? I saw three spots just down past 193rd, and they just *had* to double-park by me?

I sighed again and got into the Corolla, hoping the driver would rematerialize soon. It was already 11:30 and I had to get over to Seton Falls Park before Mrs. Truth did her mojo.

To distract myself from the tedium, I grabbed my smartphone and called Katie.

After five rings, I got voicemail: "Hi, it's Katie! Do the thing after the beep!"

"Hey, Katie, it's Bram. Congrats on braving the mighty sushi—I saw the video. I also want to apologize for subjecting you to the dead body that prompted it, even though it did lead to sushi, which is, in my experience, yummy." Shaking my head, I tried to rein in the babble. "Anyhow, wanted to talk to you about that coffee. Call me back when you get a chance."

After I ended the message with Katie and spent the better part of a minute wondering how stupid I sounded on that message, someone ran out of the Chinese food place with a big shopping bag in his hand. He headed for the car that had blocked me in, gave me a little apologetic wave, and drove off.

For the third time, I sighed, wishing I could just afford a car service. Miriam had been making noises about getting me an account with one. At least then I wouldn't have to worry about parking. That was always the biggest problem; parking somewhere free or being able to pay for it. Today was Sunday, so that wasn't an issue, and at least now they were all Muni Meters that took plastic, so I didn't have to stock up on quarters or find a side street to park on.

I had twenty minutes to make a fifteen-minute drive. I went up Jerome, past the end of the 4 train—only occasionally stuck behind a slow-moving or stopped bus that I couldn't get around because of the elevated train—to 233rd Street, then turned right. There was an accident on the road that was starting to back things up, so I turned down a side street and went down 236th.

Which would've been fine, except the one-way street was blocked by a garbage truck that was stopping every ten feet.

By the time I got past the garbage truck, the accident had cleared. I'd have been better off staying on 233rd. I turned back onto that road, zoomed over to Seton Falls Park—possibly running a red light or two—

and then finally pulling up to a spot right by the High Rock Playground entrance. Since the falls were near that entrance, that was handy.

Less handy was that it was already a couple minutes past noon. I ran over to the fence to look down at the falls.

Calling it "falls" was giving it a helluva lot of credit. Basically, it was a downhill creek, and if it hadn't rained recently, there wasn't even that much by way of water. It ran between two stone walls, and there was a rock that acted as a bridge. Not that you needed it, the "falls" were wide enough to step across, but the bridge was there anyhow. There were trees and rock formations all around it.

A woman sat on that rock mini-bridge cross-legged, a black candle in front of her. That just had to be Madame Vérité. I couldn't see anything else, because there were half a dozen people surrounding her. I wasn't even sure that was a real Obsidian candle. I kinda hoped it wasn't, because then nothing would work, and she'd be exposed as a fraud, and I wouldn't have to do anything.

I went in at the playground entrance, only to be met by two dark-skinned people. "You are Mr. Gold?" the man asked. He sounded like the voice on the phone.

"And you must be Mr. Alty. Sorry I'm late, but the traffic on 233rd was horrible."

"She is *starting* the ritual!"

"Good," I said, trying to put a good spin on it. "Means I can catch her in the act." I just hoped I could stop her before she bound a loa. Last thing we needed were some pissed-off Vodou gods floating around.

I ran down the pathway that led to the falls. The people standing around Mrs. Truth were transfixed by what she was doing. Now that I was close enough to see and smell, I knew from the spicy undertone of the flame that that was definitely an Obsidian candle, and I could also smell the sandalwood.

Madame Vérité was chanting something in Latin, which surprised me—I figured a Vodou ritual would be in an African language, not a European one. Or if it was a European one, I'd have figured French, not Latin. But whatever.

As I got close, I heard the phrase *ultimam ligabis* repeated three or four times. My Latin wasn't so much rusty as oxidized—hell, aside from the Torah portion I read at my bar mitzvah, my Hebrew wasn't much better—but I knew how this particular binding spell went from when I was learning stuff with Miriam when I was a kid. That phrase meant "final binding," and it was a refrain that ended the spell.

Panicking I ran toward the rock and said, "All right, that's enough, this has to stop!"

A few people turned to look at me with confusion—a funny-looking Jew barreling into their ritual was not on the agenda—but most ignored me.

The candle flickered as she picked up the rope. The red ribbon was tied in the middle, and she held the part with the ribbon over the candle.

The flame burned the ribbon, and in that moment, I knew we were screwed.

Bracing myself as the cold spring breeze mutated into a big wind, I wondered if I had any weapons in the car that would do any good against a god.

Just as I realized the answer was, "Hell, no," the wind got worse and cumulous clouds appeared overhead. Gasps and cries of amazement came from the crowd.

And then the clouds went away and the candle flickered and went out.

Madame Vérité opened her eyes, and she looked very confused. So did everyone else.

Probably I did, too. I only caught the tail end of it, but that *was* a binding spell she was saying, and based on what Medawe told me, she had the right ingredients, and it was noon on the equinox.

But no loa was bound. And neither was anything else; the spell just kinda fizzled.

She stared right at me. "What have you done, outsider?" she asked in an exaggerated Haitian accent that half the time sounded more like a fake Scottish accent. "Why have you ruined my ritual?" She said "oot-sider" and emphasized the third syllable of "ritual."

I hadn't done a damn thing, of course, but she didn't need to know that. I reached into my back pocket and pulled out a small booklet. To the untrained eye, it probably looked like a set of temporary tattoos bound into a small vinyl case. But each of these stickers had a restriction sigil on it that would prevent anyone it was applied to from using any magick or magickal item. Only a wardein or a member of the Curia could remove the restriction.

To my annoyance, I only had one left. Luckily, I only needed one.

As I removed the final sticker from the booklet, I said, "My name is Bram Gold. I'm a Courser, and what you're doing here isn't approved by the Wardein of the Bronx. I'm afraid I'm going to have to confiscate the spell components and report this to Wardein Zerelli. You'll be hearing from her *real* soon now."

"You're not taking my t'ings!"

I shrugged. "You're welcome to try and stop me." I didn't really do menacing very well, but I've found that matter of fact-sounding threats were way more effective than ones that tried to sound mean and nasty.

And I really hoped that was true today, because my bruised ribs did *not* want a fight.

Luckily, these were all just ordinary folks who didn't want any trouble. True, they were greedy pischers who wanted a god to do their bidding, but not enough to engage in fisticuffs over it. So they didn't do a thing as I walked right up to the mini-bridge and slapped the sticker on Mrs. Truth's arm.

The sigil disappeared instantly as if it was never there.

"What was that?" she yelled as she shrunk away from me and batted at her arm where I'd placed the restriction.

"Just a little something to keep you away from magick until the wardein can talk to you."

"You got no right to do this!" She bent over to pick up her Obsidian candle. "These are *mine*, and you can't—"

Suddenly, she stumbled backward. "What the hell—?" I noticed that she lost the fake Haitian accent for those three words. Getting her faux speech pattern back under control, she asked, "Why can I not touch my t'ings?"

"Like I said, the restriction I just put on you keeps you away from magick." I bent over and picked up the Obsidian candle, the sandalwood, and the rope (the ribbon was ashes) and cradled them in my arms. "Expect to hear from the wardein."

Turning my back on Madame Vérité and ignoring the nasty looks I was getting from her followers, I walked away from the falls and up the hill to the playground and the exit.

The Altys were waiting for me. Trevor had a big smile on his face. "Thank you, Mr. Gold!"

His wife, though, wasn't smiling. "What is to stop her from doing this again in six months?"

I was about to say the restriction would, but that only lasted for about a week. "The wardein. I'm going to be bringing this stuff to her, and she'll sanction Madame Vérité."

Ms. Alty looked dubious. "And what good will that do?"

Shuffling the items I had cradled in my left arm, I grabbed the candle with my right. "See this? It's an Obsidian candle. It's why the spell had any shot of working. Only place you can get one of these is at an officially licensed magick shop, and the microsecond she's sanctioned, no shop'll sell her squat. Can't do the ritual without it."

"What if she has more of them in her closet?"

I shook my head. "These things have a half-life—after a day or two, they disintegrate. That's the thing about magick. More powerful it is, the more unstable it is."

Trevor looked at his wife and said, "Stop pestering the man, Marguerite! He did his job and stopped that horrible woman."

"I suppose." She reached out a hand and said, "Thank you, Mr. Gold."

I shuffled the items in my arms again and returned the handshake, then also shook Trevor's hand. "You're both welcome. I'll email you the invoice."

With that, I went to the car, put the stuff in the trunk, got into the driver's seat, and immediately called Miriam.

"Hello, Bram."

"Hey, Miriam, I've got good news and bad news. Well, okay, it's not really *good* news, just news: you gotta sanction somebody." I gave the quickie version of what just happened with Madame Vérité, promising to email her the full details.

I heard her fingers clacking on a keyboard. "I'll get that sanction out now, in case she beelines for a shop. Although, with the restriction on her, she won't be able to touch anything in a shop, but still, best to let the managers know. I'm just glad you stopped her before she cast the spell."

"Well, see, that's the bad news, I didn't."

"Oh, fuck."

"No, no," I said quickly, "it's okay, the spell didn't work."

"So she sucks at spellcasting, how's that bad news?"

I shook my head, even though she couldn't see that over the phone. "She doesn't suck at it. Based on what I saw and heard when I got there past the last minute, she nailed the spell just fine, and she had an Obsidian candle, rope, a ribbon that she burned, and sandalwood."

"Which spell did she use, Hembadoon's?"

"No, actually, it sounded like Silverio's, believe it or not."

Miriam sounded as surprised as I felt when I heard Mrs. Truth rocking the Latin. "Yowza. And it didn't work?"

"Yeah, and we're starting to get a pattern here. We got the unicorn tapestry, we got that crane down at the Met, Hugues mentioned a djinn that got loose yesterday, and now we got this. That's three binding spells coming unraveled and one not working at all. It's freaking me out a little bit."

"I'm a lot more freaked out by your rogue vampire. But I'll see if anyone else is reporting binding spells gone bad."

"Thanks, Miriam."

"Thank you for not calling me 'Mimi' once." I could hear her grinning over the phone.

"Hey, least I could do after almost fucking up the werewolves. When can I bring by the spell components?"

"Bring 'em by tonight before your debauchery."

I chuckled. Sunday nights, a bunch of Coursers all gathered at a bar in Woodlawn. I didn't make it every week, but I figured Hugues was gonna be there toasting his daughter's graduation tonight, and I didn't want to miss that. "Sounds like a plan. Later."

After ending the call, I started the car, threw it into gear, made a U-turn on 233rd, and wove my way around double-parked cars in the right lane and cars waiting to make a turn from the left lane on that major thoroughfare before hitting the Major Deegan Expressway and taking it to my place in Riverdale.

On the way, the phone rang, but I couldn't really pay attention to it until I stopped.

Once I pulled into the driveway in front of the garage, I put it in park and grabbed the phone. (I didn't park the car in the garage, as that was valuable storage space.) There was a missed call and a voicemail, both from Katie.

I played the voicemail. "Hey Bram! I am so glad you called. I was kind of chickening out, so I'm really glad you took the step, because I kinda got nervous. Sorry, sometimes the brain weasels take over, you know? Anyhow, I'm actually on my way to that coffee shop right now, so if you're free, you could join me. Or not, I totally understand if you're not free. Call or text and let me know! Thanks!"

Smiling, I quickly composed a text: *"Just finished a job. Meet you there in ten."*

I opened the garage, which revealed several stacks of plastic totes in the back, a dozen plastic shelving units on the right-hand side and in the middle, and a big pile of empty boxes on the left-hand side. I put the Obsidian candle, rope, and sandalwood in one of the empty boxes piled on the side, then put the box on a shelf.

As I did so, the phone beeped with a text from Katie: *"Great! See you there!"* Plus a smiley face and a heart and a coffee cup.

I closed the garage door and headed over to Riverdale Avenue, which was one of the main drags with commercial stuff on it, ranging from restaurants to drugstores to doctors' offices to banks. A new café had opened up on the corner of Riverdale and 236th Street, and I walked inside to see Katie already sitting with both a latte and a tablet in front of her.

She looked up at me as I entered, smiled brightly, and rose. "Hi, Bram! Thanks so much for coming!"

"Thanks for inviting me," I said, smiling right back. "Nice to get together when it isn't business."

That got her to frown for a second. "I guess it is business for you, isn't it?"

"Very literally. I'm gonna get some coffee."

"Okay." She smiled again and sat back down with her tablet.

I ordered a regular coffee, paid, and brought it straight to the table.

Katie had been watching me, and when I sat down across from her she shook her head. "Wow. I don't think I've ever seen that before."

I blinked. "Seen what?"

"Someone just get a black coffee in a café without putting anything in it. No latte, no macchiato, no espresso, just a straight up black coffee with no dairy, no sweetener. That's so — so — "

"Boring?"

She chuckled. "I was gonna say old-fashioned."

"Thank you. In both my professions, it's best to keep the caffeine no-frills. Just pour into the mug and then pour down your throat, no fuss, no muss."

"Both professions?" She squinted in confusion. "You're not just a Courser?"

That threw me for a loop. I thought everyone knew that I was a doctor. "Nope, I'm also an MD I work two days a week at Montefiore's ER."

"Wow. I had no idea."

"It pays a few extra bills, and keeps my shingle polished, as it were. Besides, it's handy to help give first aid to other Coursers under the table, y'know?"

"Makes sense." She sipped her latte. "Thank you so much for coming. I've actually been thinking about asking you out for a while now. Miriam and Anna Maria kept telling me to just ask. I was hoping you might ask me, but they told me that was a lost cause."

I sighed. "Yeah, well, I'm not good at flirting. Or being flirted at, apparently. There was this woman in med school, Sara Mankiewicz, who apparently had the hots for me the whole time, and I completely missed it."

"When did you find out?"

"At her wedding."

Katie almost snarfed her latte. "Oh my God, really?"

"Yeah. She just took her vows with some putz from her neighborhood, and she was dancing with all her med school friends, and when she got to me, she told me right there on the dance floor that if I'd just asked her out, I'd probably be the one marrying her instead of the putz."

With a small smirk, Katie asked, "Why didn't she ask you out?"

I pointed at her. "The exact question I asked!" I laughed. "Did she not get the memo that it's the twenty-first century? I mean, you did."

"I did, yes. And boy, was it not easy."

I sipped my coffee. "Because I'm so oblivious?"

"Well, no, because of my anxiety. Honestly, for a long time, I only left the house on the nights of the full moon."

"Oh." I couldn't think of anything intelligent to say to that.

"I'm lucky—I inherited the house I live in from my parents, and it's all paid off. I make enough money from freelance work I can do from home to pay the taxes on the house and for food and stuff."

Wow. I had no idea of any of this. Luckily, I had the presence of mind not to say that out loud. I felt like enough of a schmuck as it was. "What do you do?"

"Transcriptions, translations, editing, some production and design work. For a long time, I'd go weeks without ever going outside and only opening the door for deliveries of groceries and mail and things—at least until full moon time. Miriam was the one who convinced me to start seeing a therapist. It's because of her — the therapist, not Miriam — that I've been doing the fish pictures and the live videos and things. It helps me engage with other people, even if it's only online. I've even met a few people that way."

"That's great." I smiled. "I gotta admit, there are days when those fish pics make a crappy day better."

"Aw, thank you, Bram, that's sweet."

"If you don't mind me going all doctor on you, are you on any meds for the anxiety?"

"I have Xanax, but I only take it when things get really bad."

I nodded. "Good. That means it's not as bad as it could be, if you don't have to take something every day. And Xanax generally works, as long as you don't drink any alcohol."

She shook her head. "I never do anyhow. I don't like the taste of alcohol, and I've always been able to taste it in anything I drink. Back in college, before the anxiety got so awful, I was always the designated driver. Now I can't even drive — gave up my license about a year after my parents were killed."

"Killed?" Recalling that lycanthropy was sometimes inherited, I added, "Please tell me it wasn't a Courser."

"No, but they were killed on the night of a full moon. They used to go out into the backwoods of Van Cortlandt Park or Pelham Bay Park and run around all night. One night, someone found them and shot them."

"Damn, I'm sorry."

"Thanks. I've been kind of a mess ever since." She finished off her latte, then said, "Enough about me, tell me some more about you. Why'd you become a doctor? And how'd you become a Courser?"

"The two are kinda related, actually." And then I told her all about growing up the child of two doctors and the golem and my aunt and Hugues.

By the time I was done, I had finished my coffee. "Want another?" I asked her.

Katie hesitated. "I want to, but — I need to get back home. This is way too much people-ing. First the sushi restaurant yesterday, now this — I need to get back home where it's quiet and safe."

I held up both hands. "I totally get that. You okay to get home on your own?"

"Yeah, it's a short walk, and I can get my steps in." She grinned. "That's another thing my therapist suggested, going for walks. I'm using one of those apps that counts steps."

"Nice. Walking's good for you. I should probably do it more myself."

We both got up and someone immediately grabbed our table. We tossed our cups into the garbage, she put her tablet in her purse, and we both went outside.

For a second, we just stood there staring at each other.

Finally, I opened my arms. "Hug okay?"

She let out a happy-sounding sigh. "Absolutely."

We hugged, and I said, "Let's do this again sometime."

"I'd like that. Maybe next week?"

"Sounds good."

She headed down Riverdale Avenue and I headed up 236th Street and I was home in about five minutes, a spring in my step.

Should've realized all the times she chatted with me was her flirting. Or at least expressing interest. Well, maybe I could make up for it. Not sure how much time for dating someone I'd have in this life—it was one of many reasons why my social life has been kind of a wasteland—but at least Katie understood what I did for a living. And her anxiety meant she probably wouldn't want to be going out much.

When I got home, Rebekah was on her way out the door. She was, unsurprisingly, holding another box full of flyers. To my equal lack of surprise, neither her socks nor her shoes matched.

"Oh, hey, Bram! Can you take a few of these and put them up? Elvin Mathis is speaking at Manhattan College on Friday."

I vaguely recalled seeing a news item about him on one of the televisions in the waiting room at the hospital when I was working a shift. "That's the guy angling for the reservations to declare themselves independent from the Union, right?"

"I think he's got great things to say. I really support his cause."

"Well, I think you're both nuts—but it's also good that he's talking about this stuff. He pushes for independence; it might at least lead to smaller improvements."

My cousin stared at me over her plastic-framed glasses like I was nuts. "It's not about small improvements, Bram, it's about changing things for the better."

"All the better changes in the world happened in small doses. The big changes usually involve body counts."

"You're wrong, it's the big changes that matter." She shook her head. "Look, I gotta go put these up in that new café over on Riverdale. Take some?"

I nodded and held my hand out, smiling to make sure there were no hard feelings. It wasn't the first time we'd argued about this stuff, anyhow. She was young, she'd figure it out eventually. "Sure. And hey, the coffee there's pretty good, you should try some." I instantly regretted saying that, as the last thing my cousin needed was a stimulant.

As she handed me about a dozen flyers out of the box, she said, "Oh, did you hear? Ben Palmer died!"

I blinked. "Really?"

"Yeah. I only found out because he was the one who was going to put up Elvin while he's in town. He convinced the college to let him lecture."

That didn't surprise me. Palmer was a rich guy from one of the older families in Riverdale. The Palmers had owned the same mansion in north Riverdale since the Bronx was mostly Jonas Bronck's big farm, and Ben used his money for serious activism. I knew that Rebekah had gotten to know him pretty well, since their social-justice paths crossed a lot.

"I'm sorry about that. You okay?"

"Yeah. I mean, no, not really, but that's why I want to push this lecture, in his memory, y'know?"

"All right. I'll drop these off next chance I get," I said, holding up the handful of flyers.

"Thanks. Talk to you later."

She started up the street in her mismatched footwear, her uncombed hair flying around in the breeze.

Loved that kid.

As I walked toward the front door, my phone started playing "Daytripper."

"What's up, Miriam?"

There was silence for a second. "You still aren't calling me Mimi."

"Consider it my present for convincing Katie to ask me out to coffee. We just got back from that new place over on Riverdale."

"That's great! I'm really glad she finally asked you, and I'm *really* glad you accepted. Mostly because if you didn't, I'd have to kill you, and I'm sorta kinda fond of you."

"Sorta kinda, huh?"

"Well, you keep calling me Mimi—sometimes. Anyhow, I'm actually calling on business. Ben Palmer died."

"Uh, yeah, I just heard about that from Rebekah. News travels fast."

"This is bigger news than you think. Palmer was an immortal."

I blinked. "What?"

"Just like Warren, he goes back to the colonial Bronx. He built a free bridge across the Harlem River to compete with the King's Bridge, back in the day. The King's Bridge charged a toll, and he thought passage should be free."

"Doing noble causes back then, too, huh?"

"Something like that. Point is, that's two immortals from the colonial Bronx killed in a couple of days. I don't like this one bit. Can you check the crime scene? See if Lyd can let you in? I'll pay your usual fee."

"Uh, yeah, sure." I wasn't too keen on asking Toscano for another favor after Warren's body, but once I told her it was spook shit, she'd probably be okay with it. "I'll let you know what I find."

I ended the call and shuddered. I was starting to come around to Miriam's notion that the crazy vamp killing immortals was a much bigger problem than messed up binding spells.

Chapter 6

THE GOOD NEWS WAS THAT TOSCANO WAS THE PRIMARY DETECTIVE ON the case, which made it easier to go up to the Palmer mansion and ask her to look around. She gave me the hairy eyeball and groused when I told her it was more spook shit, but she told me to put on gloves and booties and let me look around the house so long as I didn't touch anything.

The bad news was that this didn't do me a lick of good. It was a much nicer death scene than Warren's, but pretty much the same thing: dead body with two puncture wounds on the carotid, very little blood, and no sign of a struggle. I didn't expect the latter with Warren—he was usually hammered, especially at night, so anybody could've just walked up to him and whacked him—but here, it probably meant that Palmer knew his killer.

And if Palmer was an immortal going back three hundred years or so, it would be perfectly reasonable for him to know a vampire.

I walked out, ignoring the dirty looks from uniforms and crime scene techs, not knowing any more than I did when I went in, except that it looked like a vamp got him, too.

After I was done, Toscano followed me out onto the street. This part of Riverdale was mostly winding, badly paved streets with no sidewalks and a number of really big houses. The house my parents owned up until my father's inability to maintain a garden became an issue was a few blocks from here.

"So what the fuck was that all about, Brammy?" Toscano lit a cigarette as she asked the question, figuring that being away from the crime scene was an opportunity to suck nicotine.

"You really wanna know?"

"Warren was a skell nobody gave a fuck about, really. Palmer's hot shit, and I'm gonna have people lookin' over my damn shoulder. So yeah, I really wanna know."

I sighed. "Look, Lyd, all I can tell you is that it may be a vampire."

"Seriously? Like that asshole I busted who tried to kill Mike?"

Snorting, I said, "Kinda." The asshole in question had a beef with Miriam's dad when he was the wardein. He broke into the house on Seward and tried to attack Miriam—this, of course, was in her pre-wheelchair days. She took him out without breaking a sweat, and Mike called Toscano. "If this really is a vampire, I promise, I'll let you know if I find it."

"You better." She took a drag on her cigarette. "I hate this shit."

"I don't much like it, either."

We babbled at each other for a few more minutes until she was done with her cigarette, then she went back inside to work on processing the scene some more, while I walked back over to the Henry Hudson Parkway service road to catch a bus back down to my part of Riverdale. Parking was never easy on these old streets—generally folks parked in their garages and driveways—and that problem would be metastasized by the cops and crime scene nerds, so I'd just taken the bus up here (after buying a new MetroCard at the deli around the corner, since the one I had didn't have even one fare left on it, much less two).

When I got to the bus shelter, a strikingly attractive African-American woman was sitting on the bench. Her skin was incredibly smooth, like mahogany, and she wore her hair in a purple snood. A matching purple shawl with a pattern of flames and streaks draped her shoulders, and her legs were crossed under a tan skirt, showing off her black boots.

Just as I pulled my smartphone out to check the MTA's app that told you where the buses were and how long you had to wait for the next one, the woman spoke in a beautiful, rich voice, with enough of a hint of an accent to show that English wasn't her first language, but not enough of one for me to place it. "Anne DeLancey will be the next victim."

I blinked. "Excuse me?"

She got to her feet and walked over to me, the boot heels clopping on the sidewalk. "Warham Mather and Benjamin Palmer have already been killed. The next target is likely to be Anne DeLancey."

Okay, this was starting to get weird, especially since she used Warham rather than Warren. "And you are—?"

"Someone who is grateful for the service you did for the loa earlier today."

"Oh, you live in Edenwald?"

She smiled, showing magnificent teeth. And seriously, that smile just lit up the whole street. She wasn't very tall, but she had presence oozing out of her pores. "No, but I have many there that I consider friends."

"And why would Anne DeLancey be targeted?"

"For the same reason why Misters Mather and Palmer were. She is an immortal, who was born Anne van Cortlandt in the late seventeenth century."

"How do you know about all this?"

The smile grew wider. "I know many things, Abraham Goldblume. Including that you prefer to be called Bram Gold."

"Depends on the circumstances. Look, I don't know who you are—"

"No, you do not. Nonetheless, you may trust that I speak the truth. As I said, you did the loa a great service today. Bonita Soriano has been an irritant for some time, but Wardein Zerelli's sanctioning of her should put an end to her meddling."

"That was the idea," I said neutrally. Obviously, this woman was plugged into my world. "Look, can you at least give me a hint as to—"

"Your bus is coming."

I turned around and saw that a Bx7 bus was on its way down the service road toward the bus stop.

"Yeah, okay, I—" I turned back only to see that she was gone.

I shook my head. Probably a spellcaster. I thought I knew all the ones in the Bronx, but maybe she was new.

Well, new to the area, anyhow. She obviously wasn't new to the game.

Sighing, I got onto the bus and headed back home. I hadn't gone upstairs before, heading straight to Palmer's house, so I took the time to scritch Mittens and refill his food and water. Then I sat down at the computer to send invoices to both Rodzinski and the Altys. I also caught up on other email, including a nice note from a reverend who hired me to stop a lamprey a while back, and one from Hugues reminding me that I'd better be at the Kingfisher's Tail tonight to toast his little girl. I also checked a few social media sites and noted that Katie had posted her daily picture of her fish tank. She'd even mentioned me in the caption, though not directly. *"A friend told me these pictures brighten his days sometimes,"* she wrote, *"and I hope it does the same today!"*

I also wrote up what little I learned at Palmer's place and emailed it to Miriam, along with an invoice for a token amount—it wasn't like it took that much time or I accomplished much, but if I didn't charge her, she'd give me a hard time about it—then followed it up with a phone call.

"What is it, Bram?"

"So I just sent you an email. Not much at Palmer's place—it's Warren all over again."

"Puncture wounds on the neck?"

"Yeah. Lyd'll probably tell me more once they have an official cause of death, but even though this is a press case, it'll be a couple days before the autopsy's done."

"What's your medical opinion?"

I snorted. "That he's dead. I'm not a pathologist, Mimi, I'm a GP, and Lyd wouldn't let me get close enough to do a proper exam of the body—which was fully clothed. All I can tell you is that there wasn't much blood pooled under the body, which indicates a vampire, since they subsist on the stuff."

"Fine, sorry, I had to ask. Hey, wait a sec, you had all night with Warren. What did you think of his body?"

"That it smelled like crap even before it was dead. I didn't want to get near him, and besides, I had bruised ribs and bending over hurt like hell. Sorry."

"No, no, it's fine, I just—" She let out an exasperated noise. "I don't get this, Bram. I have no idea why immortals are being targeted. I have no idea why a vampire is going on a rampage. It just doesn't make any sense."

"Probably a newbie vamp, thinks he needs to prove himself worthy of the name or some kind of bullshit like that."

"Then why go after these two?"

"Three, apparently."

"Three what?"

I sighed. "This is why I called—I didn't put this in the email, but I met this woman near Palmer's house. Claimed that Anne DeLancey, formerly Anne van Cortlandt, is next on the vampire hit parade."

"Who is she?"

"No clue, just said she was grateful for the service I did the loa by taking Madame Vérité's toys away."

"Well, Anne van Cortlandt is also immortal—though I didn't know about the name change."

I grinned. "Thought you were supposed to have files on all this stuff."

"Yeah, and you know how well Dad organized them."

"As I recall, the files are arranged in strict order of when he touched them last."

"Pretty much." Miriam let out an annoyed sigh. "I've automated everything I've come across, but Warren's death is the first time I've had to even deal with any of the immortals we have wandering around."

"How many are there?"

"At least a couple more here, plus others around the country. They're all that way by magickal means, but here's the thing—there's nothing about how the ones up here became immortal. Most of the others we know about were cursed or are tied to some kind of magickal object or event or something. There's a guy down in Florida who won't die until he falls asleep, so he just drinks coffee and soda all day and night. But I haven't the first clue how or why Warren or Palmer or van Cortlandt—or, I guess, DeLancey—became immortal in the first place, or what magick is involved."

"Well, given how far back they go…"

"Yeah. I mean, we all knew about Warren because he talked about it all the time to whoever dropped a coin in his cup and stood still for too long, but—" She sighed. "I'll keep digging into Dad's files, maybe I missed something. Thanks for checking out Palmer."

"No problem." I noticed that it was getting onto early evening. "I'm gonna grab a quick nap before I head to Woodlawn. Can I bring the loa-binding components by tomorrow?"

"Sure. And have fun tonight. Give Hugues my best." She chuckled. "I'd really love to be a fly on the wall for those things."

"It's not that exciting," I said. "Just a bunch of Coursers getting drunk. No different from any other group of co-workers getting drunk."

"I guess. I just miss pub-crawling with you."

"Ha! What you really miss is my singing."

"Actually, that is the one part of going pub-crawling with you that I do *not* miss. In fact, if I never ever hear you sing 'Wild Rover' ever again, it will be too soon."

Grinning, I said, "You realize this means I have to sing it for you next time I'm at the house, right?"

"I'm the wardein, Bram. I've got, like, hundreds of magickal items in the house. You even try it, and I will totally turn you into a newt."

"Meanie." I laughed, and so did she. "Remember when we got thrown out of the Slaughtered Lamb?"

"'We' didn't get thrown out of anywhere, boychik, you got thrown out for accusing the bartender of being a Medusa."

"He had weird hair," I said defensively.

"No, he had a big afro."

"It looked weirder after the tenth beer." I shook my head. "All right, I'm gonna go nap. Let me know if you find out anything about the immortal gang."

"And you let me know if your Courser buddies have any vampire gossip."

"You bet."

◄—THE BRONX—►

Around nine PM that night, after a refreshing nap and an even more refreshing shower, I called a cab company and had a car take me over to Woodlawn. No way I was going to drive, as I was guaranteed to be too impaired to operate a motor vehicle within an hour of my arrival. Less if Hugues was already there toasting his daughter. And mass transit would take too long, as it required two buses to get from Riverdale to Woodlawn, on a Sunday schedule no less.

As a general rule, neighborhoods in New York were always changing, and Woodlawn was no exception. A tiny wedge between the Bronx River Parkway, the Yonkers border, Van Cortlandt Park, and Woodlawn Cemetery, this neighborhood of narrow streets and small houses started out as an enclave for German and Italian immigrants in the early twentieth century, but by the 1970s or so became almost exclusively populated by Irish immigrants.

Up and down Katonah Avenue—the only street inside the neighborhood that was commercial—were dozens of pubs. A lot of them catered to émigrés from particular counties in Ireland.

One place, in between a bakery and a private house, was the Kingfisher's Tail. Six days out of the week, it was a County Wicklow haven, where folks who'd emigrated from that county came to hoist a few.

Sundays, though, the owner only opened the bar to Coursers. Brendan Sheehan's family came to the U.S. when he was ten years old; he became a Courser when he was twenty; and he retired when he was thirty-five after blowing out his knee chasing down a rabid werewolf. His parents owned the bar, and he'd run it with them after he retired, taking over when they died. For twenty-five years now, the Kingfisher's Tail was known as a Courser bar, at least on Sundays.

When Hugues first took me here after I turned twenty-one, I saw Sheehan standing behind the bar, his salt-and-pepper hair flopping over his face. He had said to me then, "Nobody came on Sundays. They'd all been out Saturday night and spent Sunday morning confessing their sins at church. Sunday night, they're still repenting, so I figured let's boost business and give my old lads a place to hang their scythes."

I had immediately turned to Hugues. "We get scythes?"

He had glowered at Sheehan. "What you gotta be puttin' ideas in the child's head for?"

Sheehan had just grinned and grabbed a bottle of rum with one meaty hand and poured it into a glass, followed quickly by using those huge paws of his to pull a light beer from the tap, and had put them in front of Hugues without his having to ask for it, which was the coolest thing ever to twenty-one-year-old me.

Of course, tonight when I walked in, it was *my* usual that Sheehan poured as soon as he saw me enter: an amber beer, though I seriously considered ordering a single malt in Warren's honor.

The Kingfisher was your basic hole-in-the-wall. Small sign over the blue door in lettering that was really hip when it was first painted in 1977, with a silly drawing of a bird that sorta kinda looked like a kingfisher next to it. Sheehan had touched up both the lettering and the artwork over the decades but refused to change it. "Then no one would be able to find the place," was his usual rejoinder on the subject.

Once you pushed open the blue door—which you sometimes needed to throw your shoulder into, as the damn thing kept sticking— you saw an old wooden bar-top taking up the right-hand side of the narrow space, with tiny round tables all around the floor arranged in no particular pattern or order, making it impossible to walk in a straight line anywhere in the room. Luckily, few people ever were capable of walking in a straight line when they were in here, so it all worked out.

The one and only change Sheehan had made to the place over the decades that wasn't straight up maintenance was replacing the stools at the bar and the cheap wooden chairs at the tables with wireframe chairs that gave you back support. Dunno about the regulars who were here from Monday to Saturday, but the guys who were constantly nursing nagging injuries like ribs bruised by crazed unicorns appreciated that little bit of ergonomic assistance.

When I entered, the first thing I noticed was that a bunch of the tables had been pushed together so Hugues could hold court. I figured he was carrying on about Antoinette's graduation.

The second thing I noticed was how warm it was. It had gotten about ten degrees colder outside, and I regretted not wearing something thicker than my denim jacket.

I approached the bar where Sheehan stood. His salt-and-pepper hair had gone completely white over the past nine years, and had also thinned considerably, but it still flopped over his face. He had my beer poured by the time I snaked my way through the tables to the bar.

Abby Cornwell was asking, "So did she look beautiful in her cap and gown?" Cornwell was one of three women in the bar. Amusingly, we had one blonde (who was tan), one brunette (who was mixed-race with coffee-colored skin), and one redhead (who was incredibly pale). Cornwell was the blonde. There were a dozen men—thirteen now that I came in, fourteen if you counted Sheehan—which was about the ratio in general of male to female Coursers, as it happened.

"Jesus, no," Hugues said, his flat face forming into a frown, "she looked like she was wearin' a damn tarpaulin, okay? They all did!"

Sal Antonelli held up a glass of red wine near his acne-scarred face, framed as it was by a hairdo that was just shy of a pompadour and sideburns down to his jawline. "How borin' were the speeches?"

"Completely." Hugues shuddered and sipped more of his rum. "The salutatorian talked in a damn monotone, and the valedictorian sounded like someone fed her helium before the speech, okay? I could not even say what the speeches were about."

I came over to join the group with my beer. "I'm gonna go out on a limb and say they were about the future and the importance of education."

"Why you say that?" Antonelli asked.

"They're all about that."

Hugues frowned. "When you get here, child?"

I sighed, having long since given up getting him to stop calling me that. "Just now. Obviously, I'm behind on drinking, since you're facing the door and didn't see me coming in."

"I was tellin' my story!"

"Hey, it's fine, it's not like you taught me to be aware of my surroundings or anything."

There weren't any chairs around the table, but Eddie Mohapatra got up from his. "Here, Bram, take mine."

"No, I can't—" I started, but he waved me off.

"It's fine, I need to get home to Indira and the baby. Little Martine is sick."

Hugues pointed at Eddie's diminutive form. "I am only forgiving this transgression because you have a daughter, okay?"

Eddie bowed his head. "Thank you. Congratulations again to Toni. I'll see the rest of you around."

Everyone wished Eddie good night, and he headed out. He had gotten out of his seat without pushing it back—you can do that when you're five four—but I had to pull it out to get my taller frame into it, which I did after shrugging out of my jacket and draping it over the back. Eddie had left his Coke unfinished. Guy's got a sick kid at home, and he still puts in an appearance for Hugues's celebration. Sweet guy.

Hugues went back to his pontificating. "Now the worst part of the whole thing, okay? That was the keynote. The man was some kind of descendant of the man who founded the university—"

"Albert Gallatin?" That was Dahlia Rhys-Markham, the brunette among the trio of women in the bar, and also the one we all wanted as our partner on trivia night. Seriously, she knew everything about everything. I made a mental note to ask her what she knew about immortals in the Bronx later.

Or maybe tomorrow. Later, we were unlikely to all be upright.

"How the hell should I know the man's name? I was falling asleep during the speech, okay? Started droolin' out my mouth onto my nice suit."

I held up a hand. "Wait a sec, you were wearing a *suit*?"

"Of course, I was wearin' a suit."

"You *own* a suit?"

"I do now." He grinned. "It was Toni's graduation, okay? You got an issue with that, child?"

Shaking my head, I said, "No, no issue at all, I'm just impressed that you spent more than ten bucks on an article of clothing. That must've been traumatic."

Hugues just snarled at me and said, "Someone shoot this child with a crossbow."

"Hey, none of that!" Sheehan cried out. "You know how hard it is to get blood outta the floor? You wanna kill Gold, do it outside."

"*Thanks*, Brendan, appreciate the support." I shot him a mock-annoyed glance.

Antonelli said, "Actually, Gold's right, you usually dress like shit."

"Shoot him, too!" Hugues yelled.

Everyone laughed, and Hugues talked about the graduation some more, and then I had another beer, and then Dahlia started talking about her son's high school graduation and how it was the first time she and her ex-husband spoke in ten years, and then I had another beer, and then Antonelli talked about his own high school graduation when a snake ate the principal, which lasted right up until I pointed out that that was the third-season finale of *Buffy the Vampire Slayer*, and then he admitted that he didn't actually graduate high school, so he told the story of why he dropped out instead, and then Dahlia left when I ordered another beer, which annoyed me, as I wanted to ask her about immortals, and then I had a bunch more beer. Also, beer.

At one point, not long after Hugues passed out and was snoring in his chair, the blue door got shoved open to reveal a barrel-chested Latino gentleman with a crew cut and a perpetual scowl: Bernie Iturralde. I tensed and flinched at the same time at his arrival. His blue trench coat was streaked with stains of various colors as it swooshed behind him like a second-rate cape. I figured he kept the blood and dirt stains from his work as a Courser on the coat to make himself look tough, but to me it just made him look like a grown-up who didn't know how to do his own laundry.

He went straight for the bar and everyone got a little quieter. He didn't bother to take his coat off and hang it up like everyone else had.

"Shit, this a fuckin' funeral, or what?"

Sheehan poured him his usual tequila. "No, just got quiet after Baptiste passed out."

"Good, means I don't gotta listen to him talk about his fuckin' daughter all night."

Cornwell and the other woman who'd come, a redhead whose name my beer-induced brain could no longer recall, both said they had to leave and headed out the door.

"Hey," Iturralde said, "you fuckers hear about the vamp?"

"What vamp?" Antonelli asked.

"We got us a vamp on a motherfuckin' killin' spree. Got Ben Palmer, and I heard he got that homeless guy who said he was immortal."

That got everyone started.

"Ben Palmer died?"

"Who the hell's Ben Palmer?"

"Rich dude up in Riverdale."

"Jesus, that homeless guy who drinks fancy bourbons or something?"

"Scotch, I thought."

"You know anything 'bout it, Bram?"

That last was from Antonelli. I'd been hoping to stay out of it, but Antonelli looked right at me.

I sighed and tried to get my beer-addled brain to stop swimming. "I'm actually the one who found Warren's body. He's'a homeless guy, and he really is immortal. Or was, I guess. And so's Palmer."

"Palmer was a fuckin' immortal?" Iturralde asked, incredulous. "Jesus fuckin' Christ."

"So I'm not even sure this is even a vampire. I mean, sure it looks it, but we don't even know COD yet."

Iturralde frowned. "Cash on delivery?"

I laughed out loud, though it wasn't *that* funny. Yay beer. "No, cause of death. Sorry, doctor term."

"What-the-fuck-ever. They both got fuckin' puncture wounds in their fuckin' necks. We gotta do somethin'. Ever since my parents got—"

I winced, and half the bar finished the sentence for him: "—killed by a jiang shi!" Iturralde never went more than twenty minutes without mentioning that Chinese undead creatures killed his parents. He claimed it was also why he always wore turtlenecks.

That woke Hugues up, and he blurted out something in French.

"Welcome back," Sheehan said with a chuckle.

"What's goin' on?"

Antonelli said, "Bernie wants to kill vampires."

After slugging back all of his tequila and pointing at the shot glass by way of requesting another shot from Sheehan, Iturralde asked, "Who fuckin' *doesn't* wanna kill vampires?"

Hugues sat up. "I prefer something challenging. Besides, who would even be paying for that?"

"Vamps, I'll kill for free. After my parents, I'm always ready to go ten rounds with a fuckin' vamp."

"You wouldn't be goin' two!" Hugues said.

"Hugues is right," I said, "and we don't have proof. Not only that, I'm not too sure a vampire *could* kill an immortal, much less two."

Antonelli asked, "You sure Palmer's an immortal?"

"That's what Miriam told me."

"Yeah, well," Iturralde said, "what the fuck does she know?"

I whirled on him, which just made my head swim more. "'Scuse me?"

He held up a hand. "Look, I know she's your friend and all, Gold, but let's face it, she got tossed in the fuckin' deep end. She barely knows her ass from her elbow."

"An' the pot calls the kettle black," I said. "Look, we don't know for sure *what* killed those two."

"Maybe you and the wardein don't, but I do. Look, I know you fuckin' people like to talk shit about vamps, but they're still fuckin' *vampires*. They live on blood. That makes 'em bad guys in my book."

John McAnally—a tall, wiry, pale specimen who was a regular at the pub during the week, as well—spoke up for the first time all evening. "Bernabe's right, for all that he's blaspheming. Vampires are evil and must be stopped."

"This is a job, Johnny," Hugues said, "and I for one won't be hunting anything that might try to eat me unless there is a payday at the conclusion."

"At the very least," Antonelli said, "we should keep an eye out."

"Jesus shit, what does that mean?" Hugues shook his head and dry-sipped his drink. "Brendan!"

Without missing a beat, Sheehan said, "Another one coming up."

Hugues regarded Antonelli with a look I got a lot when I was apprenticing with him. "'We should keep an eye out.' We should *always* be keepin' an eye out! But that don't mean we go off half-cocked."

I swallowed some more beer and then said, "And if you do go off half-cocked, Miriam's gonna come down on you like a ton of bricks."

"Why," Iturralde said with a sneer, "*you* gonna tell her? After all, your head's so far up the wardein's ass, your fuckin' nose is stickin' outta her fuckin' belly button."

I tamped down my initial response—which was to punch him in the solar plexus, the same thing I wanted to do the first time I met him, and every other time I saw him since—and instead just said, "I won't *need* to tell Miriam anything if you go and do something stupid like you did in Castle Hill."

"That fuckin' vamp was askin' for it!" Iturralde snapped, and he jumped off his bar stool and started moving toward me.

"Hey!" Sheehan said. "Not in here."

"Or anywhere else, thanks," I said quickly. "I started the weekend going three rounds with a unicorn."

"Oh yeah," Antonelli said, "I heard about that. The Cloisters, right?"

Amazingly, that got us off the subject of vampires. Within seconds, I was telling a rapt bar full of Coursers about my adventures on 180th and then Rodzinski being a schmuck and then me calling Velez. I may have slurred a few words while doing so because beer, but I think I told it okay.

McAnally said, "Mr. Velez said it was hard to get the unicorn back in, you say?"

"Yeah." I gulped down the last of my latest beer, as my lips and throat were dry from telling the story. "Why?"

For a second, McAnally looked away. Then he stood up and looked abashed. "What I speak of does not go beyond these walls."

With a pointed look at me, Iturralde said, "*I* don't tattle."

"What are you, six?" I shook my head. "But I won't say anything, either."

Everyone else agreed, and then McAnally cleared his throat. "Father Geenty has a failinis that he captured some time ago."

Iturralde frowned. "The fuck is a failinis?"

"It's a dog that can win any battle and turn water into wine by splashing in it," I said, dredging up a lesson I learned from Mike Zerelli a long time ago.

McAnally nodded. "The Father kept it in a binding for emergencies."

Antonelli snorted. "What, if he runs outta communion wine?"

"I did not presume to ask," McAnally said tightly. "But my point in telling the tale is that it is quite similar to what Abraham just told. I was forced to corral the beast, and then the Father hired Miss Fofanah to restore the binding spell. She mentioned the difficulty she had in restoring it, just as Mr. Velez did."

Hugues glowered at me. "Why were you hirin' Velez, anyhow, child? Thought you and Vanessa Fofanah were tight?"

I looked away. "She's—she's pissed at me."

Antonelli chuckled. "Still?"

"What did you do to her?" Hugues asked.

"I don't wanna talk about it."

Then Guthrie and Chatwal told a story about a shahapet infestation that they had to clear out, and that changed the subject again, thank goodness.

Eventually, closing time rolled 'round. It was just Hugues, me, Guthrie, and Iturralde left—Chatwal had just stayed long enough to help Guthrie tell the shahapet story, then he went home, leaving his husband to stay social.

Me, Iturralde, and Guthrie had to help Hugues to the street. There were a bunch of private cabs all up and down Katonah Avenue to get drunks home safely. We poured Hugues into one of them, then Guthrie walked off—he and Chatwal lived in Yonkers, about a twenty-minute walk, and he preferred to hoof it home.

After Guthrie wandered away, Iturralde stared at me. "I'm goin' after the vamps, Gold. They need stoppin', and I'm the guy to stop 'em."

Then he got into a cab.

I sighed. This was very not good.

But I'd deal with it in the morning. Right now, I needed to try to remember my address so I could tell the cabbie where to take me so I could sleep off all this beer.

Chapter 7

THE NICE THING ABOUT BEER IS THAT YOU CAN DRINK A TON OF IT, GET A nice buzz on, but the next morning, you're not hung over. I've been pretty lucky—I've only been hung over three times, and they were all in med school. Safety tip for civilians: never go drinking with med students. Your liver will never be the same again.

I needed to operate a gigunda motor vehicle Monday morning, so it was for the best that the only thing I woke up with were sore ribs—the gift that kept on giving from the Cloisters' unicorn. I popped a bunch of painkillers and walked down the hill to the parking garage. It wasn't until I was halfway down the hill when I realized I was starting to get sweaty—it was too warm for the denim jacket. One of these days, I'd remember to check the weather on my phone *before* I went outside.

Removing the jacket and tying it around my waist, which looked dorky but got the stupid thing out of my way without baking me, I arrived at the lot and got the moving van out of hock, then drove it the block and a half to the truck rental place. My water bottle was still in the cupholder, the water itself nice and warm and undrinkable after being baked in the truck for three days.

The clerk who looked over the truck was an African-American woman named Darcelle. As she climbed into the driver's seat to check the mileage, she said, "Paperwork says you were bringing this back Saturday."

"Yeah, I kinda lost track of time on Saturday until after you guys closed."

"Okay, but you can just drop the truck off even after we're closed, and then enter the rental agreement number on our app. Or you could leave a message on the 800 number, and we'd mail you the paperwork."

She pointed at the sign in the window that provided that very information to anyone smart enough to read it—in other words, people other than me. "Woulda saved you two days of pay."

I blinked. "Really?" *What do you want from me? I don't rent trucks that often.*

She opened the back and then coughed. "*Damn,*" she said, making the word about six syllables.

After a moment, I got it too: the remnants of Ahondjon's charm. Mind you, it only smelled about a tenth as bad as it did Friday night, and it still stunk like rancid Limburger that had been under a magnifying glass in sunlight.

"Yeah, sorry about that," I said. I didn't volunteer an explanation, mostly because I couldn't think of one that she'd believe.

"Look, based on the mileage, you didn't hardly drive the thing. I can take yesterday off, so you only get one extra day instead of two, all right?"

"*Thank* you." I meant it, too, especially since I couldn't bill either extra day to Rodzinski.

Once we took care of everything and I paid the bill, I headed over to the bus stop on 231st to get back up the hill to my house. According to my phone, the next Bx7 would arrive in fifteen minutes, so I occupied myself during the wait by trying to figure out what to do.

On the one hand, Miriam needed to be told that Iturralde—and possibly some other Coursers—were going after vampires.

On the other hand, if the other Coursers started thinking that I would run to the wardein every time someone did something that could be construed as hinky, they'd never say anything around me.

Normally, when I had some kind of issue with the business, I'd either talk to Miriam or to Hugues, but that wouldn't really work here.

By the time the bus arrived and took me up the hill and I walked home, I wasn't any closer to a decision, so when I got inside, I called my rabbi.

Aunt Esther answered on the second ring. "What's wrong, Bram?"

"What, I can't call my favorite aunt unless something's wrong?"

"First of all, I'm only your favorite aunt when something's wrong. Second of all, you only call when something's wrong. If you just want to chat, you do it over email or text. So obviously something's wrong."

I sighed. "Fine, I do have a problem." I outlined the basics of what went down at the Kingfisher's Tail last night, focusing on Iturralde's posturing, as well as McAnally and Antonelli sorta-kinda going along with it.

"Thing is," I said after I finished, "they were also dismissing Miriam."

"What do you mean?" Esther asked.

I bit my lip. "Just what I said. Saying she doesn't know her ass from her elbow, that kind of stuff. I mean, I get it, she drives down the median age of wardeins all by her lonesome, but that doesn't mean she isn't good at the job."

"All right, Bram, now you've told me the situation. What's the actual problem?"

"Should I tell Miriam about what Iturralde and the others said?"

There was a several second pause. "For this, you called me?"

I blinked. "Aunt Esther—"

"Don't 'Aunt Esther' me, you putz. Stop wasting time with me on the phone and *call Miriam*."

"So you think I should tell her?"

"*Yes*, I think you should tell her. What I want to know is why you think you *shouldn't* tell her?"

"Because if I go to Miriam every time a Courser gets hinky, I'll—"

"—be a responsible Courser and a good friend to Miriam. And if those doofuses don't appreciate that, then they're *bad* Coursers and don't deserve your friendship or your consideration. And from the sounds of it, they're being dumbasses. Isn't the wardein's job to rein in dumbassery on the part of Coursers?"

"One part of the job, yeah." I chuckled. "Thanks, Aunt Esther, I guess I just needed some encouragement."

"No, you needed a kick in the tuchas. Now unless you want a *real* kick in the tuchas, you'll get that tuchas over to Miriam's place with an everything bagel slathered in cream cheese and lox and tell her what's going on."

Now I laughed out loud. Of course Esther remembered how Miriam liked her bagels, and of course she recommended I bring food. Yes, she was a rabbi and an aunt and a yenta, but first and foremost, she was a Jewish mother. "I will, I will."

"Smart boy. Anything else, or can I go back to my *New York Times*?"

"It's almost noon, you haven't finished the *Times* yet?"

"The first person to call me with a stupid problem, you aren't. I've been trying to read this same article for the last two hours. So if we're done?"

"We're done. Thanks again, Aunt Esther."

Next I texted Miriam, who texted back that she was home. I paused long enough to give Mittens some desperately needed scritches (I'd say it was even money who needed them more, him or me), in addition to more food and water, then headed out to Seward Place via the bagel shop.

When I arrived at her house, I got to make it further than the foyer this time. Walking past the staircase—which was now outfitted with a chairlift for those rare occasions when Miriam used the house's second floor—I entered the living room to find her sitting at the computer desk reading over something.

"Hey, Mimi! As promised, I have bagels." I set the bag and my coffee down on the glass table in front of the sofa.

Miriam just grunted, which meant I'd need to wait until she was finished reading before she'd even properly acknowledge my presence. An immersive reader, was Miriam.

Finally, she finished and wheeled herself over to the coffee table. By that point, I was already halfway through my poppy seed bagel (which I ate with nothing on it), while Miriam's everything bagel was sitting on the flattened paper bag.

"Oh God, I need this bagel." She took a bite with her eyes closed and made nommy noises before putting it back down and then sipping the mug of tea that was in her wheelchair's cup holder. "That hits the spot. Thanks, Bram."

"Least I could do after screwing up the werewolves."

"Yes, this is the absolute least you could do," she said with a nod. "For starters, you couldn't even be bothered to get a plate."

"So I could add to your dirty dish pile? No chance."

Miriam glared at me. "It's a pain to load the dishwasher."

"And what was your excuse when you let the dirty dishes take over the kitchen before the accident?"

Now she grinned. "Oh, pure laziness. I just have a *better* excuse now."

I chuckled and sipped my coffee. "So you said you wanted to know what we gossiped about at the Kingfisher last night."

"Uh-oh."

Frowning, I asked, "What do you mean, 'uh-oh'?"

"The last time you actually told me what happened at the Kingfisher, it was Iturralde gloating about Castle Hill and I had to sanction him—*and* listen to his abusive voicemails and read his abusive emails for the entire month he was sanctioned."

I sighed. "Well, your instincts aren't bad. And it's even about Iturralde and vampires again."

Before I could tell the story for the second time in an hour, Miriam's phone chirped with a generic ringtone. Even as it did, mine vibrated—I had turned the volume off when I was in the bagel shop.

Miriam frowned at the display, then answered it. "This is Wardein Zerelli."

Obviously, it was someone in the game.

I pulled my smartphone out of my pocket, and saw that I had two text messages.

Before I could look at them, Miriam said, "Wonderful, that's all we need… What's the address?… Okay, I'll be there as soon as I can." She put the phone down. "Can you give me a lift to Shakespeare Avenue?"

"Uh, I guess so, why?"

"A Courser killed a vampire."

Suddenly, I had a gut feeling that those two texts were from fellow Coursers. "Who, Iturralde?"

She shook her head. "No, Eddie Mohapatra."

I nearly dropped my phone. I did drop my jaw. "Eddie?"

Miriam sounded as confused as I felt. "He's the one who called. Reported it right away."

Staring down at my phone, I activated it. The two text messages were from fellow Coursers: one from Iturralde, the other from McAnally. That didn't bode well, since the two of them were at the top of the vampire hit brigade.

Iturralde always texted in all caps with minimal punctuation. *"HEY GOLD YOU GOTTA TALK TO ZERELLI CUZ MOHAPATRA KILLED A VAMP AND I DON'T WANT HER COMING DOWN ON HIM NOT FAIR."*

McAnally was a bit more coherent. *"Edward killed a vampire on Shakespeare Avenue. He called me right away and I advised him to report to the Wardein. I thought you should know, since you were the one who put this together."*

I didn't put anything together, but if that was what McAnally believed, fine. I also noticed that Eddie left out that he called McAnally before he called Miriam, but I figured it wasn't necessary for her to know that. In fact, it was probably better that Miriam thought Eddie was responsible.

I dashed out the door to walk to my house to retrieve my car. By the time I turned into Seward Place with the Corolla, Miriam's wheelchair was at the edge of the driveway. I made a three-point turn, helped her into the car, folded the wheelchair and put it in the trunk, got back in, and drove off. I've given Miriam enough lifts since the accident that I could do the get-her-into-the-front-seat-and-fold-and-put-away-her-wheelchair routine in my sleep. In fact, once I pretty much did, when she needed me to take her somewhere at three in the morning.

Unlike me, Miriam had an account with several local car services, but for trips to places involving things like dead vampires, she preferred to keep as many civilians out of it as possible.

As I drove down the Major Deegan Expressway through mild midday traffic, Miriam was fondling her smartphone. "The address we're going to is an abandoned building right by the Cross Bronx, but it's on the same block as a church and a post office, so I don't know how long we'll be able to keep it under wraps. But I thought I recognized the address—it's 1542 Shakespeare, and that's had a nest of vampires squatting in it for a few years now."

I nodded. Eddie may have known that too and went there looking for trouble.

Except that didn't make any sense. Eddie never looked for trouble.

"Also," Miriam added, "if you say one word about how awful the Cross Bronx is, or how awful Robert Moses was for building it, or how many neighborhoods were bisected by it, or how much traffic is on it, or any other damn thing, I will beat you with a stick."

Putting my right hand over my chest while steering with my left, I said in a mock-outraged tone, "I have no idea *what* you're talking about, Mimi. What makes you think I'd go on about how a power-hungry city planner destroyed half the central Bronx with a stupid expressway whose sole purpose is to get people through the Bronx and out of it with no regard for the people in it?"

"You are in serious trouble as soon as I find a stick, boychik. I should never have lent you that book."

I chuckled. Miriam had lent me a copy of a book about Moses, the city planner who was responsible for a lot of the asphalt silly straws that made up the expressways of New York City.

It took about twenty minutes to get to the address, and I spent it telling Miriam about what was discussed at the Kingfisher's Tail.

"So Eddie wasn't even there for the conversation about vampires?"

I shook my head. "But Eddie's always been pretty plugged into things. He could've found out on his own."

"Yeah."

I pulled in front of the rickety, boarded-up brownstone on Shakespeare Avenue between Featherbed Lane and the Cross Bronx service road. It was between another similar brownstone that looked occupied and a small parking lot that, according to the sign, was used by the church that was a couple doors down. The brownstone itself had a bedraggled white wooden fence next to the stoop, a pile of garbage cans on the other side of it.

Usually a brownstone in New York City evokes images of Manhattan's Upper West Side and Brooklyn's Park Slope: magnificent pieces of architecture that were built in the nineteenth century. This place, though, had none of the charm you saw in those famous structures—it was just a boxy, brown-brick building.

Three Coursers were all on the stoop. Iturralde looked pissed, McAnally looked worried, and Eddie looked resigned. The first two were sitting down, while Eddie was standing, but since Eddie was only five four and the other two were freakishly tall, they all looked like they were the same height. Eddie was wearing a plain T-shirt and jeans; McAnally was, as always, in a nice button-down shirt (sleeves rolled up) and slacks; while Iturralde was still wearing that damn coat over a turtleneck, even though he had to be roasting.

I double-parked, got out, pulled out Miriam's wheelchair, and helped her into it.

Eddie had stepped forward right when we pulled up, but he was nice enough to wait until she was settled in her chair before approaching all the way. Bowing his head, he said, "Wardein Zerelli."

Miriam nodded. "Eddie. How are Indira and Martine?"

"The baby's running a fever, unfortunately."

Iturralde rolled his eyes and got up from the stoop. "Oh, for fuck's sake."

Gazing past Eddie, Miriam stared at Iturralde. "Is something wrong, Bernie?"

"Look, I just wanna make sure that Eddie doesn't get railroaded, here. This was a good kill."

"And I'm just supposed to take your word for it?" Miriam asked in her mock-sweet voice, which always scared the shit out of me.

Iturralde, though, wasn't bright enough to be scared. "You should. I actually *know* about vamps, ever since my pa—"

Even McAnally rolled his eyes. "Jesus, Mary, and Joseph, to bring up your parents at a time like this…"

Before Iturralde could turn to yell at McAnally, Miriam said, "Actually, Bernie, your parents were killed by jiang shi. Yes, they're similar to vampires in some respects, but they're not the same thing."

"The point is, something happened here, and you're standin' around askin' about his wife and kids, for fuck's sake."

I shook my head. "It's called being polite, Bernie, you should try it some time."

He ignored me and stared daggers at Miriam. "You even know what you're supposed to be doing here, Miriam?"

"Oh, I know exactly what *I'm* supposed to be doing here, Bernie—what I'm confused about is what *you're* doing here. Did you kill the vampire?"

"No, I—"

"Because when I got the call that a Courser killed a vampire, my immediate thought was 'What did Bernie do *this* time?' Most of the vampire deaths in my demesne since I became wardein have been at your hands. So if you didn't kill this one, why are you here, exactly?"

"Moral support. Me and Johnny, we wanna make sure Eddie's okay, and that you don't treat this like you did Castle Hill."

"Fine, go be morally supportive and *quiet* over there." She pointed at the stoop. "Eddie, let's go for a walk."

She and Eddie started moving slowly toward the Cross Bronx service road. Not too many pedestrians, especially on a Monday afternoon, and the traffic noise from the expressway gave them a certain amount of privacy.

Once they were out of earshot, Iturralde looked at me urgently. "You talk to her in the car?"

I regarded him with annoyance. "No, we used semaphore the whole time. Of course I talked to her in the car."

"So Eddie'll be okay?"

"How the hell should I know?"

"C'mon, you actually like her for some reason, you gotta know how she's gonna think. I sure as shit don't. She ain't nothin' like her old man—now *that* was a wardein. Zerelli knew what the fuck he was about. After Castle Hill—"

I cut him off sharply. "Hang on, Bernie, she did the right thing after Castle Hill. In fact, if anything, she went easy on you. Remember when you went over her head to the Curia? All you did was make your sanction last another two weeks."

Iturralde held up both hands. "Hey, look, this isn't about me, it's about Eddie. He's got a wife and kid to support; he can't afford to get sanctioned, all right?"

"Funny how when Miriam brings up Indira and the baby it's proof that she's a lousy wardein, but when you bring it up, you're being a good friend."

"I *am* his friend. She ain't."

"No, she's the wardein. If he didn't do anything wrong, he'll be fine."

"Ain't nothin' wrong 'bout killin' a vamp."

McAnally finally spoke up. He'd been glancing up the block at Miriam and Eddie talking at the corner. "From what Edward told me, it was self-defense."

"What the hell was he doing here, anyhow?" I asked.

Indicating the abandoned brownstone with his head, Iturralde said, "This shithole's been a vamp squat for a while now."

McAnally added, "Edward wanted to question one of the vampires he's used as an informant with regard to the immortals who were killed. He attacked, and Edward was forced to defend himself."

"Where's the body?"

Again, Iturralde shook his head toward the brownstone. "Still in there. Ain't like it's gonna make the place smell *worse*. Ain't like it's the first corpse in there, neither."

Miriam and Eddie started heading back toward us.

She took a glance at the dozen or so stairs that led to the brownstone's front door, then shook her head. "I'm just gonna take Eddie's word for it that Figueroa's alone in there and dead."

I assumed Figueroa was the vampire.

"I can verify that if you wish, Miss Zerelli," McAnally said. "When I arrived, the vampire was lying dead in the building's vestibule. His neck was snapped."

Nodding, Miriam said, "Thank you, John, I appreciate that. And that matches what Eddie just told me."

I was impressed. Snapping a person's neck isn't as easy as it looks on television, and Eddie wasn't the most impressive physical specimen in the world. Then again, I'd never actually seen him in a scrap; I only knew his rep and his drinking habits on Sunday nights.

"Because of Eddie's history, I'm willing to believe that it was self-defense."

"Gee, how nice," Iturralde muttered.

I winced. I could tell that Miriam heard him but chose to pretend that she didn't.

She went on. "However, Eddie also was acting on his own, without a client, or a particular cause. He wasn't charged with investigating the deaths of Warren Mather and Ben Palmer, but their deaths were what prompted him to question Alvaro Figueroa, who then attacked him, unprovoked."

"He was scared," Eddie said quietly.

I nodded. "Probably worried that some nutjob would use this as an excuse to hunt vamps." I was staring right at Iturralde when I said that.

"That," Miriam said, "is *not* happening. I'm not sanctioning Eddie, though I am putting him on restriction for the time being. Any existing contracts may be fulfilled, and he can still purchase magickal items as needed. But no new contracts until this matter is resolved."

"I understand, Wardein," Eddie said with a bow of his head. "Thank you."

"You're *thankin'* her?" Iturralde threw his hands up. "You're takin' food outta his mouth, lady! And his kid's!"

"Until we know for sure what happened to the immortals, I'm not taking any chances. People going off half-baked information will just result in more people getting killed beyond Figueroa."

"Who gives a fuck, he's a vamp!"

McAnally put a hand on Iturralde's shoulder. "That's enough, Bernabe."

"It ain't even close to enough. Vamps killed those people, and we gotta—"

"Do *nothing*," Miriam said sharply. "Let me be abundantly clear, Bernie—vampires are off-limits until we know for sure what happened to Mather and Palmer."

"We *know* what happened!" Iturralde shouted.

Her tone getting quieter even as Iturralde's got louder, Miriam said, "No, Bernie, we don't. We know what it *looks* like, but we also know how bad vampires are at violence, and we know how hard immortals are to kill. There's still too many unknowns here, and just jumping to conclusions has already resulted in one death, and I'm not going to let people go off half-cocked killing *anyone*. As of right now, vampires are off-limits to all Coursers in this demesne. If a contract comes up that involves interaction with a vampire, the Courser will have to run it by me before taking the contract—or, if in the course of a contract, a Courser must approach a vampire, that too must be run by me first. Anyone who violates these instructions will automatically be sanctioned for a year."

"Oh, for fuck's sake, seriously?"

Miriam glared up at Iturralde. "One more comment, Bernie, and I'll sanction you just for the hell of it. Now if you'll just shut up for a second, we need to get Figueroa's body taken care of. Bernie, John, I'm officially hiring you for that job—dispose of the body before somebody from that church down the street notices the smell when they park their car."

"Excuse me, Miss Zerelli," McAnally said, "but you just informed us that we may not approach vampires."

"Living ones." Miriam smiled. "Dead ones are fine."

Iturralde suddenly looked outraged. Based on the look on his face, I think he realized that Miriam could have been setting him up to sanction him for approaching Figueroa's body without asking her permission first. But Miriam wasn't that devious or vindictive—though I wouldn't blame her for doing it to Iturralde just on principle—and besides, she wouldn't have included McAnally in the job if she just wanted to nail Iturralde.

"Eddie," she said, "go home. Take care of Martine. I'll let you know when I can lift the restriction."

"Again, Wardein, thank you. And I'm sorry." Eddie reached out his hand, and Miriam returned the handshake.

Without another word, Eddie got into his car, which was parked across the street, and drove away.

"I'll leave you to it, gentlemen," Miriam said. "Send me the bill when it's done. Bram?"

I nodded, and we headed back to my car. I got her into the passenger seat and put the chair in the trunk.

The whole time, Iturralde was giving both of us the hairy eyeball, until McAnally said, "Come, Bernabe, let us do our appointed task."

"Yeah, whatever."

They went up the stoop stairs, Iturralde's stupid coat swooshing behind him, and I drove us down Shakespeare to Featherbed.

As soon as I made the left turn onto Featherbed—which was a funny half-oval shape, probably left over from when it was a road used by farmers in colonial times—Miriam said, "Bram, I need you to find out who's killing these immortals. I hereby give you permission to approach any vampires you might need to in order to solve this."

"O-o-o-okay." I wasn't entirely surprised at this, but I was a little nervous about this, too. "You sure you want me to handle this?"

"You were the one who found Warren, and you're the one I sent to check Palmer. It makes sense to just keep you on it. Besides, I trust you to actually *listen* to me."

I winced as I turned right onto University Avenue. "Look, Bernie is Bernie."

"He wasn't like this when Dad was alive. You know how Eddie was? All polite and deferential and stuff?"

"Eddie's like that with everyone."

"Right, well, that's how Bernie was with Dad."

I blinked. "Really? *Bernie?*"

"Really. He didn't turn into an asshole until Dad died. Then again, half the Coursers in the demesne turned into assholes then."

Shrugging as I pulled into the queue of cars waiting to go left onto Burnside Avenue, I said, "I dunno about that."

"I do. I'm only thirty years old, I'm in a wheelchair, and I have a uterus. Most of these jerks could probably deal with one of those, maybe two, but all three? I can't walk, so I don't know what it's like to be in the field, I'm too young, I don't really know anything, and this is men's work, not women's work."

I only didn't roll my eyes because I was keeping a close look at the oncoming traffic, waiting for a break so I could turn left onto Burnside. "Oh, come on, the best Coursers I know are women."

"Because they have to bust their ass twice as hard to be considered half as good. Honestly, there's a reason why I try to give Abby and Dahlia and Siobhan and Trina as much work as I can. I only gave that body disposal to John and Bernie because time is of the essence and they were there anyhow. We can't leave a vamp body just lying around."

I *finally* was able to make the left turn, and I maneuvered around the double-parked cars on Burnside. "Speaking of jobs, I think the first thing I should do is find Anne DeLancey."

"Good idea. I still haven't found Dad's file on her. Of course, what I *really* would like to know is who that woman was who gave you DeLancey's name."

"You and me both." I drove down the steep hill of 179th Street that took us down to the entrance to the Major Deegan. "You and me both."

Chapter 8

AFTER I DROPPED MIRIAM OFF AT HER PLACE, I HEADED HOME. WHEN I got inside after I parked the car, I noticed that Rebekah had left her door ajar. With a sigh, I closed the door all the way. This was generally a safe neighborhood, but why take chances?

Something smelled funny in her apartment—and familiar, too, but I couldn't place it. Shaking my head and closing the door, I wondered why she couldn't keep her own place as clean as she kept mine.

Then again, nobody paid her to clean her own place...

I headed upstairs to my second-floor apartment, shrugged out of my denim jacket, went to the bathroom, made sure to scritch Mittens—which only woke him up for a second, curled up as he was in repose on the blue chair—pulled my leftover sandwich from Saturday out of the fridge, and went to my computer to catch up on email and stuff, including Katie's daily fish tank photo and a note from Aunt Esther asking if I'd talked to Miriam like I said I would.

After replying to my aunt, I went to see what I could find out about Anne DeLancey.

In fact, I found four Anne DeLanceys who lived in New York State, but I was pretty confident that it wasn't the one in Ticonderoga. The others were all closer: Nyack north of the city, Patchogue out on Long Island, and one right here in the Boogie Down.

It was pretty likely that the last one was the right one—but not necessarily. I mean, sure, Palmer and Mather had history in the Bronx and still lived here, but that didn't mean it necessarily had to be true for her. Besides, I had no idea why immortals were being targeted, or why they were in the Bronx—or, honestly, anything. I only knew about DeLancey because a woman I don't know told me about her.

Point being: best to check all four of them.

First, though, I wanted to catch up on my other online stuff, and also finish my sandwich.

An email from Hugues reminded me that I also wanted to pick Dahlia Rhys-Markham's brain about immortals. Unfortunately, her phone went to voicemail, so I composed an email and sent it to her, asking her what she knew about the Bronx's immortal population.

That done, I started digging into my four Annes.

The one in Ticonderoga turned out to be a college student. I found pictures of her online, and she looked twenty. While immortals were well preserved for their ages, both Mather and Palmer looked middle aged at the very least. Plus, I found a massive online footprint for the woman—fairly typical of a twenty-year-old—going back to her teen years, including some prepubescent pictures of her posted by her mother. So she probably wasn't our immortal.

Anne DeLancey of Nyack, New York had moved, though she was still listed as living in Nyack. But she'd moved to San Francisco a year ago. It was possible she was being targeted, but California was a bit out of my range.

Patchogue's Anne DeLancey was in a car accident six months ago and was still in a coma, as far as I could tell. That made me worry that she *was* the immortal, and she'd already been attacked.

However, the one nearby fit the bill. I found a picture, and she looked the same as the other two victims, like she was in her fifties or so. Her online footprint was very tiny, which you'd expect from an immortal who'd had to reinvent her identity every few decades.

And she lived nearby, in an apartment on 203rd Street, just off the Grand Concourse. She was the building's superintendent.

First thing I did was try the phone number she had listed. It rang twice then went to voicemail. It was a computerized voice saying I'd reached that particular number and I could leave a message at the tone.

"Uh, well, if this is Anne DeLancey—the former Anne van Cortlandt—then this is Bram Gold, and I need you to get in touch with me as soon as humanly possible." I gave my cell number and then ended the call.

Still not sure if that was the right person, but her place wasn't far. Couldn't hurt to drive over there and check her out. If that crapped out, there was always Patchogue…

Just as I was about to put the phone back in my pocket, it rang with "Late in the Evening" by Paul Simon, which meant it was a number not programmed into it. Looking at the display, I saw that it was a 718 number, which was assigned to the four outer boroughs of New York. That didn't necessarily mean a local, as it could've been a cell phone that was acquired by a resident of one of the non-Manhattan boroughs in the past and they kept the number after they moved away.

Not that I got too many out-of-town calls in any case. I didn't recognize the number, but that didn't mean anything. I often got calls from unfamiliar numbers—generally potential clients—and I also had a hard time remembering to put new people's numbers into my phone and an even harder time remembering people's numbers. (The Zerelli house on Seward has had the same landline for the entire thirty years I've been alive, and I've called it more times than I can count. Still couldn't tell you what it was, except that it had a 718 area code.)

Anyhow, while lots of people don't answer unfamiliar calls, it was my best way to get new clients. So I answered it.

And boy was I sorry.

The fake-Haitian accent of "Madam Vérité" sounded over the tiny speaker next to my ear. "Is this Bram Gold?"

"Speaking," I said slowly, though I recognized her awful voice right away.

"I hope you are satisfied, young man. You have earned my wrath."

"Uh-huh."

"I have been turned away from all my vendors. They will not even speak to me! And I still cannot touch anything in the shops! They say I am sanctioned by this war-deen person. How am I to do business like this?"

"Not really my problem. Also, if you don't even know who or what the wardein is, then you've got no business doing any kind of magick."

"Don't be tellin' me what I can and cannot do, young man!"

"I'm not, Wardein Zerelli is. You take it up with her. Good luck getting anywhere, though."

"You haven't heard the last of me!" With that, she ended the call.

"Okay, then." I put the phone back in my pocket. Mrs. Truth certainly talked a good game.

I texted Miriam to let her know that Madame Vérité wasn't taking her sanctioning lying down, and also that she didn't know what a wardein was. I also passed on her phone number.

Would love to be a fly on the proverbial wall for *that* conversation.

Climbing into my car, I drove over to the Henry Hudson Parkway, taking it north a bit before getting on the Mosholu Parkway south, then turning onto the Concourse, which started at the Mosholu here in Norwood and went all the way down to 138th Street in Mott Haven.

It took me about ten minutes to find a parking spot in the area—basically, I had to keep driving around until someone pulled out. I finally nabbed a spot on 202nd, a block away from the apartment building.

Walking up the Concourse, it only took me a minute to get to the building on the corner of 203rd. It was a large red-brick building, with a courtyard entrance in the center: you walked up three stairs and went through the courtyard to get to the front door. Just to the right of that courtyard, though, was a recessed door that was down a few steps from the sidewalk, with the word "Superintendent" stenciled on the door and a doorbell next to it.

There was also a small window that was open about half an inch with no screen in it. My first thought on seeing that was that there was no way Anne DeLancey had pets. Mittens was the laziest cat in the universe, but if I opened a window even a crack without a screen down, he'd leap onto the sill and jump out with visions of chasing squirrels or birds dancing in his walnut-sized brain—and likely fall to his doom from one flight up.

Before I could even approach the doorbell, though, I was startled out of half a year of life by a black shape that flew out the window.

Ducking instinctively and throwing my arms up, I looked to see that it was a bat. An actual, honest-to-goodness bat. It flew quickly down the street, and it sure looked like a bat.

It went half a block to the intersection with the Concourse just as the traffic camera flared. The bat flew off into the late-afternoon sky, while I made a mental note of that traffic cam.

First, though, I needed to get inside, fast. If she was like any other New Yorker, she locked her door. And the person I'd normally go to in order to get inside would be the super.

Of course, it was possible that everything was fine, and that that bat wasn't part of some plan to hurt DeLancey, but I wasn't about to bet any money on that.

Still, it was worth a shot, so I figured I'd ring the doorbell.

No answer.

I knocked on the door—and it opened with a tiny click, and slowly fell open.

Shaking my head, I went inside. Apparently, DeLancey was the kind of superintendent who always left her door unlocked.

Right inside the door on the right was a narrow kitchen with a crummy electric stove that was vintage 1977 or so, very old linoleum floors, Formica counters, gaudy yellow wallpaper, and a refrigerator that was about as old as the stove. There was a plate with two pieces of toast on it, only one of which was buttered, a knife and butter dish next to it.

Then I heard a moan.

Turning around, I moved down the hallway. The left side was just one long, unbroken wall, decorated with three different, pretty generic-looking landscape paintings. On the right were three doors, one to a bedroom, one to a bathroom, one skinnier one that was probably a closet, and then the hallway opened up to a wider space that served as the living room. It was full of furniture that was all avocado or flower-print, a glass coffee table, and a woman dying on the floor.

I ran over to who I presumed to be Anne DeLancey—she certainly looked like the picture I'd found online. She was prone on the floor of the living room, puncture wounds in her neck, pale as a proverbial ghost. She was still alive, but the blood was barely seeping out of the wounds, which didn't make sense. If her heart was still pumping, the blood should've been gushing.

Then again, maybe immortal blood flowed more slowly?

"Ferris..." she said in a hoarse whisper. "May... next..."

Then she gurgled and stopped breathing.

Immediately, I tried CPR, but to no avail.

Collapsing on the floor against the ugly green couch, I sighed. I wondered if I might've been able to save her if I hadn't taken so long to find a damn parking space. Or if I'd actually gotten my ass over here sooner instead of wasting time checking email and scritching my cat.

Dammit.

I looked around, and sure enough there was a landline. I found a tissue and then picked the phone up with it, using another tissue to push the number 9 and the number 1 twice.

"Hello," I said after the 911 operator answered, "my super, I think she's dead!" I gave the address and then hung up before I could answer any more questions.

Aside from the body, I hadn't actually touched anything else. Well, okay, the front door with my knuckles, but that was it. While it was possible that some trace evidence of me was on her, there wasn't really any way for me to get rid of it. I'd just have to hope that wouldn't bite me on the ass later.

I got out of there and headed back toward the Concourse, using my foot to get the door shut again.

I pulled out my phone and called Toscano.

"Jesus, Brammy, you gettin' psychic or somethin'? I was just gonna call you."

I blinked. "Uh, okay. What's up?"

"Nice try. You first."

"Okay." I'd been hoping that she'd provide some info about Palmer's death that would shed some light on the ever-murkier deaths of Bronx immortals. "Well, we've got another dead body just like Mather and Palmer—Anne DeLancey in the super's apartment at 214 East 203rd. I already called 911."

"Shit, that's the five-two," she said, referring to the 52nd Precinct. "All right, thanks for the heads-up. I'm guessin' it's the same vampire?"

"Yes and no. The main reason why I called was because there's a traffic camera in the intersection half a block away from DeLancey's front door on the Concourse. I need whatever footage from it you can get me from about twenty minutes ago."

"Do I even wanna know?"

"Maybe?" I sighed. "Look, something flew by that camera that may give me a hint as to what it is killing these things. I *think* it was a bat."

"Which tracks with the whole vampire bullshit. Well, I got news, too. We got a prelim on Palmer's autopsy, and the ME says she thinks the COD is total organ failure. She hasn't cut him open yet, but just based on the X-rays and such, every organ looks like it was disrupted. Which is weird, 'cause I figured a vampire'd kill by draining all the blood. Then again, the ME also figured the puncture wounds were postmortem, but wouldn't she say that anyhow if the blood got sucked?"

"They would, yeah. But one thing I know for damn sure now, Lyd— it's *not* a vampire."

There was silence on the other end of the phone. By this time I'd gotten to my car on 202nd.

As I beeped the car unlocked and climbed in, Toscano finally said, "What the fuck, Brammy? What about your bat?"

"That was my main clue that this *wasn't* a vampire."

"Can't they turn into bats?"

"Not even a little bit. And even if they could, it wouldn't be a bat that small unless the vampire in question was a newborn."

"All right, now you've completely lost me."

I took a breath and started the car. One-handed, I pulled out of the spot and went toward Valentine Avenue, still holding the phone with my other hand. My Corolla was too old to have Bluetooth and I kept forgetting to get a headset. "Okay, shape-changing is possible for someone who's got, like, phenomenal mojo. I mean, super-powerful. There are maybe ten magick-users in the world that powerful. And even they have to obey the laws of physics. Let's say we're talking one of those ten and they got turned into a vampire. Even if they did decide to turn into a bat for whatever reason, it would be a bat with the same body mass. So say it's a hundred-fifty-pound woman, she'd change into a hundred-fifty-pound bat."

"All right, I guess that makes sense." Toscano sounded very reluctant to say that much.

I turned down 203rd, passing by DeLancey's place. No sign of ambulances or cops yet.

As I turned right onto the Concourse to head back to the Mosholu, I went on. "No, whoever did this is trying real hard to make us think it's a vampire. The bat was just a little extra flair. It means whoever did this knows what they know about vampires from watching old Hammer films, not reality."

"Hey, I like those movies. Christopher Lee's still the best Dracula, you ask me."

I let out a tiny chuckle while I waited at the light to turn onto the Mosholu. "Nah, Bela Lugosi now and forever."

"You know he was a drug addict, right?"

"If I factored drug addiction into liking actors, I wouldn't like any."

"Fair enough."

"*Anyhow*," I said, dragging the conversation back on track, "the puncture wounds, the lack of blood, the bat—it's all trying to get us to look for a vampire. If we hadn't been sidetracked by that, we might've been on the right track before two more people got killed. Now I just gotta figure out what the right track *is*."

"Maybe." Toscano let out a ragged cough, then said, "Look, I'll get you that footage, but if the bat isn't a vampire, what's the point?"

"Just want to make sure it *was* a bat and not something else."

"Yeah, okay. I'll let you know what the final autopsy results are."

"Thanks, Lyd."

"An' I won't even give you shit about talkin' on your phone while drivin', neither."

With that, she ended the call.

I shook my head as I dropped the phone into the center console. Knew I wouldn't be able to get over illegal behavior on Toscano. I really needed to get a headset for my phone.

Right after I got an assistant.

Hell if I know who I'd hire for something like that. Rebekah would have been the obvious choice, but I doubted that she'd have the time, plus organizing was never her strong suit, exactly.

At the red light at Mosholu and Gun Hill Road, I called Miriam. I got her voicemail, so I filled her in on DeLancey and also that we were *not* looking at vampires as the culprits.

My phone had beeped while I was in the midst of leaving the message. By the time I was done with Miriam's message, I was on the Henry Hudson Parkway. It wasn't safe to even look at my phone until I got off at 246th Street and got stopped at a red light on the service road.

Looking at the phone then, I saw that the call had come from Dahlia, and she'd left a voicemail. I played it on speaker as the light turned green.

"Hello, Bram. Was hoping to catch you on the phone, but I'll send an email. Short version, though, is that, besides Mather and Palmer, there are several other immortals who reside in the Bronx, but there are two others who are contemporaries of those two: Anne Van Cortlandt and John Ferris. I do know that they all were part of the eighteenth-century Bronx community, but beyond that, I'm not sure what all else they might have in common—besides the obvious, in any case. I'll put more in the email. Hope this helps! Talk soon—maybe get some lunch at Palace of Japan again?"

Okay, well, that was useful. Especially given DeLancey's—née Van Cortlandt's—final words.

I turned into my driveway to see a familiar woman sitting on my stoop. She was wearing the same snood, blouse, skirt, and boots she wore yesterday at the bus stop. No shawl, though, as it was a lot warmer today.

This time I picked up my phone and took a picture of her before I got out of the car and said, "You again."

"You were too late to save Anne DeLancey." That was all she said. No greeting, no salutation, just jumping right in with the accusations.

Then again, I felt like making a few accusations of my own. "That only happened half an hour ago. Mind telling me how you know so much?"

"Why does it matter?"

I glowered at her. "It matters a lot if you're the one who did it. That's twice I've bumped into you after encountering a dead immortal, which means you've been near two-thirds of the crimes in question. For all I know, you were nearby when Warren was killed, too."

"I can assure you, I was very far from this city at that time. I only became aware of what was happening after you stopped Bonita Soriano before she could bind the loa. It was then that I sought you out—and learned of what happened to Warham Mather."

"Yeah, well, this is getting serious. I just missed whatever killed De-Lancey by five minutes. I got to *watch* her die."

"Did she say anything to you before she perished?"

I blinked. "Gee, I thought you knew everything."

She gave me that perfect smile again. "I know many things, far more than is comprehensible to mere mortals—or even to immortals. But I am unaware of what Anne DeLancey's final words may have been."

Against my better judgment—something about this woman just oozed trust, though how drop-dead gorgeous she was probably entered into that—I told her. "She said 'Ferris may next.' Since there's a fourth immortal from the eighteenth-century Bronx named John Ferris, I'm guessing she said that he may be next."

"Unlikely," the woman said, "as John Ferris died during the draft riots of 1863."

I shot her a look. "How the hell do you know that?"

"Ferris died saving innocent lives during the riots. Some of those lives belonged to people who worshipped the same gods as those who have been defrauded by Bonita Soriano of late."

So that meant practitioners of Vodou. "And this matters to you because—?"

She smiled again. "My point, Bram Gold, is that John Ferris is dead, but he had a descendent named May Ferris, and she became immortal following her ancestor's passing. She lives in the area known as Throggs Neck. And you might wish to hurry this time."

I sighed. On the one hand, this was actionable intel. On the other, this woman had continued to not tell me who she was, which was starting to piss me off. "I think maybe—"

"Hey, Bram!"

I turned to see Rebekah coming toward the house. "Hey, kid." Then I turned back to face my mysterious stranger. "Maybe we should take this—"

But she was gone. Again. Dammit.

Rebekah walked up to me. She was holding a bag from the grocery store on the corner. Her socks matched, but her shoes did not. Small victories. "Who're you talking to?"

I just stared at the now-empty stoop for a second. "Nobody, apparently."

We went inside. "You okay, Bram?"

"Yeah, just a weird case that keeps getting weirder."

"Okay. Aren't you late for your shift?"

I blinked, then pulled my phone out of my pocket and saw what time it was.

Crap.

"Thanks, kid," I said as I ran upstairs to change. I had maybe twenty minutes before I needed to be at Montefiore to work my ER shift.

Chapter 9

My night shift at the Montefiore ER went from 6 PM until 2 AM and I showed up right at 6:07 on the nose. Yes, maybe I should have blown it off to check on May Ferris, but there had been twenty-four hours between each murder, and I'd used up all my good will with my supervisor, Dr. Cho Park, the last four times I called in "sick" last minute for an ER shift thanks to Courser business. Park had been looking for an excuse to get rid of me, anyhow, as he viewed me as a dilettante. And it's hard to find another doctor gig when you get fired for not showing up for your only-twice-a-week job.

I'd get a few hours' sleep after my shift and deal with May Ferris first thing in the morning.

The one thing I did do was text the picture I took of my mysterious informant to Miriam.

The first few hours were pretty standard: just the usual collection of ailments and broken bones and accidents.

Then around nine, we got a call that there was a big-ass pileup on the Bronx River Parkway near Gun Hill Road. We were the closest ER at only ten blocks or so away, so we'd be getting most of the patients. Me and the other doctors and nurse practitioners on duty went around the ER, which was set up like a big wheel, with curtained sections all along the outer walls and the clerical desks in the center. We quickly got people in process to be treated and either admitted or released in order to clear beds as fast as possible.

The first wave from the accident was the simple stuff: concussions, lacerations, bruises, scratches, broken bones, and the like. I got to talking to one guy who had some cuts and scrapes, but who also was having trouble focusing his eyes. The name on his chart was Vito Fernelli, but he was Asian. I figured either he was adopted, or he's got a *really* entertaining family tree. I didn't bug him about it while I examined him, though, as he was just in a car accident, and didn't need to be asked the same question he was probably asked seven or eight times a day.

"It's weird, I've always been 20/20," he was saying while I gave him the once-over. "Never had blurry vision before. It's weird."

"So you said." I wasn't about to complain about him repeating himself given the head trauma. "Do you remember what happened?"

"Some of it? I mean, I was driving up the parkway, and there was the usual slowdown when you got to Gun Hill—seriously, they need to add a lane to that exit ramp or *something*—and then suddenly the ground started to shake."

Nobody else I'd seen had mentioned that. "What, like an earthquake?"

"I dunno, maybe? I mean, I lived in New York since I was two, so I've never been in one. I guess. Anyhow, the ground shook and then the pavement split open—and then next thing I know my car's on the divider, the rear end smashed into the guardrail, and EMTs are dragging me out of the car."

"Okay. You may have a concussion, so we're gonna get you a CAT scan to see if there's any obvious brain injury, and you're gonna need to see a concussion specialist."

"Uh, all right."

We went over a few other things, and then I left him in the care of the nurses while I went to the next patient, a salt-and-pepper-haired woman named Kamilah Vasquez.

She had a broken arm. I gave her a once-over, too, but aside from the arm, she seemed to be fine. A few more tests needed to get done, but there was a line for that tonight.

I asked her what happened—which was both a way to tickle my curiosity and also determine if there was any amnesia or blackouts, like what Fernelli experienced—and she said, "No, it was amazing! The pavement just—just cracked open!"

"Did you feel the ground shake before that?"

Nodding, she said, "It was just like San Francisco. I was on vacation there when I was a girl and that earthquake hit in '89."

"Oh, come on, you're not old enough to have been alive then."

She chuckled. "Nice try, Doctor. I was eight."

"Didn't that quake postpone the World Series that year?"

"You're damn right it did—we had tickets to the fourth game! But they postponed it a week, and we had to fly home. You know, I still haven't been to a Series game?"

"Me either." Of course, in my case it was because I didn't follow sports. I only knew about the '89 Series because I remembered my mother—who was a huge baseball fan—talking about it. She talked about other baseball-related things, but I didn't care about any of those. Postponing for an earthquake, though? *That* was interesting.

Anyhow, it was obvious that Kamilah didn't have any amnesia issues, but just in case: "So what happened after the ground shook and the pavement split?"

"The car in front of me hit the brakes, and so did I, but I turned right so I wouldn't hit him—but I crashed into another car and got bounced around a little."

I glanced at her arm. "More than a little."

"No, I wanted to call 911, but my arm was in so much pain. The ambulances came pretty quick, though."

I finished my exam, and left her alone.

The next wave came soon after that—the really bad injuries, and the people who were trapped in their cars and had to be carefully and safely removed by the fire department.

I wound up assisting Dr. Banerjee, a surgeon who'd been called down to assist in the emergency. She needed to remove several large pieces of what used to be a windshield from various places on the legs of a teenager named Jamal Crewey. I wasn't any kind of surgeon, but Banerjee needed another pair of hands, and, as Park put it so incredibly sweetly when he ordered me to help her out, "Yours will have to do, I suppose, Abraham." When the ER's a zoo like this, you dance where they tell you.

While Banerjee was prepping, I asked Crewey if he remembered what happened. At this point, I'd gotten the story from several people, and was forming a picture in my head.

"You don't need to question him, Dr. Goldblume," Banerjee said while she prepped. "He's been cleared for a concussion."

"Yeah, but it might take his mind off his leg."

"Ain't no thing," Crewey said. "Y'all gave me the *good* motherfuckin' shit. I ain't feelin' *nothin'*."

I smiled under my mask. "Glad it's working. So what happened?"

Banerjee gave me an annoyed look, but I ignored it.

"It was some motherfuckin' shit. Motherfuckin' road jus' *opened* an' shit. Right under my motherfuckin' Escalade. An' there was *fire* an' shit."

"Fire?" This was new. Then again, the other patients I talked to were all approaching the part where the pavement split open. Crewey was the first one I'd talked to who was on top of it.

"Yeah, some crazy motherfuckin' shit. I thought there was, like, sewer lines or some shit, but this was some motherfuckin' *fire* up in there."

"All right, Mr. Crewey," Banerjee said before I could ask another question, "let's get you set."

The anesthesiologist went to work on Crewey, and I did some more prep work.

Banerjee got everything out of Crewey's leg, and then I treated the wounds while she went on to another patient who needed cutting.

The worst part of the night was not long after I finished with Crewey. An older man named Valery Nechai, who'd come in unconscious, had woken up, and I gave him a once-over. He answered all my questions, but he had rather a big one for me: "Please, Doctor, where is my wife? She was driving the car."

"Not sure—what's her name?"

"Ana Nechai. She is a very careful driver. I do not know how this could have happened."

I gave him an encouraging smile. "Well, the pavement split open out of nowhere, Mr. Nechai. I don't think they cover that on your driver test. Just in case they brought her in without her ID, what does she look like?"

"She is short, only one-and-a-half meters, and very thin. White hair to her waist."

"She the same age as you?"

He nodded.

"Okay, I'll check, see if I can find out where she wound up."

"Thank you, Doctor."

First thing I did was head to the one of the desks in the center of the ER and talk to Bekenya. There were four clerks working this shift, but Bekenya was the one of the four who liked me the most. Mind you, most of the clerks hated the doctors, but I was only part-time, and I also actually treated the clerks like human beings. The other clerks mostly just figured that was an act to try to cash in with favors later, and they treated me with the same disdain that they did anyone with "MD" after their names. Bekenya, though, saw it for the genuine charm and friendliness that it was. I've always found it's better to be nice to people. Doesn't cost me anything and it usually makes it easier to talk to them.

"Hey, Bekenya."

"Hello, Abraham." That was the other thing. Bekenya called me by my first name. Every other medico was "Doctor Whoever." "What may I do for you?"

"Got a husband who was part of the Bronx River pileup looking for his wife. Ana Nechai." I spelled the last name.

"I see a Valerie Nechai."

"That's Valery—that's the husband. No other Nechais?"

Bekenya shook her head.

"Check the Jane Does—she's five feet tall, white hair, skinny, sixty-two years old."

Scrolling through the unidentified women checked into the ER, Bekenya found nothing that matched. One was close, but it turned out to be a woman who was brought in earlier this afternoon before the mess on the parkway.

"If you want," Bekenya said, "I can call the other ERs, see if one of them have her." There were several other hospitals in the area to which the patients could have been sent. And that was how I know that Bekenya genuinely liked me—she never would've volunteered to do that for anyone else.

"Thank you. Mr. Nechai's in twenty-three right now, although they're taking him for tests soon."

As I said that, two paramedics were walking by. I knew one of them, Ash Perrin, a lithe transgender. Ash had a new partner, a burly African-American man with brooks stitched into the chest of his blue shirt. It was the latter who said, "Mr. Nechai? It's not Valery Nechai, is it?"

"Um, he's in twenty-three. Why?"

Ash exchanged glances with Brooks and said, "Shit."

"What is it?" I asked, though I could guess the answer based on the looks on their faces.

Brooks said, "We had a DOA at the scene. ID said Ana Nechai, and listed her husband Valery Nechai as her next of kin."

"You didn't treat the husband?" I asked, confused.

Ash said, "She was thrown clear of her car. After we pronounced her, we figured out which car was hers, and we found out that her husband was in the passenger seat and had already been taken here. We were just gonna go do the paperwork now."

"Dammit. Okay, thanks, Ash. And thanks, uh—"

Brooks put out his hand. "Ralph."

I returned the handshake. "Abe Goldblume. Helluva night, huh?"

"Yeah."

I went back to give Valery Nechai the awful news about his wife. I don't think I'll ever get used to telling people that their loved ones are dead.

Truthfully, I hope I don't. Getting inured to stuff like that is what might turn me into Bernie Iturralde. If that happens, I'm gonna have Miriam just turn me into a newt and have done with it.

By the time 1:30 am rolled around, things had gotten back to something like normal. I spent my last half hour on-shift looking at some of the people who'd been waiting semi-patiently. Their place in the queue was bumped down a lot by the pileup. I treated them while trying not to think about how devastated Valery Nechai was at the death of his wife.

At 2:07, I clocked out and drove back home. I was a loopy, disjointed combination of wired and tired. The wired part was handy, as it meant I could operate a motor vehicle. But the tired part meant that my brain was pinballing all over the place when I really wanted to focus on why the pavement split open on the Bronx River Parkway. That was not a natural phenomenon, and the fire that Crewey saw pointed to it being very much a supernatural one. And it was one that claimed—according to Bekenya right before I clocked out—eight fatalities, including Ana Nechai.

Damned if I knew what it was, though. That was a Miriam question, but I wasn't suicidal enough to try calling her at 2:00 AM when it wasn't actually an emergency.

And I needed a good night's sleep so I could hopefully save *one* of the Bronx's immortal population in the morning.

As soon as I pulled into the driveway and turned the ignition off, all my energy seemed to shut down with the car engine. I stumbled my way upstairs, in no shape to even compose the email to Miriam. I barely had the wherewithal to set my alarm for 8:00 AM.

My head hit the pillow, and seemingly half a second later, the alarm went off. That was, on the one hand, a sign of how exhausted I was, and on the other that I really needed more than five-and-a-half hours of sleep.

When I woke up, my ribs were aching worse than they had since Friday night. The tippity-tap of rain on the bedroom window, punctuated by a crack of thunder and flash of lightning as I rolled over in the bed, told me why. Nothing like the high pressure of a storm outside to exacerbate bone pain.

As I sat up gingerly, grateful in the knowledge that there were more painkillers in the medicine cabinet, I noticed Mittens curled up at my feet.

I blinked, rubbed my eyes, and looked at the foot of the bed again.

Sure enough, there was Mittens. When he was a kitten, Mittens used to jump up on the bed, but by the time he was three, he'd stopped doing that. He'd only ever jumped up on the bed like that twice since then: when someone tried to tap into the ley line on 125th Street and when that dimensional portal got opened up on Orchard Beach.

I really hoped that whatever got him to become a foot warmer again was related to immortals dying and parkways splitting open and not something *else*.

I got my coffeemaker going, then took a quick shower, pausing enroute to swallow some pills. By the time I was dried off and dressed, the coffeemaker had finished making B-movie monster noises. I poured myself a nice hot cup and then sat at the computer to compose an email to Miriam and wait for the painkillers to kick in so moving didn't feel like someone was running over my chest with a steamroller. I'd follow it up with a phone call after I caffeinated my brain.

Once I got her all the info about the parkway weirdness, I checked my email. Surprisingly, I got one from Toscano. She usually kept to the phone with me, since she preferred to keep our interactions verbal and without a paper—or pixel—trail. Having said that, this came from her personal email, not her NYPD one.

Turned out to have an attachment: a still from the traffic cam on the Concourse near Anne DeLancey's place.

It looked exactly like a bat.

Toscano's email accompanying the picture read: *"Brammy: Here's what you were looking for. Det. Alves got a look, and he's an animal nut. Said it was definitely a vampire bat, if that helps. If it doesn't help, well, tough shit, it's still a vampire bat. — Lyd."*

Okay, then.

As I sipped more coffee, I started doing research on ways to reverse animal possession. By the time the caffeine had finally kicked in, I knew that the best I could do myself was temporarily halt the possession. To reverse it completely, I'd need a spellcaster.

My next step was to dig up info on May Ferris. Sure enough, there was someone by that name who lived on Dare Place in Throggs Neck. Unfortunately, she had even less of an online profile than Anne DeLancey—only picture I found was her driver's license photo. The only email address I could find for her was a prodigy.net address, which didn't bode well, as Prodigy was bought out ages ago.

I tried calling the number listed for her, but it gave me three tones and a message that the number was out of service. So I tried emailing the Prodigy address—which immediately bounced back as being no longer active.

Finally, I grabbed my phone to call Miriam. Only then did I notice the missed call and the voicemail, both of which were from Katie. She had called in the midst of the craziness at the hospital. I was so zonked after the shift ended that I hadn't even really looked at the phone until now.

However, the voicemail wasn't going anywhere, and I had an immortal to try to save. I called Miriam, who answered on the first ring and said without preamble: "You're up early."

"Gotta head down to Throggs Neck to talk to May Ferris, since she doesn't seem to be reachable via the usual twenty-first-century methods. Speaking of which, did you get my email?"

"Looking at it now. I heard about the thing on the Bronx River Parkway, and it's only part of the problem."

I didn't like the sound of that at all. "What do you mean?"

Miriam blew out a breath. "The City Island Bridge collapsed last night."

"The new state-of-the-art bridge that they just built?"

"Mhm. It's as structurally sound as any bridge you're likely to find. Or it was, anyhow. Also, the plant life in Ferry Point Park went brown and died last night—grass, trees, shrubs, flowers, everything. And both those things happened at the same time that the parkway split open."

"Anyone killed?"

"Besides the eight at the parkway? No, not that I read, just some injuries. This is bad, Bram. I'm talking to the other wardeins, but nobody's reported anything else odd, so it's probably local. What worries me is that it could be related to all the problems we've been having with binding spells. What if something's gotten loose that's more dangerous than a unicorn?"

Absently rubbing my still-sore ribs, I said, "Not sure there is anything more dangerous, but yeah."

"By the way, I've been trying to get ahold of Madame Vérité, but she's proven elusive."

"I did tell her that the only way the restriction was coming off was to talk to you."

"Well, listening to people who know what they're talking about isn't something she seems to have had a lot of experience with."

"Yeah." I shook my head. "Look, I need to head to Ferris before she's killed, too. And I need to stop at Ahondjon's first. Mrs. Truth got my last restriction, and I also need to get something to disrupt our killer's control over the vampire bat."

"Smart plan. I've put the word out that it's definitely not a vampire, by the way, and reinforced the restriction on vampire-related jobs."

"Good."

"As for the bat they're using to frame the vamps, you should see if Ahondjon has a Peruzzi Charm. They're best for freeing animals from possession."

"You sure? I was gonna go for an Osborne Amulet."

"They can't cover every kind of possession. The Peruzzi's more broad-ranging."

"Yeah, but I can only use the charm once and then it disintegrates. The amulet lasts for years."

"Gee, really? I didn't know that; what with being wardein and all."

I winced. "And for my next trick, I'll tell my grandmother how to suck eggs. Sorry, Mimi, not enough sleep after a shitty shift."

"It's okay. Anyhow, the amulet's more expensive and you'll just lose it after today anyhow."

I didn't say anything in response to that, to the point where Miriam said, "Bram? You still there?"

"Yeah, just trying to dredge up some outrage at that accusation of me losing the amulet, but I can't seem to manage it."

"Well, you are tired." Her tone turned mischievous. "Plus, y'know, I'm right."

"There is that." I sighed.

"Oh, almost forgot—I got that picture you texted last night. I didn't recognize her, but I'm running her through the database, see what turns up."

I smiled. This was why I loved Miriam. If this was her dad—or van Owen, for that matter—I wouldn't have been able to text the picture, I'd have to print it out and hand it to them, and if they didn't recognize her, that would be the end of it. Maybe Mike would look through some of his files, but van Owen would trust his memory. (To be fair, his memory was pretty good.)

But Miriam had made an effort since becoming wardein to digitize and automate as much as she possibly could. In fact, the database I searched to find out about disrupting animal possession was the one she created. Best research tool around.

"All right," I said, "I'm gonna get going."

"Good luck, Bram."

"Thanks, Mimi."

"Don't call me—" I cut off the call before she could finish chastising me for the nickname.

I refilled Mittens' water bowl and food dish, grabbed my denim jacket and my big-brimmed outback hat, and then headed downstairs.

Getting to Ahondjon's shop took much longer than usual. I'd expected some slowdowns due to the rain—precipitation always was good for tying up traffic into knots—but I soon realized there was more to it than that as I sat in the bumper-to-bumper mess on the Mosholu. The Bronx River Parkway basically broke in half. I turned on the AM radio in my car, since it wasn't safe to search my phone while driving in stop-and-go traffic. It was tuned to an all-news station, and I quickly learned that they'd closed the parkway in both directions between 233rd Street and Allerton Avenue. Those were the two exits on either side of Gun Hill Road, where the disaster happened. This meant the traffic was spilling over to the other north-south thoroughfares, including the Mosholu.

I played Katie's message on the phone's speaker while I sat in the barely moving traffic. "Hey, Bram! Just wanted to thank you again for the coffee. We *definitely* should do it again soon. Thanks!"

Eventually, I worked my way to Jerome Avenue and got a metered spot near the shop. After putting money in the Muni Meter and sticking the ticket on my dashboard, I went through the newsstand, nodding to the Pakistani guy behind the counter, and went down the steep metal staircase to see Ahondjon sitting behind the counter arguing with Madame Vérité.

Great. Just what I needed.

As soon as I came in, Mrs. Truth turned around and her face — already pretty well twisted in rage — got downright apoplectic. I tried very hard not to laugh in her face at the ridiculous expression on it, made even sillier by the clear plastic rain bonnet she was wearing to protect her coiffure.

"You! This is *your* fault!"

Ahondjon, whose dark, round face was a mix of grumpy and constipated — about like usual, honestly — said in his accented voice, "You know this woman, Mr. Gold?" Ahondjon always addressed people formally.

"We met."

"This man is responsible for my being denied my rightful ability to engage in commerce!" she yelled, pointing a finger with a very long, red-polished fingernail at me.

"Only indirectly, as I'm the one who told Wardein Zerelli that you tried to bind one of the loa."

Now Ahondjon's face was the one twisted in anger. "You did *what?*"

"I was conducting business for my community!" She was still screaming.

Ahondjon, though, wasn't much for volume. Instead, he got quieter. "Madam, you have precisely seven seconds to walk out that door, or I will phone the police and have you arrested for trespassing. Leave my store and never return."

Madame Vérité was actually quivering with rage now, but she stomped toward the staircase — as well as anyone can stomp on three-inch heels, anyhow — and grabbed an umbrella out of a bucket by the door. "You have not heard the last of me, Bram Gold!" With that, she went upstairs, clutching the umbrella like a sword.

"Lucky me," I muttered. I had no idea why she had both the bonnet *and* the umbrella, but whatever. Maybe she got her kicks poking people on crowded streets in the eye with the tip. I preferred to stick with the hat—the wide brim kept me about as dry, and it left my hands free. My line of work, you often needed both hands…

"What manner of accent was that?" Ahondjon asked as I walked up to the counter.

"Fake Haitian. She was actually born in the DR, but the community that she said she was serving is mostly Haitians."

"Mostly imbeciles if they follow her."

"Yeah, well."

Ahondjon smiled, showing his perfect dentures, since life growing up poor in Nigeria did not give him access to decent dental care. "So what may I do for you today, Mr. Gold?"

"Three things. One, I need a new booklet of restriction sigils. I used my last one on your most recent customer." I jerked a thumb toward the door.

"Of course. What else?"

"I need a Peruzzi Charm."

"You are in luck. I only have one left—the new shipment will not arrive until next month." He moved toward the shelves in the back. "And the third thing?"

"A minor complaint."

"If this is regarding the item you purchased last week, Medawe informed me of your issue, and it has been duly noted."

I sighed. That meant he was going to ignore me. I just had to hope that the Peruzzi Charm wasn't as stinky as the talisman that made the unicorn docile.

He pulled what looked like an ice pack off the shelf. Looking more closely at it, I saw that it was a bag similar to what they made ice packs out of but was a solid blue instead of white with instructions written on it. There was also a seam down the middle.

"You activate this by breaking the seal between the two sides. Easiest is to just snap it with your hands. The two elements will mix and the charm will activate."

"How long does it last?"

Ahondjon shrugged. "It will vary depending on the weight of the animal, the strength of the spell, the animal's lung capacity—"

"So you have no clue."

He smiled. "None."

"Fine." I took out my debit card and he ran it. While the machine contacted my bank to make sure my balance could cover the cost, I asked, "Out of morbid curiosity, you have an Osborne Amulet?"

"About a half dozen, why?"

"How much would that run me?"

He quoted a price that my current bank balance could not cover, especially with the added expense of the restriction sigils, which were *not* cheap. Well, maybe if Rodzinski and the Altys had paid me, which they hadn't yet, and if I didn't have to pay my ConEd bill and the rent on my office. I was starting to get why Miriam was pushing me toward the Peruzzi.

As I signed the receipt, Ahondjon said, "Oh, how did the Dozarian talisman function?"

"It didn't. Not," I added quickly as I handed the receipt back, "that it didn't work, I just didn't get to use it. The client changed his mind."

"Well, I hope it comes in handy at some point."

I smiled as I took the Peruzzi charm and the booklet. I placed the former in my jacket pocket and the latter in the back pocket of my pants where the old one had been. I'd actually misplaced the Dozarian, but I didn't see any good reason to tell Ahondjon that. The talisman only worked on divine minions, paralyzing them for a few seconds. The client in question had pissed off an Inca deity named Cavillace, but it turned out to be a lovers' quarrel—the client was *another* Inca deity, Coniraya. They made up, I got a nice kill fee, and reimbursement for the Dozarian, which I'd already paid a pretty penny for.

Would've been a useful thing to have around if I'd remembered where the stupid thing was.

I said my goodbyes to Ahondjon and went back upstairs to the wet street. Mercifully, the rain had lightened to a drizzle. I tossed the charm into the passenger seat, started up the car, and headed out.

I took Kingsbridge Road to Fordham Road, and then got on the Bronx River Parkway—south of the mess on Gun Hill, it was fine—and took that to the ever-hated Cross Bronx to the Throgs Neck Expressway. And before you ask, that was the official name of the highway. The section and the neighborhood were originally named Throggs Neck, but Robert Moses—yes, that jackass again—officially shortened it when the Throgs Neck Bridge and the expressway were built because he thought the original name was too long to fit on signs. That may be the single stupidest reason anyone has done anything ever. Anyhow, you ask any ten residents how they spell it, you get fifteen different answers, but me, I like to stick with tradition where possible and practical. And also to stick it to Moses.

Even with the lighter rain, the traffic was kind of a mess, and getting there was not as simple as it should've been. Then again, my travels today took me from the northwest corner of the Bronx to the borough's southeast corner. The Boogie Down may not be as big as Queens or as populous as Brooklyn, but it's still plenty big, and the roads aren't really designed with the idea of going from Riverdale to Throggs Neck.

Then again, the roads aren't designed to let you travel within the Bronx. It's all designed with ease of getting to and from Manhattan. Something else we can thank Moses for.

Anyhow, I eventually made my way to Pennyfield Avenue. On the way there, I went through a neighborhood that looked like every third area in the Bronx: lots of two- and three-story houses, with one apartment on each floor, mostly made of red brick, with awnings over both the windows and the front doors that were a sun-faded bright color like red or brown or green. The Bronx was littered with places like that—my own house was set up that way, in fact. Every immigrant group who came to New York had a bunch of people who migrated to the Bronx, and these it'll-do houses were perfect. Not the best buildings in the world, not luxury homes by any means, but serviceable places you can live in without being embarrassed.

Of course, once you got a little further into Throggs Neck, you got some private roads and nice houses and such with views of where the East River met up with the Long Island Sound. As I drove down Pennyfield, I could see the bridge, cars driving to and from the Flushing and Bayside neighborhoods of Queens.

Dare Place was one of six cul-de-sacs that used to be private streets. The streets were alphabetically named, with Dare being the fourth one up, between Casler and Eger.

My Corolla barely fit on the road, and it was two-way, thanks to being a dead end. The houses on the road all had a great view of the water.

The street was a mishmash of very old and very new houses. May Ferris's address was one of the former, a squat brick-and-stone building, only one floor, set in a bit from the street. Luckily, there was a driveway that had space for two cars, and only one actual car in it—

a big sedan that looked like it was at least thirty years old — so I pulled my Corolla in next to it, hopped out, and knocked on the door.

A short middle-aged woman with close-cropped dark hair and light brown skin answered the door. She had bags under her eyes, like she hadn't slept in a while. "Can I help you?"

"I'm hoping I can help you."

"Look," she said, backing off, "I really don't have any interest in questions about God, so—"

I held up both hands. "Oh, no, I'm sorry, not a Jehovah's Witness. Just a semi-observant Jew." I pointed to my oversized nose. "The schnozz gives it away."

She gave a small smile. "So should the hat and jacket have done. Proselytizers tend to be more formally dressed."

"No proselytizing for me. I'm a Courser."

She raised an eyebrow. "Who are never formally dressed. I always thought you were better off being called Slayers."

"Well, we don't always just kill things."

"Not based on the Slayers — or, rather, Coursers — I have met in my time."

"Which goes back to the draft riots, yes?"

For the first time since answering the door, she relaxed. She let the door open all the way, revealing a modest living room with a green couch, a blue chair, and a wooden end table. I could see a kitchen off to the left and a hallway leading to more rooms in the back. "Very well, you obviously know who and what I am. What is your business?"

"My name's Bram Gold, and I'm trying to figure out why three other immortals are dead."

"That would make two of us, then. Come in, Mr. Gold, and perhaps we may figure it out together."

Just as she stepped aside to let me into the living room, a vampire bat came out of nowhere and dive-bombed her.

Chapter 10

It wasn't like I should've been *surprised* that a possessed vampire bat was going to try to kill Ferris, since that was, y'know, the whole reason I drove to Throggs Neck in the first place.

And yet, here I was, completely caught off guard when one came howling through the doorway out of the rain and into Ferris's house.

We both swung our arms at it, but it moved quickly and darted around. Suddenly, I wished I *had* brought an umbrella, so I could swat the beast.

The bat dove toward my head and I flailed in a manner that was at once graceless, silly looking, and effective, as the bat got knocked back out into the rain for a second. It also did a number on my aching ribs, and knocked my hat to the floor.

Ferris had stumbled back further into her house and was now sitting on the green couch, hand over heart, breathing heavily.

I reached into my denim jacket's pocket for the Peruzzi Charm—and it wasn't there. Like the prime dumbass that I am, I took it out of my jacket pocket and threw it onto the passenger seat of the car so I wouldn't forget it, and then proceeded to forget it anyhow.

A gold-furred, shorthair cat came galloping out of one of the back rooms of the house into the living room just as the bat flew back inside. The cat—which looked like an Abyssinian—got up on its hindlegs for a second and hissed mightily at the bat.

The bat hovered for a second, and I took advantage of the lull to say, "Be right back!" and run out to the driveway.

"Where are you going?" came a plaintive, breathless cry from the living room. Not that I blamed her. She probably focused a lot more on my departing while she was being attacked than she did on what I said.

Naturally, the rain had picked up again and I was pretty much drenched from head to toe in the time it took me to navigate the twenty feet from Ferris's front door to the Corolla. Reaching into a wet denim pocket, I fumbled for the button on the keychain that would unlock the car, swearing that my next car was going to be one of those fancy-shmancy ones that unlock just by walking near it with a key fob.

Snatching the Peruzzi Charm off the passenger seat, I ran back into Ferris's living room, just in time to see a flail of arms and legs on the couch. Ferris was trying desperately to keep the bat away and not entirely succeeding. I heard a yowl and saw a flash of gold fur and realized that the cat was in there, too.

I had no idea how the bat was going to kill Ferris, but Toscano mentioned disruption of organs, and at the very least, the bat had to bite the neck to keep up the illusion of it being a vampire responsible, so there probably had to be contact.

Whatever, that was about to stop.

I held the charm in both hands and pulled the ends downward until I heard a snap.

A second later, the whole place smelled like the beach at high tide. Looked like I was going to have to have *another* talk with Ahondjon about his wares making with the stinky that he would ignore.

However, the bat suddenly flew up to the ceiling and settled on a brass light fixture. It hung upside down and didn't move.

The cat immediately ran out of the room, probably offended by the smell.

Based on her wrinkled nose, Ferris was equally offended, but more willing to tough it out. "What *is* that?"

"A Peruzzi Charm. That bat's possessed, and the charm broke the possession. The bat's probably both confused and exhausted, which is why it's just hanging out there, but this charm's only temporary."

She regarded me with disdain. "You had the charm in your car?"

"I—I forgot to bring it in. Sorry."

"Yes, well, it's just good for all of us that Henry came to assist me. I doubt I would have been able to fend off that creature for long without his help."

I assumed Henry was the Abyssinian. "You have a carrier for Henry?"

She nodded, figuring out why I was asking right away. "Of course. I'll fetch it and a towel for you."

Since I was dripping on her wall-to-wall, I appreciated that second part.

Reaching behind the couch, she pulled out a black mesh bag on wheels. After handing it to me, she went into the same hallway Henry had run down.

I unzipped the cat carrier along the top and put the charm inside it. Then I walked over to stand under the light fixture. The bat looked like it was sleeping, or at least breathing slowly, its wings moving ever-so-slightly.

After pulling the flaps of the carrier top apart, I nudzhed the bat off the fixture and into the carrier. I zipped it shut as fast as I could, and just in time, as it started flapping around. How much of its sudden agitation was because it was knocked off its perch, and how much was because I was dripping on it was an open question. It was definitely a legitimate bat response, and not a result of possession, as the charm was still intact, and still smelled horrible.

Ferris came back with a towel, which I eagerly took from her. As I patted down my hair and face, Ferris sat back down on the couch, again putting her hand over her heart.

My doctor instincts took over, as I noticed that her breaths were shallow and rapid. "You all right?"

She shook her head. "I've felt strange since that monster attacked me."

"Oh, come on, it's just a bat who was possessed."

"The monster to whom I refer, Mr. Gold, is the person who did the possessing."

I patted down my clothes as best I could, then sat down next to her and reached for her arm. "May I?" I asked before actually grabbing her arm. "It's actually Dr. Gold—I'm a GP in addition to being a Courser."

She blinked. "That shows impressive foresight, Mr. Gold. Or, rather, doctor."

"Blame my parents." I checked her pulse, which was racing to beat the band. She was also running a fever. Her glands felt okay, and her breaths were still fast and shallow, and that was the extent of what I could reasonably do in her house. "It could just be the stress of what just happened—and what already has happened to Warren, Ben Palmer, and Anne DeLancey. And it could be the aftereffects of the bat's attack on you—it may not have actually killed you, but it may have gotten the job started at least, and this could be a side effect. I'd like to do a full exam, if you don't mind. I also need to get the possession permanently off that thing"—I pointed at the cat carrier, in which the bat was still flapping about agitatedly — "before the charm wears off."

"And where would this examination take place?" she asked raggedly.

"I've got a home office, and I think you'll be safer there than here, since whoever's doing this knows where you live."

"That is reasonable. I believe I will require some assistance, however."

I helped her to her feet. She kept a coat rack near the front door that included both a raincoat and a couple of umbrellas. I helped her into the former and grabbed one of the latter, and also picked my hat up off the floor. I held the umbrella open over her head while she locked up the house. I was already soaked, and the umbrella was really only wide enough to cover her.

I put the cat carrier in the trunk, figuring the bat would prefer the darkness, and also because the smell wouldn't be so bad if the charm was back there.

Ferris pretty much fell asleep the moment she settled into the passenger seat, which was probably for the best. Her breaths were slowing down and getting deeper, which was a good sign, at least.

Before starting the car up, I texted Velez to see if he was free to break the possession on the bat. I figured I owed him for van Owen bitching at him.

The rain was now coming down in sheets, and we were also well into that great misnomer, rush hour. Every single highway between Throggs Neck and Riverdale was backed up, and so it took me almost two hours to get home. By that point, the rain had finally stopped, and it was completely dark out. At some point during the ride, Velez had texted me back to say he'd meet me at my place.

Ferris woke up when I pulled into the driveway, and said she was feeling a lot better.

"Let's get you upstairs." I got out, went around to the other side of the car, and opened the passenger door, helping her out.

"Thank you, Dr. Gold."

"It's a third-floor walkup, unfortunately," I told her as I unlocked the front door. My apartment was on the second floor, but my private exam room was on the third floor. It also had a wide-open space that I mostly used for working out, but also where any magick stuff got taken care of when necessary.

I slowly walked up the two flights with Ferris, then unlocked the upstairs and led her into the exam room. I told her to sit tight and relax and I'd be right back. First, I went into the workout room and grabbed the plastic folding table that was propped up in a corner. I unfolded it, pulled out the legs, and stood it upright, so Velez would have a surface to work on when he unpossessed the bat. Then I headed downstairs to retrieve the cat carrier from the trunk.

Just as I got downstairs, Velez was pulling his 3000GT up right behind my car in the driveway.

As he climbed out of the two-seater, I rolled my eyes. "You leave it there blocking the sidewalk, you're gonna get a ticket."

"Yeah, but your buddy at the five-oh can fix it, right?"

"Not again."

"Whatever, yo, I'll just add it to your bill." He gave me a big grin at that.

"It's adorable that you think I'll pay that. Just hope the cops aren't on the ball tonight."

I popped the trunk, and both Velez and I turned our heads away at the sudden release of Peruzzi Charm funk.

Hand in front of face, Velez said, "You have got to find your ass another magick shop."

"Yeah, yeah." I grabbed the cat carrier and we both went upstairs. The bat had finally calmed back down, at least, and it seemed to be napping like it was on the light fixture before I disturbed it.

Velez went up the stairs as slowly as Ferris did, and by the time we got to the top, he was wheezing. "You got some water? Or a fuckin' elevator?"

"What'd I tell you about exercising more?"

"That's for fat people. My ass is big-boned."

"Your body is big-boned. Your ass is fat. Anyhow, I'll get you some water."

The top floor had been a full three-bedroom apartment once upon a time, but while I'd turned the living room, dining room, and one of the bedrooms into the big workout room and the other two bedrooms into my exam room, I left the kitchen and both bathrooms as they were, the former with a refrigerator filled with lots of bottles of water. You'd be amazed how often folks who came up here needed to hydrate—most of those folks being me after a workout, of course.

I handed the carrier to Velez, who extended his arm to keep it as far from his nose as possible, and he went over to the table I'd set up. I opened the fridge to find only one bottle of water left. Knew I forgot something.

Walking over to the table, Velez had placed the carrier on it, and also slung the across-the-shoulder satchel he'd hauled upstairs with him. It contained his spell components. "It'll be, like, twenty minutes or some shit to set this up."

"Knock yourself out," I said as I handed him the water bottle. "Can you also do a provenance, see who cast it?"

"A'ight, but it may not work. It don't always."

"I know. Try it anyhow, it's worth a shot."

"Your ass is payin' for that, too. That one I really will add to the bill. Even if it don't work, I still gotta burn the roots, which means I gotta replace 'em."

"Yeah, I know how the spell works, Velez. Just add it to the invoice, okay? I'll be in the exam room with the person the bat attacked."

"Lucky him."

"Her. It's an immortal, May Ferris."

"So what the hell you need to check her out for if she can't die?"

"That thing you're depossessing tried to break her no-dying streak."

"Shit, they used Westerback?"

I frowned. That was a new one on me. "Westerback?"

Velez shook his head. "Spell that kills an immortal by usin' a creature of the air."

"And you can break that?"

"Nah, but I ain't gotta. I break the possession, Westerback ain't gonna work no more. They gotta start all over."

"Good."

"A'ight, I'm'na get to work. You go check up on Immortal Lady."

"Right."

Velez pulled pestles and herbs and roots and lighters and other stuff out of his satchel. I went back to the exam room. Ferris was lying on the bed, staring up at the ceiling.

"How you feeling, Ms. Ferris?"

"All things considered, Dr. Gold, I have been better. Just this morning, in fact. I feel very much what I imagine running a race might feel like."

Nodding, I grabbed my stethoscope and immediately did all the usual stuff for an exam. In the end, her heart rate was elevated, though I chalked that up to the day's stress. Her EKG read normal, but her blood pressure was unusually low, which contradicted my stress idea. Thing is, I had no idea what her baseline was. She'd been immortal since the nineteenth century, so she'd never actually had her blood pressure taken in her life. There were no medical records to compare to.

I heard Velez's footsteps coming down the hallway, so I said, "Excuse me," and smiled, then met him out there.

"I got good news, and I got bad news."

I sighed. At least there was *some* good news, though it would be nice to just once get only good.

Then I remembered something Hugues told me during training. *"Ain't never no good news, child. If there was good news, they wouldn't be hirin' us."*

"What's the bad news?" I preferred to rip the bandage off quickly, as it were.

"Provenance didn't work. Gonna take me weeks to get new karkalla from Australia, too."

I waved off his complaints. "I told you I'd pay for the damn spell. What's the good news?"

"Whoever it is the spell couldn't figure out who it was? Don't know a damn thing about what they doin'. Nobody taught this fool how to reinforce a spell, so they cast it twice, thinkin' that'd make it stronger."

"That mean you had to break it twice?"

"Nah, 'cause that would mean casting it twice *would* make it stronger. Only had to break it once, it just popped twice. And the charm's a pile'a dust now, so your big room over there don't smell like ass no more."

"So we're dealing with an amateur." I wasn't entirely sure that constituted good news, though the spellcaster not knowing the ropes explained the incomplete knowledge about vampires.

And then the ground shook.

It was only for a second, but it scared the living crap out of me. The Bronx was built on a gigunda piece of bedrock called the Fordham Gneiss. My neighborhood of Riverdale is on one of the highest spots in the city. So we're on a big hill made out of seriously solid rock — that's why my building doesn't have a basement, the rock is too solid to go under the surface — and yet whatever just happened to shake the Earth, we felt through all that.

This did not bode well. New York has had earthquakes before, but they were quick and painless — like a big truck backfiring. For this, I had to brace myself against the wall to keep from losing my footing.

It was over after three seconds, and Velez and I exchanged freaked-out looks.

"What the *fuck* was that, Gold?"

"My money's on an earthquake."

"No shit."

I checked the exam room to make sure Ferris was all right.

She was standing up now, still looking kinda shaken, but also determined.

"You okay?" I asked.

"No," she said, "but not for health reasons. If this keeps up, Malsum will be free."

I stared at her, having absolutely no idea what, exactly, that meant.

Before I could ask, though, she said, "You must get in touch with your wardein. I believe it is a gentleman named Zerelli?"

"Not for ten years — his daughter Miriam's the wardein now, and she lives nearby. I'll give her a call."

"Have her come here right away, if she is proximate."

I winced, glancing at the doorway to the staircase. "Yeah, that's not really an option. It's okay, though, Plan B will work, too. I'm assuming that this Malsum person is connected to your fellow three immortals?"

"Yes. And also the dire omens that have ravaged the peninsula these last few days."

"I figured. C'mon downstairs, let's set up a video chat with Miriam and you can tell us *all* about it."

Chapter 11

WE WENT DOWN TO MY LIVING ROOM ON THE SECOND FLOOR. VELEZ CAME with, even though his work was done. I considered kicking him out, but he seemed genuinely freaked out by the earthquake, and to not let him find out what was going on would be just mean. So I formally introduced him to Ferris as I invited the pair of them to sit down on the couch.

Mittens was in the big blue chair, and even as I scritched his head, he *mrowed* in annoyance that I hadn't fed him in *minutes*. He was probably also upset about the little earthquake.

I fetched my laptop from the home office and offered my guests drinks—Velez took another bottle of water, while Ferris asked for tea. I put some water on the stove and pulled out my supply of tea bags from the cabinet.

I called Miriam from the kitchen while waiting for the water to boil and my laptop—which was now on the coffee table in the living room—to boot up.

She answered on the second ring and said without preamble, "Bram, I don't have time to talk right now, so unless you've got something important—"

"I've got May Ferris alive and well, I've got the no-longer-possessed bat that tried to kill her resting comfortably in a cat carrier, and she's about to tell me all about what's actually going on, and I kinda figured you'd want to hear it."

A four second pause, then: "Okay, fine, I'd say that counts as important."

"Can you fire up your webcam? I figure that'll be easier than the three of us schlepping up to Seward Place."

"Three? You're counting the bat?"

"No, Velez. He's the one who freed the bat. I figured it would be churlish to exclude him from the juicy part. 'Sides, I have a feeling we may need more spells cast before this is over."

"You're probably not wrong. All right, give me a few to settle things out—that earthquake was definitely *not* natural, and I've got a few fires to put out. I'll start the video chat when I'm ready."

"You got it."

It only took Miriam about five minutes to finally call in, by which point I had made Ferris's tea.

Once Miriam's face appeared on my laptop's fourteen-inch screen, I said, "Wardein Miriam Zerelli, may I introduce May Ferris, last immortal standing." Only after I spoke did I see that Miriam looked even more stressed than usual. Her hair was sticking up in odd spots, though she had tried to tame it with a barrette or two, and her skin looked even blotchier than usual.

Not that I could really blame her.

Ferris gave the laptop screen a small smile. "It is a pleasure to make your acquaintance, Madam Wardein. I met your father when he was a young man training to replace your grandmother. I was unaware of his passing until Dr. Gold informed me. You have my deepest condolences."

Miriam smiled right back. "Thank you, and please, call me Miriam. 'Madam Wardein' makes me sound like a supervillain."

Ferris frowned. "A what?"

"Never mind," Miriam said quickly. "José, it's good to see you."

"S'up."

"So," Miriam said to Ferris, "Bram informs me that you have something to tell us."

"Quite a bit. I should apologize, first of all, for not coming to you sooner, but our task was always a solitary one, to be kept among the four of us. We had dealt with any issues ourselves, and there hadn't been one in decades. I honestly had assumed that your father was still wardein, and my memory was that he'd recently taken on the task, which was obviously faulty."

By this point, I'd sat down on the blue chair and Mittens had jumped into my lap. The stupid, twenty-pound moggy missed my genitals by about an inch. I was stroking his gray fur and he was purring while I spoke. "So there aren't any other immortals floating around waiting to be sucked dry by possessed bats?"

"There are not. I am, as you so eloquently put it, Mr. Gold, the last immortal standing, and the only one keeping Malsum from freeing himself. And I do not know how much longer I will be able to maintain the spell alone."

Velez asked, "What the fuck is a Malsum?"

"That's one of the Algonquin gods, right?" Miriam said.

Ferris nodded, then took a sip of her tea. "Bear in mind that, while I have many more years than any of you, the tale I am about to tell is older still. I was not present for the events I will describe to you. I will endeavor to speak the same words to you that Warham, Benjamin, and Anne spoke to me after Uncle John's tragic death during the Draft Riots."

"Understood," Miriam said.

"In the year of our Lord sixteen hundred and forty-one, a member of the Weckquaesgeck people—I think they are referred to as Wappingers in this age? In any event, a young Wappinger killed a wheelwright named Claes Rademaker by taking an axe to his head. It was a revenge killing, as the Wappinger who committed the murder did so in response to his uncle being killed by Dutch traders. Rademaker himself had nothing to do with the previous killing, but the young man felt that all Dutch should pay."

"Vendettas are always fun," I muttered.

"I assume you are employing sarcasm, Dr. Gold, as 'fun' is not a word that applies to this situation."

"It doesn't, no. Sorry, it's been a long week."

"For all of us." Ferris took another sip of tea. "The Dutch, thankfully, did not choose to wage war in response, but the one who killed Rademaker had a nephew of his own, a young man named Teattanquer, who grew up to swear revenge as well. However, he preferred to wield magick as a weapon rather than an axe. He attempted to raise Malsum."

"And that's bad?" I asked.

Miriam answered that one. "Very. According to both the myths and the files belonging to past Wardeins of the Bronx, Gluskap and Malsum were twins. Gluskap was the good twin, Malsum the bad twin, starting with killing their mother during childbirth by bursting out of her side rather than coming out the normal way."

"Charming," I muttered.

Ferris said, "The wardein is correct. Gluskap and Malsum were in constant conflict, which ended when Gluskap killed him and drove his magick under the earth. He remained there until the turn of the eighteenth century, when Teattanquer cast a spell to raise him up. He was opposed by the Reverend Warham Mather, who cast a spell to bind Malsum."

That actually got me to stop petting my cat for a second. "Wait, that old drunk was powerful enough to bind a god?"

"For a time, and only by sacrificing his own mortality."

"Not gettin' old?" Velez said. "Shit, that don't sound like no kinda sacrifice to me."

Giving Velez a withering look, Ferris said, "Try it, Mr. Velez, before you sing its praises. Immortality is a cruel burden. Of the four of us, only Benjamin truly took to it, using his longevity and wealth to further the goals he viewed as important. For the rest of us, it became increasingly difficult to keep our lives discreet. Anne and I preferred to live quietly, while Warham chose to remove himself from society all together. In fact, casting the spell when he did cost him dearly at the time."

"What do you mean?" Miriam asked.

"Warham was a reverend, well respected in the communities of Lower Yonkers, Eastchester, and Westchester. A Colonel Heathcote was charged with uniting the frontier communities of what we now call the Bronx under the Church of England, and he saw Warham's practicing of magick as satanic. He refused to induct Warham into the living of the church." Ferris sighed. "I remember when Warham first told me of it. It was two-and-a-half centuries removed, yet he felt the slight as strongly as he had the day Heathcote refused his petition to join the living."

"Wait," I said, leaning forward and letting Mittens jump to the floor, "you said Warren cast the spell alone?"

"Yes, and that was sufficient—at first. But Teattanquer was determined, and years later, he made a second, more powerful attempt. Warham needed to reinforce the spell." Ferris turned to look at Velez. "You spoke earlier of how the person who is trying to free Malsum now was ignorant of the nature of spellcasting, that casting it twice would do nothing to reinforce it."

"Yeah, so?"

"The notion does have its roots in truth. A person casting the same spell twice is akin to singing a song twice as loudly and assuming that the song is stronger, yet it is in fact the same song. However, a second spellcaster may cast the spell on top of it, which *will* serve to reinforce — more akin to two people singing a song in harmony and thus making the song more powerful."

"Kinda already knew that," Velez said.

"We all did," I added quickly, "but I like that metaphor better than the one Miriam's dad used when he explained it to us as kids. So when Teattanquer tried again, that's when your uncle and Palmer and DeLancey stepped in?"

"Not all at once. Benjamin reinforced the spell the second time, and Anne and Uncle John did so a decade after that. That third attempt was when Teattanquer was an old man, and he died in his final failed casting of the spell to free Malsum."

Miriam asked, "And you've had to maintain the spell all these centuries?"

"Shit yeah, you wanna go keepin' a fuckin' *god* under wraps," Velez said.

"Is this the first time someone has tried to break the spell?" I asked Ferris.

"Since Teattanquer died? Yes, it is. But we remained vigilant, as there were a few natural occurrences and unrelated incidents that risked freeing Malsum. The spell covers a large portion of the peninsula, but there are spots where it is weak."

"Let me guess," I said, "by the Gun Hill Road exit on the Bronx River Parkway? Ferry Point Park? City Island?"

Ferris nodded. "Yes. The incidents that occurred there were Malsum's attempts to break through the weakened spell. We were first alerted to the danger when someone cast Babb-Jobson."

That got Velez's attention. "For real? Didn't think anybody was pullin' that one out."

Frowning, I said, "I don't know that one."

Miriam said, "It disrupts binding spells. At least when it works, which it only does about half the time, which is why it isn't in common use anymore."

"It had no effect on our binding," Ferris said. "Quadruply reinforced as it is — or was, at least — it was simply reflected back."

Velez put his head in his hands. "Oh, shit."

I rolled my eyes, and Miriam did the same.

Ferris now looked confused. "I do not—What is it?"

"It wasn't reflected back," I said, "it had a cascade effect on *other* binding spells. Basically, half the binding spells in the area became unraveled, and casting binding spells became twice as hard." Absently, I rubbed my ribs, still sore from one of those unraveled binding spells.

Quietly, Ferris said, "I hadn't realized that."

"No reason why you should have," Miriam said. "But what's done is done. What matters now is keeping Malsum imprisoned. I assume we need to reinforce the spell?"

Ferris nodded. "I believe it will only require two more spellcasters rather than the three we had. Malsum's power is much less than it was, as there are few who still worship him. But I do know that my own efforts will be insufficient before too long. And whoever casts the spell will have to sacrifice their mortality—their very humanity."

"You sure *look* human," Velez said.

"There are many things that are now denied me, Mr. Velez. I no longer enjoy food, I cannot procreate, my ability to experience pleasure is stunted—it is a hellish existence, one I only agreed to because the alternative was the death of thousands. Today, it would be millions should Malsum be loosed, for even weakened, the population of this peninsula—of this city—would be helpless before him."

Miriam was frowning. "So we'd have to find two spellcasters who would be willing to make this sacrifice."

Velez raised both hands. "You ain't got one here. I don't give my ma some grandkids, my ass is disowned."

"Yeah, I'm guessing there's gonna be an issue with anyone we ask," I said. "But you never know. We should start making phone calls."

A voice came from the front door, which I didn't hear open. "There will be no need for that, Bram Gold."

I looked up and saw my mystery woman. She had the same outfit on again, including the purple shawl, since it was a little colder. I wondered if this woman ever did laundry, or if she was a spellcaster who made her clothes never get dirty. Or maybe she just had three copies of the same set of clothes.

I didn't ask her about that, though, since I was focused on something more basic. "How the hell'd you get in here?"

"Quite easily," she said with her honeyed voice. I wanted to be pissed at her for invading my home, but just those two words, and I was all at ease.

Ferris was standing up now, her jaw set, her fists clenched. "Such as she may go where she pleases. She is, after all, a god."

I blinked. "Excuse me?"

Bowing her head in acknowledgement to Ferris as she walked the rest of the way into the living room, the woman said, "May Ferris is correct."

"Of course I'm correct. I've spent the last century and a half maintaining a spell to imprison a god. I'm quite well versed in all those that still walk this world, including Egungun-Oya."

I just stared blankly, as the name didn't ring a bell, but Miriam came to my rescue. "I wasn't aware that the Yoruban goddess of fate and divination was living in the Bronx."

"I live in no one place, Miriam Zerelli, but rather spend time in any place in which those who worship dwell."

I nodded, putting it together. The Vodou practiced by Madame Vérité and the people she was binding the loa for is derived from West African religions, including the Yoruban pantheon. "*That's* why you were helping me out."

Egungun-Oya nodded. "Yes. I'm one of the loa that Bonita Soriano was attempting to bind to her will."

"What," Miriam said, "that mess in Seton Park?"

"Yeah." I shook my head, confused, though now I knew why her clothes never got dirty. "So what are you doing here now?"

"Offering my services. The spell cast by Warham Mather and reinforced by Benjamin Palmer, John Ferris, Anne DeLancey, and May Ferris is no longer sufficient to contain Malsum. Rather than ask any more good people to make the same sacrifice that the five of them made, I offer instead to cast the spell myself."

"You can't," Ferris said. "You have no mortality to sacrifice."

"The spell only requires the *power* of such a sacrifice," Egungun-Oya said with a sweet smile. "I already *have* such power."

"We got one problem, though," Velez said.

"Only one?" I asked with a snort.

"God lady here can't reinforce the spell. She gotta cast a new one."

That didn't make sense to me. "Why not?"

"Same reason you don't put Mentos in your soda pop."

Miriam added, "Spells involve the interaction between a person and various forces in the aether. Different people interact differently with them. Gods aren't actually people, so their method of interaction is different. If Egungun-Oya tries to reinforce Ms. Ferris's spell, it would backfire. There'd be the backwash of so powerful a spell failing *and* Malsum would be free again."

Egungun-Oya — who at this point had moved into the living room and was perched on the arm of the couch — shrugged. "Then I will cast a new spell. It should be powerful enough to keep Malsum trapped."

"'Should'?" I shuddered. "You're not sure?"

"Ain't no 'sure' in this business, Gold, you know that," Velez said.

"Okay, fine, so assuming it does work — won't there be a pause between the spells when Malsum is free?"

"It will only be a few minutes," Ferris said, "but Malsum will be able to act. In fact, he is already preparing to do so. His attempts to break free have borne some fruit, and he is gathering his forces at several places where he might break through."

I swallowed. "He has *forces*?"

Egungun-Oya smiled. "All gods have forces. It is what makes us gods."

Miriam said, "In Malsum's case, he can control wolves. Which means he might be able to control werewolves. Dammit. Ms. Ferris, where are those places he's gathering his forces?"

Ferris looked at me. "Do you have a map of the peninsula?"

I nodded and sat down on the couch between Egungun-Oya on the arm and Velez on the other half of the couch. Ferris was still standing. I made the video chat window smaller so it only took up a small corner of the monitor, then called up a map of the Bronx on the rest of the screen.

Ferris knelt down in front of the coffee table and pointed to six spots on the map. "Here, here, here, here, and possibly also here and here."

For Miriam's benefit, since she couldn't see where on the map Ferris was pointing, I said, "The definites are the parade ground in Van Cortlandt Park by Broadway, the Gun Hill Road exit on the Bronx River Parkway, the City Island Bridge, and Ferry Point Park. The maybes are the shopping mall in Co-op City and Bronx Community College." I looked at Ferris. "I'm guessing it's not a coincidence that Ferry Point Park, the City Island Bridge, and that part of Gun Hill were hit before?"

Shaking her head, Ferris said, "There are two sigils that can weaken the spell. If you link the four locations they make one of the sigils—all six will make another."

Miriam, I noticed, was looking away and writing something. After a second, she held up a piece of paper. I maximized her window so we could all see it better. She had drawn two different symbols, which looked roughly like the results of two connect-the-dots games with those locations.

"These two, yes?" Miriam asked.

"Yes."

Miriam put the piece of paper down. "The six-point one is a pretty common disruption symbol. Given that we're dealing with an amateur, I think that's the more likely of the two. The four-point one is fairly obscure."

"Yeah," Velez said, "that six-point one was one'a the first things I learned, but I ain't never seen the other one."

"All right." Miriam folded her hands in front of herself on her computer desk, which usually meant she was making a decision. "Egungun-Oya, how long will you need to prepare the spell?"

"I will need to assemble the components."

"José, can you assist with that?" Miriam asked.

"Uh, yeah, I guess."

Egungun-Oya gave Velez her biggest smile. "I would be very grateful for your assistance, José Velez."

"Yeah, okay." Velez was squirming on the couch, which I would've enjoyed the hell out of under different circumstances.

"Assuming we may gather said components with dispatch," Egungun-Oya said, looking back at the laptop, "I can be prepared within twenty-four hours."

"All right," Miriam said, "we'll need to time this right. I'll gather up as many Coursers as I can and send them to those six locations. They can deal with whatever minions Malsum sends through when Ms. Ferris's spell goes down."

I was really pissed off that I didn't know where my Dozarian talisman had gotten to. It would've come in real handy right about now. Aloud, I just asked, "Where do you want me?"

"My place," Miriam said. "I need you, Abby, Eddie, and Dahlia in the basement to guard the werewolves. I hope I can get them all here."

Miriam's grandmother had converted the basement of the house on Seward Place to a dungeon with several cells in case creatures needed to be imprisoned. I nodded and said, "Not that I object, but why those three in particular with me?"

"Because of all the Coursers in the demesne, you four are the only ones I trust not to kill the werewolves."

I couldn't argue with that. So I argued with something else. "We sure Malsum'll be able to control them?"

"Like José just said, there's no such thing as 'sure' here. But Malsum is a wolf-god; I can't take the chance that he'll be able to use Anna Maria, Mark, Tyrone, and Katie for his own ends."

Egungun-Oya said, "You should heed your wardein's words, Bram Gold. Malsum is fully capable of taking possession of any lycanthropes." Then she looked at the laptop. "Are there truly only four within your demesne?"

"That I know of. Trust me, I've looked. I'll also talk to van Owen, Katz, Annichiarico, and Kearny, warn them, too."

I nodded. Those were the wardeins of, respectively, Manhattan to the south, Long Island (including Brooklyn and Queens) to the east, northern New Jersey and parts of eastern Pennsylvania to the west, and the Hudson Valley to the north.

Egungun-Oya stood up and beckoned to Velez with a gesture. "Come, José Velez. Let us assemble what is necessary."

"Uh, yeah, sure."

I chuckled. I'd never seen Velez look this uncomfortable.

At my chuckle, he shot me a look. "Kiss my entire ass, Gold. And hey," he added, looking at the laptop, "I'm gettin' paid, right?"

Miriam nodded. "Assuming we survive, José, send me a bill for your time on this."

Velez shuddered. "Yeah."

So did I. I'd dealt with all kinds of nonsense since Hugues started training me, but the potential for nastiness here was worse than anything I'd seen since the last time Shostakovich blew through town.

"Hey, Egungun-Oya."

She turned and smiled sweetly at me. "Yes, Bram Gold?"

"I appreciate you helping me out, but this goes a little above and beyond recompense for stopping Madame Vérité."

"Many of my people live in this borough, Bram Gold. I do this for them."

With that, she departed, Velez following her out the door. This time I saw her actually *use* the door, which was a nice change, and probably for Velez's benefit. Idly, I wondered if she was gonna ride with him in the GT.

Ferris put a hand to her head and sat back down on the couch.

I sat next to her. "You okay?"

She nodded quickly. "Malsum. Dr. Gold, may I use your upstairs space? It is quiet up there and better for the meditations I must engage in to maintain the spell. The barriers are weakening, and it will require everything I have to maintain them until that woman is ready."

"Absolutely. The door's still unlocked."

"Thank you." She got up slowly and walked to the front door. "I will also cast a warding spell so that I will not be disturbed, and also be protected from any of Malsum's minions that he may send after me. I will allow you, Mr. Velez, and the wardein to penetrate those wards."

Miriam wasn't likely to get up there, but I thought it was kind of Ferris to include her. "What about Egungun-Oya?"

Ferris snorted as she opened my door. "The warding spell cannot keep out gods, only slow them down. Which is why I must be sure to maintain the spell. If Malsum should be freed, I suspect I will be his first target."

"Yeah. Good luck."

"Thank you, Dr. Gold—for everything. You saved my life today."

I nodded as she left the apartment and headed upstairs.

Then I turned to look at Miriam. "This is bad, isn't it?"

"Let's hope not. I'm gonna call Mark and Tyrone. Can you call Katie and Anna Maria? Then if you could call Abby and Dahlia and get them to my place. I'll call Eddie, I want to tell him that his restriction is lifted."

"He'll appreciate that. So will Indira."

She smiled raggedly. "Yeah. We can do this, Bram."

"You trying to convince me or yourself?"

"Yes."

I chuckled. "That's what I figured. Ferris should be okay on her own. I'll ask Rebekah to keep an eye on her when I head over to your place."

"Best not. She said she was setting up a warding, right?"

I snapped my fingers. "Right. At the very least, I'll ask her to call me if she hears anything weird up there."

She nodded. "Let's make those calls. Be here in five?"

"You bet." I ended the video chat and then pulled out my phone. I sent a text to Rebekah, then called Anna Maria.

Chapter 12

THE GOOD NEWS: WE GOT IN TOUCH WITH ANNA MARIA, TYRONE, AND Mark, and they agreed to come straight to Miriam's. Anna Maria and Mark were both single—the former by her choice, the latter by the choice of the rest of humanity—so they got there pretty quick. Tyrone had his daughter that evening, so he had to arrange things with his ex for her, which took about an hour.

More good news: I got in touch with a friend at the Wildlife Conservation Society, the people who ran the five zoos in New York City (not just the Bronx Zoo and the Central Park Zoo, but ones in Queens and Brooklyn, as well as the Aquarium). She agreed to send someone to take in the poor vampire bat that was stuck in a cat carrier upstairs. This was not my first possessed animal, which was why I'd cultivated the contact at the zoo. The bat deserved to be taken proper care of, not just let loose.

We had three Coursers at each of the six locations Ferris had given us as weak spots. Miriam had seriously considered not hiring Iturralde, but it turned out that only twenty-two Coursers were available, and that included calling ones in Manhattan, Queens, Westchester, New Jersey, even Brooklyn. She didn't have the luxury of screwing Iturralde, though I get why she was tempted. Not sure if that counted as good news or bad news, but at least we were ready.

But there was bad news, too: I hadn't been able to get in touch with Katie.

We were sitting in Miriam's living room. Our host was wheeling herself in with a tray of cookies. Tyrone had just come in and joined Anna Maria and Mark on the couch. Abby was sitting in an easy chair, Dahlia in a rocker, and me and Eddie both standing. Well, Eddie was standing, I was pacing, checking my phone every two seconds.

"I'm sure she's fine," Mark said.

"Who's fine?" Tyrone asked, as he took a cookie off Miriam's tray.

"Katie," I said. "She hasn't returned my voicemail message or responded to any of my texts or messages."

Anna Maria swallowed her own cookie. "Maybe she took a trip?"

I shook my head. "Nah, she doesn't really leave the house much. Besides, she posted her daily fish tank photo this afternoon."

Mark rolled his eyes. "God, is she *still* doing that? I had to unfollow her, I was going to *kill* someone the next time I found Nemo."

I gave Mark a death glare but managed to refrain from biting his head off—literally or figuratively. Still, there was no call for him to be *quite* that much of an ass about it.

Not that that ever stopped Mark.

I decided to call Katie for the fortieth time, and it went straight to voicemail again. "Dammit."

Miriam had been fondling her own smartphone, and then put it down and said, "All right, I just got a text from José. They've got everything they need, and they're heading back to Bram's place. Egungun-Oya will cast the spell in a little under an hour, and Malsum's window to try to get out will be about fifteen minutes while she does that. We need to get you three downstairs."

Holding up a finger, Tyrone said, "Hold up. I wanna know exactly why you got a jail cell downstairs."

"I don't." Miriam smiled. "I have six. They came with the house."

Anna Maria grinned. "Kinky."

That got Mark to wince. "Oh, yuck."

Dahlia then spoke up. "Don't get your hopes up. The wardein has always had to have facilities for imprisoning dangerous beings."

"For real? *We're* dangerous?" Tyrone asked. "Ain't even the full moon for another three weeks."

"Lycanthropy means the full moon triggers a transformation, but it's not the only time you can transform," Miriam said. "There are several instances of werewolves who figured out how to trigger the change on their own."

Mark shuddered. "Why in *God's* name would anyone want to do that?"

"Takes all kinds, Mark," I said, while staring at my phone trying to will Katie to send me a text.

Miriam went on. "Malsum has the ability to control wolves. He may be able to take possession of you, force the transformation, and enslave you to his will."

"Shit," Tyrone said with his usual three syllables.

Anna Maria stood up. "What the hell're we sittin' around here for? I mean, the cookies are nice and all, but if some Native god's gonna make me his actual bitch, let's get our asses locked up!"

Chuckling, Miriam said, "Abby, Dahlia, and Eddie will take you downstairs. I'm afraid you're going to have to strip. Don't worry, I put nice, cushioned seats in the cells, and the Coursers will bring you food as needed."

"Let's go," Eddie said.

After the six of them trundled off to the basement, I regarded Miriam. "I'm worried."

"I don't know what to tell you, Bram. I don't have much contact with her the other twenty-seven days, you know?"

"She said she's been doing more stuff out of the house since she started seeing a shrink—thanks for that, by the way, it's obviously done her some good—but she's still basically a homebody." I sighed. "Maybe she just stayed up all night working on a freelance gig and she's slept through the phone ringing."

Just as I said that, my phone dinged. I took it out and saw a notification that Katie Gonzalez was showing a live video.

"Aha!" I said as I touched the notification. The display changed to an image of Katie looking very sweaty and sitting in what looked like a bar or restaurant. Her hair was tied up with wet wisps sticking out everywhere, and she was wearing a skintight purple T-shirt.

"Hi everyone! So I did it! I went running! I know I've been saying I'd go running for *months* now, but today I *finally* did it! I ran the entire running track around the parade ground in Van Cortlandt Park, and I'm *so proud* of myself! That's a mile and a half, and I ran the *whole thing*! Now I need to check all these messages I got, but I wanted to go live with this as soon as I turned my phone back on because I know I've been talking the talk for ages, and now I finally walked the walk! Or, I guess, ran the run? Whatever."

"At least we know she's okay," Miriam said.

"And where she is," I added. "And that she made all her steps for today and then some. If she ran the parade ground, then that's gotta be the Tortoise & Hare she's sitting in." That little café/restaurant was right across Broadway — the western border of the park — from the statue of the tortoise and the hare from Aesop's *Fables* that was right by the one-and-a-half-mile track she'd just run.

I waited several seconds for her to call or text me, since I had a feeling that all the messages she was talking about were mine. Certainly the most urgent ones were.

But when nothing was forthcoming, I decided to go ahead and call her.

A moment later, a strange male voice answered tentatively. "Hello?"

"Um, who's this? Where's Katie?"

"I don't know, she— The woman sitting here just dropped her phone on the floor and screamed something and ran out of the restaurant."

"You're at the Tortoise & Hare, right?"

"Uh, yeah."

"Did you see where the woman went?"

"I think she ran across the street."

"Give the phone to the restaurant manager, please, I'll track her down." I ended the call and looked at Miriam. "This isn't good."

"I heard."

"Who's covering the parade ground?"

"Bernie, John, and Frank Haimraj from Brooklyn. They're the only two people who can stand to be near Bernie for more than five—"

But I was already running for the door. "I gotta get down to the park."

"Bram—"

"Mimi, those three schmucks will *kill* Katie the minute they see her. Well, all right, Bernie will, but the other two won't do a damn thing to stop him."

Miriam hesitated.

Then Abby poked her head through the doorway to the basement. "Miriam, they're all starting to change."

I stared at Miriam. "If they're changing, so's Katie."

Abby said, "You found Katie?"

"She's went for a run in Van Cortlandt, and she's still there."

Turning to Miriam, Abby asked, "Didn't you send Bernie Iturralde to Van Cortlandt?"

Miriam nodded.

"Eddie, Dahlia, and I got this. Asshat'll kill Katie."

I turned to Miriam, who threw up her hands. "Fine, fine, go."

"Thank you." I ran out the door.

We hadn't even had our second date yet, no way in hell I was letting her get shot by Iturralde. Miriam had told all the Coursers not to kill any werewolves they encountered, because they were pawns of Malsum. But Iturralde didn't listen to Miriam under the best of circumstances.

Luckily, I'd driven to Miriam's. I figured it would be good to have the car nearby just in case.

Proving that Mother Nature had a sense of humor, a big bolt of lightning flickered through the sky right as I walked out the door, and by the time I got off the patio, a clap of thunder reverberated throughout the Bronx.

It started raining as I hopped into the Corolla, and it got heavier as I went down the hill to Broadway. I parked in front of a hydrant—if I got a ticket, I'd pay it—popped the trunk, and then rummaged around inside it while the rain sluiced down my back and I deeply regretted not bringing my hat. I kept a bunch of backup weapons and talismans and such in the trunk amidst the spare tire, jack, tools, and other car stuff, and I knew I had a silver stick somewhere in the disorganized pile of crap.

Anybody who's seen a horror movie knows that werewolves don't like silver. It didn't actually burn them, though, they just were *seriously* allergic to it. The good news was that they knew the smell of it and recoiled. Silver bullets were useful if you wanted to hurt the werewolf, because you needed both the bad reaction to silver *and* the damage the bullet would do. Regular bullets still hurt them, but not as effectively, and they healed really fast. So silver was your best bet if you wanted to do actual damage.

And if you just wanted to stop them, the silver stick was for you.

I finally found it buried under the hydraulic jack, right next to the Henby talisman.

Crap, no, that wasn't a Henby, that was a Dozarian.

The Dozarian that I thought I had lost. Stupid thing was in the trunk all along.

I growled. Then again, it was about damn time the universe did something *nice* for me for a change. So I couldn't really complain all that much.

Pocketing both the silver stick and the talisman, I ran across Broadway in the rain, dodging a Bx9 bus and two SUVs, then working my way between two double-parked cars. A couple of people were standing around the Tortoise & Hare statue under an umbrella, pointing at the parade ground beyond.

As I walked up to the courtyard around the statue, I noticed a ripped purple tank top, ripped sweat shorts, a mangled sports bra, equally mangled panties, and a ratty pair of sneakers strewn about the wet ground.

"Jesus, what is that?" one of the umbrella users asked.

"Rabid dog, I think."

"Think those guys are animal control?"

I looked past the pair and saw Iturralde and McAnally standing on either side of a wolf that I knew from the coat was Katie. They were on the grass just past the running track—the same track that Katie had just kvelled about running around.

I'd never seen Katie's wolfen form look like this. She was growling and hissing, and her eyes were wild. The wet fur didn't help make her look any less scary.

McAnally had a silver stick out, but Iturralde had unholstered the rifle that he kept loaded with silver cartridges. At least he wasn't aiming it yet. Both of them were wearing trench coats and hats—if nothing else, the rain was getting some of the stains out of Iturralde's coat—while I was getting my denim jacket and hair both nice and soaked.

As I ran toward them, Iturralde said, "Gold, what the fuck you doin' here?"

"Three's better than two," I said, brandishing my silver stick and making a third point of a triangle surrounding Katie on the muddy grass. With my other hand I wrapped my fingers around the Dozarian in my pocket. "Where's Haimraj?"

"Tying up some kinda weird demon dog thing over by where the bathrooms are."

I nodded. There were public restrooms on the south end of the parade ground, right between the Van Cortlandt House Museum and the tennis courts.

McAnally added, "We saw the commotion here and came to deal with this creature."

"She's not a creature," I said, "she's a woman, and a friend of mine."

"She ain't no 'woman,' Gold," Iturralde said, "she's a damn werewolf!"

"Right now, she's a pawn of Malsum. Her actions aren't her own."

McAnally said, "Yes, we were told as much by Wardein Zerelli."

"I've got a Dozarian talisman. Give me a few seconds to activate it, and—"

Katie turned and growled loudly enough at Iturralde to interrupt me. That got him to raise his rifle and aim it at her.

"No!" I yelled out as he cocked the rifle.

"Fuck off, Gold!" His finger twitched on the trigger.

"*Don't* shoot, *please*! Let me activate the talisman and—"

Then Katie turned and leapt right at McAnally.

One second she was growling at Iturralde, then next she was airborne, and then next after that, she was on top of McAnally's prone form, blood all over her mouth and snout, and more blood gushing out of McAnally's throat.

Iturralde didn't hesitate a second time.

The park echoed with the report of his rifle as Katie jerked and then fell to the grass, bleeding from her stomach and whimpering in pain.

And then, all of a sudden, the wolf's body twisted and reformed into the naked form of Katie Gonzalez, fur falling off and mixing with both her and McAnally's blood and the rainwater and the mud. She had a nasty wound in her belly, just below the ribs.

"Jesus, what a mess," Iturralde muttered.

I knelt down next to both bodies. Katie was breathing, McAnally wasn't. Pointing at Katie's wound I said, "Put pressure on that."

"Why should I—?"

I was so very much not in the mood for Iturralde's shit right then. "I will shove that rifle so far up your ass you'll be shooting it through your eyeballs! Put pressure on the wound!"

"Look at you, all ballsy." But Iturralde did kneel down and put pressure on Katie's wound.

Meantime, I checked McAnally. His larynx, tonsils, and carotid artery were so much hamburger—I could see the brain stem, so much of the front of the throat was gone, especially with the rain washing away the blood and the gore. Because I was a thorough doctor, I checked his pulse, but there was nothing. He was dead within a second of Katie's attack.

Dammit.

Then I looked at Katie. She looked dazed, and the rain wasn't going to do her any favors, especially since she was completely exposed. Pulling out my smartphone, I called 911, identifying myself as Dr. Abe Goldblume of Montefiore Hospital. That didn't always help the ambulance get there any faster, but it certainly didn't hurt. I said there was a dead body and a GSW to the belly.

"The fuck you calling an ambulance for?" Iturralde asked. "You're a doctor, you fix her."

"One, I don't have any medical equipment with me. Two, I don't have time, especially since you're one Courser down, and I don't think Katie and that thing that Haimraj's hog-tying over there are the only creatures under Malsum's control we're gonna see here."

"Only *reason* we're a Courser down is because you made me hesitate. John's death's on you, Gold."

I had no reply to that, mostly because I couldn't come up with a way to refute it. If Iturralde hadn't hesitated, McAnally would still be alive. But Katie would still be bleeding on the ground.

I forced the ugly thoughts out of my head. Now wasn't the time, there was work to do.

Haimraj joined us while I took back over putting pressure on Katie's wound. Haimraj was a big guy, not too tall, but he made up for it in bulk. I'd heard of him—he had a rep as someone who always fulfilled his contracts, and also did a lot of *pro bono* work for folks in his home neighborhood of Brownsville—but I'd never met him before.

"What the shit happened here?" he asked with his light Caribbean accent.

"Naked chick's a werewolf," Iturralde said. "Had to put her down, but not before she got John."

I tensed, waiting for Iturralde to throw me under the bus. But he didn't elaborate.

Great, now I owed the pischer a favor.

"Shit," Haimraj said. "The mutt I hog-tied over there was a house pet that got possessed. You know how many dogs there are in New York? We got some serious shit here."

I should've realized that Malsum's ability to possess wolves also extended to dogs, since they were related. Just ducky.

We all turned at the sound of a scream. On the other side of the parade ground, a woman in running clothes very similar to what Katie had been wearing on her live video was being menaced by a dog.

She'd probably been running and then got caught in the rain but was determined to finish the run. Hell, that might have even been her dog that was now growling at her.

Katie had already started to clot—yay for werewolf healing—so I no longer had to worry about her bleeding out. And I had already called 911. I couldn't really afford to be here when the ambulance showed up and asked me questions I couldn't answer, plus I couldn't leave that other woman to be saved by these two alone. "Let's go. I've got a Dozarian talisman with me."

"Shit yeah," Haimraj said with a scary-looking grin. "Let's go kick some shit."

He eagerly ran across the grassy parade ground, Iturralde right behind him. I was starting to understand why Miriam put Haimraj with the other two.

Wiping rain water out of my eyes, I ran after them, again feeling in my pocket for the Dozarian, giving Katie one last worried look.

The demon dog leapt at the runner, and she backed off, still screaming. I could see that the dog's brown fur was streaked with red, and was wild and unkempt. Even from this far away, I could see its blazing eyes and foaming mouth.

Iturralde stopped running and aimed his rifle.

I stopped running, too, and turned around to say, "What the hell're you—"

But then he pulled the trigger.

The dog was leaping in the air when he fired, and then its head snapped back, it flipped around in the air, and then landed on the muddy ground with a squelch.

"What the shit?" Haimraj asked. "He's got a Dozarian, you didn't have to waste a round!"

The runner was now kneeling next to the dog. Its brown hair was now normal, except for the side of his head where the bullet went in, which was covered in blood. The red streaks in the fur were gone, replaced with gray, and the foam was just gone from its mouth.

"Oh my God, Pokey!" She looked up at the three of us as we ran toward the tableau. "You motherfucking sonofabitch, you killed my Pokey! What the fuck is wrong with you? He was just upset!"

I had no idea how to respond to that, partly because I wasn't the schmuck who shot her dog, but mainly because it was obviously a lot more than upset. Didn't she even notice the red streaks, the foam, and the crazy eyes?

Before anybody could say anything else, the ground started shaking and the rain got even more intense. I closed my eyes and wiped them while trying to keep my footing. Iturralde wasn't so balanced, and he fell on his tuchas right when I opened my eyes back up, which I had to admit I enjoyed seeing.

And then, just as the earthquake settled back down, three different creatures appeared near us on the parade ground. They were shaped like wolves, but they were standing upright, and they had no fur, red skin, and fire came out of their eyes.

"Jesus fucking Christ, what the fuck is that?" cried out the runner, who started crab-walking away from Pokey's corpse.

Haimraj stood between the demons and her and pulled a giant machete out from under his coat. "Stay back, ma'am."

"Fuck yeah," the woman said.

Iturralde clambered to his feet.

I noticed that there were runes on Haimraj's machete, and that struck me as our best weapon. "Can that thing behead a demon?" I asked him.

"That's what Mahjoub said. Ain't had a chance to use it yet."

Amy Mahjoub was one of the best magick blade dealers in the tri-state area. If she said it worked, it almost definitely worked. "Now's our chance. Bernie, distract them while I activate the Dozarian."

Iturralde glared at me, but didn't argue, probably because even his pea brain realized that he was in the best position to do that, while I got the talisman going. Once it was activated, they'd be paralyzed, and Haimraj could decapitate them with his machete of doom.

While Iturralde started taking shots at the demons, I took out the talisman. It was a sealed paper sack that activated by pulling on the tab to rip it open.

I tried to get a grip on the tab. In the pouring rain. With wet fingers. It was not going well. The reports of Iturralde's rifle echoed in my ears as I leaned forward and tried to get a grip on the tab while holding it inside my jacket. But the rain was coming down in sheets at this point, and that wasn't doing enough to keep it dry. Hell, at this point, it felt like my bones were wet, much less all my clothes and skin and hair—and the stupid talisman.

"Gotta reload!" Iturralde cried out. His rifle had seven shots, and he'd used two on Katie and Pokey. The five he'd taken had kept the demons at bay, but that was it. The bullets didn't even penetrate their skin. They were starting to advance on us, slashing with their claws.

"Shit," Haimraj said, and started wading in with his machete.

Giving up, I did the same thing I did with packages where I couldn't get a grip on the tab that was supposed to open it: I ripped the stupid thing open across the top with my teeth, hoping to hell that it wouldn't ruin the talisman.

This actually worked, miracle of miracles. A sickly-sweet smell permeated the wet air, and the demons all froze, one of them with its claws just half an inch from Iturralde's neck.

"Nice timing, Gold," Iturralde said with a shudder.

"Better late than never," I muttered.

Haimraj's nose scrunched up. "What the shit?"

Iturralde waved his hand across his nose. "That is sickening."

"Believe it or not," I said, "that's the nicest-smelling thing I've gotten from Ahondjon in months."

"You should go to Janovich's in Park Slope," Haimraj said as he raised his machete.

Right, like I was going to go all the way to Brooklyn to shop for magickal items.

Haimraj sliced through all three demons' necks cleanly with his weapon, decapitating each of them with a single swipe. Yellow ichor spurted out and onto the ground from both the neck stumps and the bottoms of the heads as they rolled and bounced on the mud.

This was why you paid the extra money for the good stuff. The only real difference between a magick blade and a regular one is that a magick one stays sharp, and it can cut through a lot more things and do so a lot more cleanly. A regular machete would've been a hack job and taken forever to get through the muscle and bone of the neck, not to mention the leathery, bulletproof skin of your average demon.

I wanted to say something comforting to the woman whose dog Iturralde had killed. She was now kneeling on the muddy ground staring ahead in what looked to my practiced, if very rain-soaked, eyes as catatonia.

As I started to move toward her, though, the ground shook *again*, only this time all three of us lost our footing. The demons' heads started rolling around, and I honestly thought the parade ground was gonna split open the way the Bronx River Parkway had the other night.

And then, all of a sudden, the ground stopped shaking and at the exact same time, the rain ended. In the few seconds it took me to get back to my feet, the clouds dissipated, and it wasn't too long before the sun started shining.

"I *really* hope that's a good sign," I muttered.

"Something's wrong." Haimraj was staring at the ground, gripping his machete.

"I don't see anything," Iturralde said.

"Your machete's clean," I said as I realized that. It had been caked in the demons' yellow ichor, but now the ichor was gone.

So were the demons. The heads and the bodies were all gone, and the ground wasn't even stained with their jaundiced blood anymore.

"Gotta love monsters that clean up after themselves when you ban them," I muttered.

"Shit, yeah," Haimraj said. "Last demon I iced, took me *weeks* to get that shit outta my clothes."

My phone beeped, while I heard a clanging sound from Haimraj and a buzzing from Iturralde. Pulling mine out, I saw that it was a text from Miriam: *"Spell successful! Malsum is still bound!"*

"Shit, yeah," Haimraj said.

"That's a damn relief." Iturralde glanced back at the other end of the parade ground, where McAnally's body and Katie's prone form were both lying. I heard sirens and a second later, an ambulance was pulling up to the Tortoise & Hare statue. "And a damn shame." He turned to stare at me.

I pointedly didn't look at him, which was pure guilt. I should've kept my damn mouth shut, just used the Dozarian—or just attacked her with the silver sticks instead of keeping our distance.

Dammit.

Of course, if I'd used the Dozarian on Katie, I wouldn't have had it for the demons, and I'm not sure we'd have come out of that unscathed without it before Egungun-Oya cast the spell.

Speaking of which, I got two more texts: one was from Miriam, the other from Velez, both telling me to get to my townhouse. Miriam wanted me to check on our Yoruban god, and Velez was more direct: *"Get your ass over here, crazy god lady just collapsed."*

Chapter 13

MY PHONE WAS EXPLODING WITH TEXT MESSAGES AS I DROVE BACK UP THE hill. Iturralde and Haimraj had parked their cars in a lot that was in the other direction, past the Van Cortlandt House, and that enabled them to leave the park without coming near the cops and ambulance. I wasn't so lucky, but nobody was paying attention to me, as they were too busy being freaked out over the earthquake that stopped the rain.

That and the naked comatose woman next to the dead body. I hated leaving her, but the professionals were on the scene, and they'd take good care of her. As much as I wanted to hold her hand in the ambulance, I had an immortal and a god in my house that needed tending to.

By the time I got to my place on Johnson Avenue, I had about a gajillion texts from Miriam, and a few from the other Coursers. I skimmed them after I parked the car, and they all boiled down to, *"All is well."*

Easy for them to say…

The other Coursers reported similar occurrences to what happened to our trio of Malsum's demons, or demonspawn mutts that went back to being ordinary pet dogs. Plus Anna Maria, Tyrone, and Mark had reverted back to their regular selves.

Lots of injuries—both Coursers and civilians—but the only fatalities were McAnally, the woman's dog, and one Yorkshire terrier that had been be-demoned. Antonelli had had to kill the dog to keep it from killing its owner. As it was, said owner had a broken arm from when she fell to the sidewalk.

All things considered, it could've been a lot worse. Which didn't make me feel the least bit better about Katie. Or about McAnally.

I ran upstairs to the third floor of the townhouse. Rebekah's door was ajar, but I didn't have time to really check and make sure she was home. Besides, if somebody tried to break in now, there was a Courser, a wizard, an immortal, and a god in the house. I didn't much like this theoretical burglar's odds.

Velez was waiting for me on the landing. His forehead was sweating and he was all fidgety. Last time I saw him like this was when he first met Katrina.

Jerking his thumb toward the door, he said, "God lady just fell down, and immortal lady don't look so hot, neither."

Nodding, I threw open the door and went into the workshop space. Egungun-Oya lay in the center of the floor, right in the middle of a perfectly drawn pentagram. Her snood was half off her hair, which had more red streaks in it than I would have expected. Her purple shawl was halfway across the floor, and her tan skirt was ripped.

Ferris was off in a corner of the workshop, sitting with her legs folded in your standard meditation pose. She was surrounded by four bowls. The one on her left was filled with sand, the one in front of her with water, the one on her right with feathers, and based on the flickering light behind her reflecting off the wall, I was guessing she had a candle back there.

Velez indicated Ferris with his head. "Immortal lady's bringin' it old school up in here, warding with that earth, air, fire, and water shit. I ain't seen nobody use that kinda warding since I was a kid."

I knelt down next to Egungun-Oya. "Has Ferris moved at all?"

"Nah. She still breathin', but that's it."

"That's something, anyhow." Egungun-Oya's belly was moving up and down very slowly, so she was still breathing, too, and I checked for a pulse, and she seemed to have one. Of course, I had the same problem examining her that I did Ferris—I didn't have a baseline for medically examining a god.

"It's gone."

I looked up and over to the corner. Ferris was getting to her feet unsteadily.

"Give her a hand," I said to Velez.

"What?" Velez stared at me. "She's warded, I can't get near her."

"She kept you, me, and Miriam safe from it. Go help!"

"Oh, okay." He ambled over to the corner to help her up.

"Thank you, Mr. Velez."

I stood up, too, my examination of Egungun-Oya having established that she was alive, probably, but damn little else. "What's gone?"

"I'm sorry?"

"You said, 'It's gone.'"

"Oh, yes." She smiled. It was the first time I'd seen her do that in our short acquaintance. "The spell. I no longer feel it. For the first time in a century and a half, I'm free of it."

"You can feel a spell?" I asked. "Like constantly?"

"Hells yeah," Velez said. "Not everything's like 'at, but somethin' with enough mojo to bitch-slap a god, that motherfucker stays *with* you."

Ferris started to step outside the warding, but as soon as her foot moved past the bowls, she collapsed.

Velez managed to catch her before she hit the floor, but he almost lost his balance and fell himself before getting himself upright.

As soon as she straightened, I gasped. Her face had gotten sallow. Velez tried to let her stand on her own, but then she collapsed again.

"Let's get her to the back," I said quickly, and the two of us guided her out of the workshop room toward the hallway to the exam room. Her bones felt brittle under her clothes, and she weighed almost nothing. When I'd guided her to my car from her house down in Throggs Neck, she felt a lot more substantial.

"It's all right," she said in a throaty whisper. "I'm finally free, that's what matters." I'd heard other people talk in that kind of whisper, and every single one of them was a patient who was dead within a week.

She completely collapsed, unable to support her own fragile weight anymore.

No way was I letting *another* person die today. "Get her into—" I started, but she reached up and grabbed my arm with a weak grip.

"No," she whispered. "It's all right. This is what I want, Dr. Gold. Thank you."

Her grip loosened and she went limp on the hall floor. I felt her neck, and there was no pulse and she'd stopped breathing.

"No, dammit!" I ripped open her blouse and started to do chest compressions, but Velez grabbed my shoulder.

"Leave it alone, Gold."

"I can't just—"

"She's *gone*. Look, you know how this shit works, a'ight? To cast that trap, she had to give up her mortality. Well, the spell's gone now, so she gets it back."

I looked down at her unmoving form. Every instinct in my body cried out to continue doing CPR, to save her the way I couldn't save McAnally or Katie. "So you're saying that you knew this was always a death sentence?"

"Fuck, yeah. Didn't you? With this shit, there's *always* motherfuckin' consequences, yo."

In all honesty, I did. Miriam's dad taught me a lot about magick. I just didn't think it through. And the last immortal in the Bronx was now dead.

"Shit," Velez muttered, and he took a step back and stared at my hallway floor.

Looking down, I saw what he saw. Ferris's body was putrefying right in front of us. Since I had ripped her blouse open, we could see it happening, not just on her head, but also her torso. Her eyes sank into her head and liquefied, her skin dried and flaked and fell apart, her tendons collapsed, her organs shriveled up into nothing, her bones disintegrated into powder. The entire process of decay on fast-forward. I was a doctor, and I thought it was pretty gross.

Velez wasn't a doctor, and he ran into the bathroom as fast as his three-hundred-and-fifty pounds could carry him. I heard the dulcet tones of regurgitation a few seconds later.

I was suddenly very glad that I had Rebekah to clean up the place. Though disposing of a body, especially one as decomposed as this, was a lot to ask, even for free rent…

While Velez was giving Rebekah something else to clean up by barfing in my bathroom, I went back to the big room. First, I blew out the candle the late May Ferris had used for her warding spell, then I went over to check up on Egungun-Oya. She was still unconscious on the floor, and since my last attempt to bring an immortal being into my exam room failed, I figured I'd give it another shot.

I grabbed her shawl and wrapped her in it, then picked her up in a firefighter's carry. She weighed a helluva lot more than Ferris, and my knees buckled for a second as I settled her onto my right shoulder. And points to me for remembering to haul her onto my right shoulder and not the left one I'd wrenched while fighting a crazy unicorn.

I brought her down the hall, stepping gingerly over Ferris's clothes and liquefied and powdered remains. The stench wasn't nearly as bad as it usually was when bodies decayed this much—but that process usually took weeks, and it was biology, not magick. Given how much magickal things had been stinking up the joint lately, I was grateful that immortal speed-decay was, at least, not as odiferous. I was getting more of an awful whiff from Velez's puke in the bathroom.

"Turn the fan on, will you, please?" I asked between Velez's groans.

His response was just to heave some more.

I laid Egungun-Oya as gently on the exam bed as I could.

For a few seconds, I just stared at her. Even unconscious, she was incredibly beautiful, though how much of that was natural beauty and how much was divine magick was anybody's guess. Her breathing was still steady, as was her pulse.

"Yo, Gold!" came Velez's voice from the hallway.

I left the exam room and came out to see Velez heading for the door. "I'm out. Need me about fifty beers. I send you the invoice or Zerelli?"

"Miriam." Let her deal with the paperwork. "And hey, Velez, thanks."

"Yeah, well, let's not do this shit ever again, a'ight?"

"Fine by me."

After he left, I took a peek in the bathroom. The place smelled like puke, but he'd at least cleaned up after himself, as there was no visible evidence of his regurgitation. Small favors.

I looked down at the hallway floor, then, and saw that Ferris's clothes were all that were left there. No dust, no liquid, nothing. Just the clothes. The body had disintegrated down to the molecular level, it seemed. Yay, magick.

Before I could pull my smartphone out of my pocket to call Miriam and bring her up to speed, the door opened. I figured it was Velez forgetting something, but wild dark hair preceded the ink-smudged face of my cousin.

"Is everything okay, Bram? I heard a lot of noise up here, and you asked me to check in if I heard anything weird up here."

"Yeah, kid, it's fine. I mean, it's not fine, but it's over. We've got a werewolf and a god who are both comatose, and we lost a Courser and an immortal."

"Wow. That's—that's horrible." Rebekah came all the way into the apartment. "Are you all right?"

I put a reassuring hand on her shoulder. "I'm fine. And hey, the good guys won. The reason there's a comatose god in the next room is that she kept another old god trapped in his prison."

Rebekah blinked. "Malsum's still imprisoned?"

"Yeah, he—"

And then I stopped dead in my tracks.

Oh, damn.

Oh, damn damn damn.

In a very ragged whisper, I asked, "How do you know about Malsum?"

"Um, well, you must've told me?"

"I only found out who Malsum even *was* yesterday. And the only communication we had was that text when I asked you to check on things. Didn't mention Malsum. So I'm gonna ask again, kid—how do you know about Malsum?"

Rebekah started fidgeting nervously. "That book on the Algonquins you lent me—had all kinds of stuff about Mals—"

"I'm not talking about who Malsum is, I'm talking about why you knew I was talking about Malsum when I said a god was imprisoned. Or why you were *surprised* when I told you that god was still imprisoned." My stomach started rumbling, and any minute I was gonna run into the bathroom and do an encore of Velez's puking. "What the *hell* did you do, Rebekah?"

She started blinking really fast. "I—I—" She shivered. "Dammit. Okay, look, this land *belonged* to the Algonquins! Malsum was only imprisoned because he was defending it against all the white invaders! It's been hundreds of years; he deserves to be free!"

My jaw dropped. "Do you know what you've *done*?"

"I'm trying to right a three-hundred-year-old wrong!" I could see tears welling up under her thick glasses.

"By killing people?" In my mind's eye, I saw Warren propped up against an oak tree, Ben Palmer dead in his living room, Anne DeLancey dying on the floor of her apartment, John McAnally with his throat ripped open, and poor Katie bleeding all over the grass. "Dammit, Rebekah, people have died because of what you've done!"

"The immortals didn't deserve to keep living for what they did."

A fist of ice closed over my heart. I'd heard Rebekah passionate about a lot of things, but to hear the fervency usually reserved for protesting murder talking about how she was *happy* that four people died...

"What about John McAnally and Alvaro Figueroa? They deserve to die, too? Does Katie Gonzalez deserve to be in a coma?"

"I—I don't know who they are."

"A Courser, a vampire, and a werewolf. Katie got possessed by your pet god and killed John. And thanks to your little trick with the possessed bat, another Courser killed a vampire named Figueroa for no good reason."

She looked away, staring at the floor. "You always told me being a Courser was risky. And vampires and werewolves are monsters! You hunt monsters!"

For a second I just stared at her. I couldn't believe what I was hearing. Unable to bear looking at her anymore, I turned away and stared down the hallway toward the exam room.

"And what about Ana Nechai? She deserve to die, too?"

"Is that another Courser?" Rebekah's tone was particularly snotty.

I turned back around and glowered at her. "No, she was an old woman who was driving down the Bronx River Parkway with her husband. Your buddy Malsum was trying to break through the immortals' spell, and it caused the pavement on the parkway to split open, and it flipped her car over. I treated her husband in the ER, but Ana died at the scene. Seven other people died in that pileup, too. That's all on *you*."

"That's not fair," she whispered.

"How is it not fair?" I was shouting, now, my heart beating like a triphammer. "I had to tell Valery Nechai that his wife was dead. How fair is it that he won't get to see the woman he married *ever* again?"

"I didn't—I didn't think that—"

"No, you didn't." I grabbed her shoulders and started shaking her. "You didn't think at all! What made you believe it'd be a good idea to fool around with magick?"

In a whimpering tone, she said, "You're hurting me."

I blinked, shook my head, and let go, taking a step back both physically and mentally. "I'm sorry." I didn't want to hurt her; she was still my cousin. But she also was the reason why Katie was being treated in an emergency room right now, why all those people were dead, and I just couldn't process it.

She said, "And you fool around with magick all the time."

"Actually, no, I don't. I fight monsters and magickal creatures and people who abuse magick. I don't actually *touch* magick with a ten-foot pole. That's what guys like Velez do." Remembering Velez's words, I added, "With this shit, there's *always* consequences."

"I was just trying to right a wrong. An ancient wrong."

"By committing half a dozen other wrongs? Pretty sure there's a cliché about that." I turned away again, back to not wanting to look at her.

A very ugly silence ensued.

What the hell was I going to tell Isaac and Judy?

She finally broke it by asking, "What happens next?" in a soft tone.

I let out a long breath. If anybody else asked that question— Hell, if it was anybody else, there'd be no *need* to ask the question, I'd have already done it.

Reaching into my back pocket, I opened my shiny new restriction sigil booklet and peeled off the very first sticker.

She tried to flinch away from the sticker, but the hallway was too narrow for her to avoid me easily. I placed it on her arm and it disappeared.

"What—what is that?"

"Gee, I thought you were a magick-user now. Don't you know?"

She whispered, "You don't have to be snotty."

"Yeah, I kinda do. Rebekah, do you *realize* what you've done? People have gotten *hurt*, more than a dozen people are dead at *least*, not to mention the property damage, the trauma..." I shook my head. "C'mon." I grabbed her arm and led to her to the door.

Locking the door behind me and hoping that Egungun-Oya didn't wake up while I was away, I took Rebekah downstairs, keeping a gentle but firm grip on her arm.

"Where are we going?" she asked.

"To see the wardein."

Chapter 14

MIRIAM SET UP HER LAPTOP IN THE LIVING ROOM SO ITS WEBCAM WAS focused on the rocking chair, where Rebekah was currently sitting, staring at the floor. I stood off to the side, out of the cam's range. Miriam wheeled herself so she was at the far left of the cam's shot, still in the video, but not the focus.

She said the date and time, and then: "This is a hearing held by Miriam Zerelli, Wardein of the Bronx, to determine the fate of Rebekah Goldblume. She is accused of practicing magick without training or licensing."

It wasn't required to record these hearings. Wardeins had the authority to carry them out, and transcripts of the hearings were to be provided to the Curia. Of course, the Curia hadn't updated any of their practices since Pearl Harbor was bombed, so their notion of a transcript was something done on a manual typewriter—or maybe a quill pen on parchment. Miriam was one of the few wardeins who actually used twenty-first-century technology in her work.

"Ms. Goldblume has cast Babb-Jobson, which failed to disrupt the binding spell it was targeted at, to wit, the quadruply reinforced spell holding the Native god Malsum beneath the earth. Said failure had a cascade effect on lesser binding spells throughout the demesne, unraveling them and keeping them from being cast."

Rebekah looked up when Miriam said that. "I didn't—I didn't know."

"You would have, had you been trained," Miriam said tartly. "Ms. Goldblume also cast Westerback on a vampire bat in order to use said animal to attempt to kill the four immortals who had cast the binding on Malsum. She was successful in killing three of them: Warham Mather, Benjamin Palmer, and Anne DeLancey."

Part of me thought that Isaac and Judy should have been here, but Rebekah was nineteen years old, technically an adult. Besides, the supernatural world was something that Isaac and Judy always refused to accept, no matter how many times Aunt Esther or I got involved with it. To this day, Isaac insists that my parents were in a car accident, even though he knew better.

Rebekah shifted around in the rocking chair, back to staring at the floor. "I don't understand why I'm here."

"I think I just explained that pretty thoroughly," Miriam said. "I've laid out the circumstances. This is your chance to explain yourself."

She looked back up. "To who? You? Why do I have to explain anything to you?"

"Because I'm the wardein of the demesne. I'm in charge of regulating and supervising all magickal activity in this region."

"Says who? What right do you have to tell me what to do? I taught myself magick, why should I have to be beholden to you when I use it? There's no law."

"No, there isn't. But then corporate regulations aren't laws, but people who break them still have to face consequences, like being fired. Restrictions on dangerous hobbies like diving aren't laws, either, but if someone breaks those restrictions, they're prevented from accessing equipment and boats and such. And if people abuse magick, then they have to face consequences as laid down by the Curia and enforced by the wardein—which is me."

Rebekah leaned forward and stuck her chin out defiantly, which I'm fairly certain was the first time she ever did that in my presence. "And what if I just get up and walk out? How are *you* gonna stop me?"

She said that last part while looking at Miriam's wheelchair, and I just stared at her in disbelief. One of Rebekah's pile of flyers about a year ago was protesting the lack of wheelchair access in certain public places—the Americans with Disabilities Act was passed in 1990, but a lot of places in the city still hadn't gotten around to complying with it— and I couldn't believe that she was pulling this I-can-get-away-from-you-because-you're-a-cripple act.

I didn't say anything, though. Technically, I shouldn't even have been here. Stuff like this was supposed to stay between the wardein and the perpetrator—another reason why my aunt and uncle shouldn't have been present. But Miriam let me stay, since this was kinda my fault. Rebekah only knew about magick because of me.

In response to her question, Miriam gave her a sweet smile. "Quite easily, actually. The wards around this house have been tailored to keep you from leaving until I allow it. And the sigil Bram placed on you will keep you from casting any magick or wielding any magickal items. You're trapped in this house."

"You can't do that," she whispered, back to staring at the floor.

"Yes, actually, I can. It's kind of my job. But you can try to justify what you did."

"Isn't it obvious?" she asked the floor. "Malsum didn't do anything wrong. He was just serving his worshippers, who were trying to get justice!" She looked back up on that last word. "We stole their land! We stole their culture, we conquered them, and then we destroyed them! It was genocide, it was the worst crime anybody could commit, and Teattanquer was just trying to avenge the wrongful death of one of his people."

I frowned. I only knew about this because I got it from Ferris. Since Rebekah's knowledge of the supernatural in the world was pretty much from all the books of mine she'd borrowed, I realized that I needed to keep much better track of what all I had up there.

She stared back at the floor. "I shouldn't be punished for reversing a great wrong, even if it was hundreds of years ago. I have rights."

That did it. I'd been grumpily sitting on the sidelines and pretending I wasn't there for the Curia's sake; I was willing to watch this crazy woman posing as my cousin just sit there and spout idiocy, but those three words were more than I could really take.

"You have rights, huh? That's kinda funny, 'cause the other day, when you were giving me those flyers about the protest in favor of Dr. Grofsky... remember that?"

She looked up, but only stared at me in reply. I, meanwhile, suddenly remembered that I never distributed those flyers like she asked, but I also didn't give that much of a damn just then.

"I told you that the people who shot at Grofsky thought they were righteous. They thought they were doing good. Remember that?"

"I—"

"Remember what you said in response?"

Miriam looked at me. "Bram, you—"

"You said that they shouldn't have the right to kill good people."

I saw tears welling up under Rebekah's plastic frames. "That's not fair, this isn't the same thing!"

"It absolutely is the same thing! Well, no, actually, you're worse than those people who shot Grofsky because they only wounded him. You actually *killed* Warren, Palmer, and DeLancey, and you tried to kill May Ferris. I *met* May, spent time with her—she was a good person who sacrificed everything to carry on the work of the guy she thought of as her uncle. And everyone in the neighborhood knew Warren. He was always polite, always asking people how they were. Hell, Ben Palmer was your *friend*. You were always talking about how good a person he was! So you killed three good people and tried to kill a fourth, so how, exactly, does that make you better than those people who shot Grofsky?"

"It's completely different!" She yanked her glasses off and palmed tears away from her eyes.

"No, it really isn't."

Miriam wheeled over to where I was standing in the corner of the living room. "We need to talk in the kitchen right now."

"You're just gonna leave me here?" Rebekah asked, half up from the rocker.

Looking at my cousin from over her shoulder, Miriam said, "You can't leave the house. And if you come into the kitchen, I'll run you over with my chair."

We stepped through the open doorway—there used to be a swinging door that opened both ways, but she got rid of it after the accident—into the kitchen.

I leaned on the counter. "I'm sorry, Mimi. I guess you'll have to edit that out?"

"God, no, I can't edit anything out of that. No, that thing keeps recording until we're done. I can't risk there being anything edited out of the official record like that; it would make the whole point of *having* an official record irrelevant. That's why it's still recording in there now, even though it's just her sitting there." She smirked. "Besides, if she says something stupid and incriminating, that helps, too." The smirk fell. "But stuff out of the purview of the hearing isn't recorded, so I dragged you back here."

Now I was all confused. Frowning, I asked, "So, wait, this isn't about the hearing?"

"Oh, it's totally about the hearing, but if anyone on the Curia asks, I took you in here to berate you for inserting yourself into the hearing."

"Um, okay." I was totally confused at this point.

"Look, there's something you need to know. When we were kids, Dad taught you all about magick and supernatural creatures and magickal objects, and all that stuff. But after he went to the Curia when I was in that stupid phase where I didn't want to be wardein, and he asked them to let you do it—"

I held up a hand. "Wait—stupid phase?"

"Well, yeah. Got over that damn quick. And thank God, too, 'cause doing this wonderful job is the only thing that's made life bearable since the accident."

I stared at Miriam with what was probably the same dopey blank expression Rebekah'd been giving us a minute ago. "Really?"

"Well, yeah, obviously." She was now staring at me like I'd grown a second head.

Not that I blamed her. On the one hand, I don't know how I could've missed this, believing instead all this time that she really wanted to teach English and was only wardein because she had to be. On the other hand, I missed that Sara had the hots for me in med school and that Katie had the hots for me now. Hell, we were one room away from my cousin who'd been living in my townhouse, and I totally missed that she was going around murdering immortals and framing vampires for it.

"Anyhow," Miriam said, "the point is, we've got a big problem."

"Yeah, I know that, Mimi, that's why I brought her here in the first place."

"It's bigger than you realize, boychik. What I was saying before we got sidetracked is that you never got to the wardein-specific lessons from Dad. And this is the first time you've brought me someone who's used magick without training or a license."

I again said, "Um, okay. What's the issue?"

"The issue is the punishment. I was hoping that she'd be remorseful or not realize what she'd done, or maybe that she only thought the bat would hurt the immortals enough to stop the spell, not actually kill them, or *something*. But she's stated her intent, and she not only doesn't regret it, she's not regretting it while flouting my authority as wardein, which means she's pretty likely to do something even stupider in the future if left unchecked."

"So, check her? I mean, I'm assuming the punishment is a more permanent example of the restriction sticker."

"No. I mean, yes, it is, if the unauthorized magick doesn't do permanent harm. But if even one life is lost, the punishment is far worse. The perpetrator is sent to the Nagashima Dimension for the rest of their natural life."

For about four seconds, I stared dumbly ahead. The anger I'd been feeling since—well, honestly, since Van Cortlandt Park had finally burned itself out and I was overcome by confusion and sadness. I wanted Rebekah to pay for what she did to all those people, but this...

"Rebekah has to go to limbo?" The dimension Miriam was talking about was, basically, empty. Just an endless expanse of nothing, with no up, no down, no features, no landmarks... just gray emptiness. A Japanese wizard named Yoshiko Nagashima discovered it back in the nineteenth century, and when European magick-users found out about it, they started calling it limbo, even though it didn't really look anything like the Limbo of Dante's Hell.

"That's the punishment for what she's done, yes."

"But she'll—" I shook my head and started pacing. The kitchen wasn't really big enough to pace in, but I managed it. "Won't she die there?"

"Actually, no. You don't need food or drink, and the aging process is slowed down there. When Nagashima discovered it, she used it for contemplative meditation. It wasn't until after the Curia was put together in the late nineteenth century that it became a place to send people who've committed violations."

"So it's like life in prison, but without the human contact."

"Yes. She committed three murders, Bram, and she's an accessory to a whole lot more, including John McAnally and those eight people who died in the pileup on the Bronx River. What's the alternative... you call up Detective Toscano and have her arrest Rebekah? How'll that go? The justice system isn't equipped to handle something like this, Bram, you know that. We have to keep it in-house. And this is the in-house punishment—which is why we're having this conversation."

"Um, okay." I needed to stop saying that.

"The only people who know about this are you, me, and Rebekah. I haven't reported this to the Curia yet. Say the word, and I'll stop and erase the recording on the laptop, and I'll release Rebekah to you. She'll become your responsibility. We'll hire a magick-user who can cast Ampuero, but you'll still need to keep a constant eye on her to make sure that the knowledge doesn't come back."

"I—" That got me to stop pacing, at least. "I—" Not that it was helping me with words.

Ampuero was a spell that blocked memories. It was incredibly powerful and difficult to cast, and only a few magick-users could even do it. Even the best of them didn't always get it perfect, and sometimes the blocks fell, and the memories came back.

"I'd have to monitor her twenty-four-seven, wouldn't I?"

"Almost definitely. Well, you or someone else qualified, whom you'd have to pay for the privilege. Another Courser, most likely."

"And if I don't do it, she's stuck in limbo. Quiet meditation's all well and good if you're a Buddhist magick-user, but Rebekah? She's all passion and directed anger. She'd go nuts in limbo."

"Or, maybe, being confronted with such endless quiet and emptiness, she'd actually calm down enough to contemplate what she'd done. That's why the European wizards started referring to Nagashima as limbo or purgatory when they found out about it—it's a place where you can contemplate your sins in solitude."

"For all the good it'll do her—you said it was for life. The only way to come back from Nagashima is for the person who cast the spell to send you there reverses it, right?"

Miriam nodded. "It's why people can go there voluntarily, but for anyone sent there, it's a one-way trip. But maybe she'll find peace there that she obviously doesn't have now. And probably she won't have if you take door number two, since at best she'll be unable to remember important things she used to know, and she'll have you hovering over her like a mother hen."

"And if any of the memory blocks fail?"

Miriam folded her arms. "Then we go back to door number one."

"Right." I looked away, staring out the house's side window at the backs of the houses on Netherland Avenue. It was as good as killing her. Was that really a just punishment for what she did?

Not that it mattered. This was the punishment. The Curia had codified all this ages ago, and it wasn't likely to change now.

I looked back at Miriam, who was kind enough to look sympathetic and loving. "I don't have a choice, do I?"

"You, in fact, have two choices."

I snorted. "You only gave me any choice at all because you're being nice to the putz who didn't notice his own cousin was a crazy woman."

"No, I'm giving you options because you're my friend and I love you and I want you to understand exactly what has to happen here. I know you love Rebekah and she's family and all, but she's fucked around with things she shouldn't, and that has to have consequences."

"It's just a question of whether or not those consequences are just to me or to me and her both. I certainly deserve having to stand over her the rest of her life. I should've paid closer attention to her, but she was already curious from talking to Esther and because of what happened to Mom and Dad, and Isaac and Judy were no help at all, and..." I let out a long sigh. "It just seemed to make sense to tell her about it all. And I shouldn't have done it. If I had, Katie would be posting fish pictures and McAnally would be alive and—"

"Get off your back, Bram. You showed compassion to someone who abused it. That's the fault of the person who did the abusing."

"Yeah." I moved toward the exit. "C'mon, let's stop keeping the kid waiting and just tell her she's going to limbo."

Miriam was blocking the doorway, though, and she grabbed my arm and looked up at me. "I'm not gonna tell you this is the right thing to do, Bram, because there *is* no right thing to do here. But Rebekah did a really horrible thing, and she has to be punished. It's the only way we keep a lid on the crazy."

"Yeah." I put my hand on hers and we locked eyes.

Suddenly, she didn't seem so stressed or frazzled. Mostly she was just the sister I never had, just like I was the brother she never had. We'd both been through hell together, and we were about to take a trip right back there.

"You can go ahead home. You don't need to stay and watch this."

"Yeah," I whispered. "Yeah, I do. I owe her that, at least."

I wheeled Miriam back into the living room and put the chair where it was before, on the edge of the webcam's field of vision.

Rebekah was still seated in the rocker, biting her nails. "What was that all about?"

"Bram was not supposed to speak. He's technically not supposed to be here, but since he was responsible for bringing your crimes to my attention—"

"They're not crimes!"

I bit my tongue, but I wanted to shout at her for her hypocrisy.

"I'm afraid that's not for you to decide, Rebekah," Miriam said gently. "The moment you decided to teach yourself magick, you violated the rules, and your subsequent actions have resulted in multiple deaths. Therefore it is my duty as Wardein of the Bronx to sentence you to banishment to the Nagashima Dimension for the rest of your living days."

Rebekah's eyes went wide. "Banishment! To Nagashima? But—but that's not—that's not—you can't—" She rose to her feet, arms gesticulating madly. "There's got to be another way! Another punishment! You can't banish me *there*!"

I winced. I'd hoped she hadn't heard about Nagashima in her self-studies, but obviously she had.

"I'm sorry," Miriam said quietly. "There is no other recourse, no other punishment on record for what you've done."

I shot her a look, as that was contrary to what she'd told me in the kitchen. I wondered if she had done that whole thing for my benefit just to ease me into accepting what was going to happen to Rebekah, or if she was lying to Rebekah now.

Not that it mattered. This really was the only way.

Rebekah turned to me. "Bram, you've gotta help me! I didn't know!"

"I'm sorry, kid. But you *did* know what you were trying to accomplish, even if you didn't know the consequences, and that's what this is about."

"Look, I'll never do it again! I promise, I'll be good, I won't touch magick *ever* again just please, don't send me away to that horrible place, *please*!"

Miriam pulled her tablet out of the side of her chair and activated the screen. There were words in an Asian language on it—I presume Japanese, since the spell originated in that country. She started to recite the spell.

"No!" Rebekah cried, and ran toward Miriam.

Luckily, Miriam wasn't stupid. The house wards were on Miriam's wheelchair as well—anything they affected kept her person safe. For Rebekah, the feeling was like trying to walk through an open doorway, only to discover there's a glass door there.

While Rebekah stumbled back from being repelled by the wards, Miriam continued to recite the spell. As she did so, Miriam pulled a tiny pouch out of the side of the chair.

As soon as she spoke the last word of the spell, two things happened.

One was that the air felt all supercharged, kinda like the way static electricity feels on your fingers when you touch something after walking on a rug but expanded out to every pore of your body.

The other was Miriam throwing the pouch at Rebekah. She threw it hard and accurately, and weirdly I was reminded of being a kid and having picnics in Seton Park with my family and the Zerellis and a few others. We would play catch, and Miriam always was deadly accurate, but had no power behind her throws. First fight I ever got into was with my cousin Morty when he said that Miriam threw like a girl. I got my ass kicked, of course, and Miriam yelled at me for getting in the way of her getting to beat him up. Pretty much set the tone for our relationship going forward, actually.

Anyhow, years of wheeling herself around gave her upper body strength that combined with the accuracy that was already there so that the pouch struck Rebekah square in the thoracic region.

Rebekah flinched, but the pouch just suddenly burst and covered her from head to toe in white powder. She looked like she'd been dunked in a vat of flour.

I could hear that Rebekah was weeping openly now — and hearing was all I had to go on, as the powder was covering her glasses. She was whimpering, sounding exactly like she did that time at Pesach dinner when she was ten and she tripped and bumped her head. "Please, no, don't do this. I'll be good, I promise."

I couldn't watch this. I forced myself to anyhow.

"Please, it hurts."

I shot Miriam a look, and she just shrugged. Neither of us were under the impression that this would hurt, but then it was usually unrepentant criminal types who got this kind of punishment, not well-meaning kids who don't think things through.

It didn't help that she said those exact words when she was ten and I treated the bump on her head at Pesach.

The powder turned black, and then it all fell to the floor in a giant heap.

Rebekah herself was nowhere to be seen.

The room no longer had that static-electricity feel. Instead, it felt like a funeral home. I knew Rebekah wasn't dead, but she may as well have been.

Miriam went over to stop the laptop's webcam from recording, then she looked up at me. I couldn't make out the expression on her face through the tears that had welled up in my eyes. "I'm sorry, Bram," she said. "I wish there was another way."

"That's not what I wish," I said. "Because what just happened to her is absolutely justified. That's how people who do what she did should be punished. She killed people, Mimi, in cold blood! No, what I wish is that I wasn't such a thundering dumbass that I didn't even *notice* that my cousin was turning into a murdering psychopath."

"She isn't a psychopath," Miriam said firmly. "She's a person who believed so fiercely that she taught herself magick in order to right a wrong. She's actually pretty damned amazing if you think about it. If only—"

"If only her cousin wasn't so wrapped up in his own life that he could've maybe paid attention?" I started pacing, which the living room was much better suited to. "I told Isaac and Judy I'd take care of her! But I didn't, I just let her clean my apartment and took her flyers and got into stupid arguments with her, and—" I stopped pacing and closed my eyes. "And now I have to come up with something to tell Isaac and Judy."

Miriam wheeled over to me and put a hand on my arm. "No, *we* have to come up with something."

I stared down at her, wiping the tears away so I could see the look of concern on her face. "'We,' huh?"

She smiled, though it didn't last long. "Yeah, 'we,' boychik. That's what friends are for, right? Besides, we've both done this before."

"Yeah, but never to family."

"Esther can help. She'll understand, and she'll help ease your aunt and uncle into it."

I put my hand on top of her hand that was on my arm. "Thank you, Mimi. Thanks especially for that talk in the kitchen. It made it easier." I wiped more tears away. "Not to say it was *easy*, but easier, anyhow." I snorted a bitter laugh. "Y'know, I was thinking of hiring her to be the personal assistant you've been bugging me to get? That would've been hilarious. 'Sorry, Bram, can't send out your invoices today, I've gotta go kill some immortals and frame the vampire community for it. Seeya!'"

She just let me carry on and smiled at me and held my hand.

Eventually, I let go of her hand, and she let go of my arm. "You've probably got, like, a hundred things to do." Then I remembered something, and pulled out my smartphone. "And I've got a shift at

Montefiore in" — I clicked on the phone's display — "two hours. Happy joy."

"Maybe call in sick?" Miriam sounded dubious even as she said it.

"Yeah, I can't call in sick unless I'm actually dying, and even then, Park would probably use it as an excuse to fire me. And honestly, I could use the distraction of an ER shift. I don't trust my subconscious not to mess with my head when I'm asleep, and I figure I've got a better chance of a dreamless sleep if I'm totally exhausted, as opposed to my current state of only mostly exhausted."

"Okay. Be safe, Bram. And text me when you get to Montefiore, and text me when you get off-shift — I'll probably be asleep by the time you're coming home, but text me anyhow, so I know you're okay."

I gave her a ragged smile. "Yes, Mother."

I didn't mention to Miriam that I kept hearing Rebekah saying, "Please, don't!" on a loop over and over in my head.

Chapter 15

THE ER SHIFT WAS NICELY BORING. NO BIG MESSES LIKE THE BRONX RIVER pileup, just the usual collection of ailments and accidents. I tried to bury myself in the work, and mostly managed it. I only zoned out once, when I was treating a guy who came in with trouble breathing. I was looking over his EKG when my brain went to la-la-land.

"You, okay?" the patient, whose name was Dale, asked.

"Uh, yeah, sorry. Just on another planet there for a sec. Family drama."

He smiled. "That's why I stick with chosen family."

"I'm sorry?"

Pointing at the person who drove him in, who was fondling his phone in one of the guest chairs, he said, "He's listed as my brother-in-law, but the sister of mine that he married isn't related to me. We've been best friends since college, but we're as close as blood siblings—closer, honestly. Neither of us has spoken to our biological siblings in years, but we're always there for each other. Anthropological term is fictive relatives."

I thought about Miriam and me growing up together, both only children who'd found each other. "Fictive relatives, huh? I like that. Thanks." I blew out a breath. "All right, let's take a look at what this little gadget's telling us about your heart."

One thing I had done right away was check to see if Katie had been brought here, but the ambulance had taken her to the Allen Pavilion in Inwood, the upper part of Manhattan. Bekenya had been kind enough to find that out for me, and also tell me that she was out of surgery and stable, but still in a coma.

Nice to know that she was stable, at least.

At the end of the shift, I drove home, texting Miriam as I got into the car, and collapsed onto my bed. I didn't even pause to scritch Mittens.

When I woke up Thursday afternoon, my ribs didn't ache. First time since the unicorn crashed into me I didn't need painkillers for breakfast. Only took six days…

Mittens had slept in the bedroom, which he didn't always do, except when I was upset or sick. I scritched him as soon as I clambered out of bed.

I put on some coffee and took a shower. Throughout the latter, I avoided looking at myself in the mirror. I literally couldn't face myself.

Sigh. I hated it when I lived the cliché.

Throwing some clothes on and getting myself some desperately needed caffeine, I headed upstairs to check on my divine patient.

I'd looked in on Egungun-Oya last night before my ER shift, and she'd still been out like a light. Still was now, too. Both last night and this morning, I did as thorough an exam as I could—again, no baseline for giving a god a physical—and let her continue to sleep it off.

I went back downstairs, sat down at the laptop, and went through my emails.

There was a note from Miriam saying that the wake for John McAnally would be held tomorrow and Saturday, with the funeral Sunday morning. Mary McAnally requested that no Coursers come to either—"*My husband was very strict about keeping his home life away from his work life, and I'd like to keep it that way,*" were Mary's exact words according to the email she forwarded to all the local Coursers. Iturralde sent a reply all to say that Sunday night at the Kingfisher's Tail would be an Irish wake, and all Coursers were invited.

I skimmed through the other emails, which included notifications of online payments from the Metropolitan Museum of Art and from the Altys, so my bank account could be taken off life support. I double-checked the first one, and miracle of miracles, Rodzinski didn't question any of the charges—up to and including paying for Velez to put the unicorn back—so I got the full amount I invoiced for. I immediately went and made a payment to Velez for his cut, along with a reminder to invoice me for the vampire bat.

I got up to pour some more coffee, and I also called Miriam.

"Hey, Bram."

"Hey, Mimi, you surviving okay?"

"Just putting out eight hundred fires."

"Like usual."

She snorted. "No, the usual is five hundred. Today's a way bigger mess. How's Egungun-Oya?"

"Still sleeping it off. I have no idea what that means, since they don't cover comatose gods in med school, but I'm just leaving her be and making sure she's comfortable and breathing."

"Good. You got the emails about John?"

"Yeah." I wandered into the living room and sat down on the blue chair. Mittens immediately jumped into my lap, narrowly missing my gonads. "I think it's probably best if I stay away from that."

"Why?"

"It's my fault he's dead," I said as I absently stroked Mittens' gray fur.

"That's the stupidest thing I've ever heard. And I had to talk to van Owen this morning, so I don't say that lightly."

I couldn't help but chuckle before growing serious again. The Wardein of Manhattan was probably responsible for several of those fires she mentioned. "Look, I made Bernie hesitate, and if he hadn't, he would've shot Katie before she attacked John."

Miriam made a *tch* noise, and I knew I was in for a lecture. "Okay, first of all? You can't 'make' Bernie Iturralde do anything. God knows I've tried."

"Well, yeah, but—"

However, Miriam was on a roll. "Secondly, even if Bernie had shot sooner, there's no guarantee he would've hit Katie, considering that even when he did, he barely grazed her. Honestly, I've seen his range scores—the broad side of a barn has absolutely nothing to fear from Bernie, believe me."

"I—"

"And thirdly, even if none of that were true, the fact is that the blame for this whole thing falls on Malsum. He's the one who possessed Katie, and it was under his direction that she attacked John."

I sipped some coffee before saying, "Yeah, but Malsum was only able to do that because of Rebekah, and she—"

"Chose her own fate. If you'd figured out what she was up to earlier, she might've turned you into a newt or something. She was a self-taught wizard, Christ knows *what* she learned, and she was willing to kill Ben Palmer, who was an actual friend of hers."

"I guess so."

"Stop guessing, it's true."

I chuckled again, which made Mittens shift position on my lap. "You sound like Esther."

"Esther's smart, so I'll take that as a compliment."

"It was meant as one." I blew out a breath. "Maybe you're right, but—"

"I *am* right."

I was finishing this sentence, dammit. "*But* just because you know it's not my fault, and I can probably talk myself into it not being my fault, that doesn't mean the other Coursers are gonna think that. I'm not sure I'll be welcome there Sunday night."

"Check with Hugues."

That didn't strike me as the best idea, as he'd probably spend the whole time agreeing with me that it was my fault. But I just said, "Fine, I'll call him."

"Good. You gonna take it easy today?"

"I'm going down to Inwood to visit Katie. That counts as taking it easy, right?"

I could hear Miriam's wince over the phone. "Don't beat yourself up, Bram."

"I'm not," I said incredibly unconvincingly, "but I need to make sure she's okay."

"Fair enough. I need to get back to putting fires out. Let me know how Katie's doing."

"You bet."

I gulped down the rest of my coffee, and that action led to Mittens jumping off my lap. It was like he knew I wanted to stand.

In gratitude for his being my lap kitty for a bit, I made sure to refill Mittens' food and water bowls, then grabbed my denim jacket and went out the door.

First I went upstairs to check back in on Egungun-Oya, who was, in fact, awake! She was sitting up on the exam bed, rubbing her eyes, a remarkably prosaic gesture for a god to be performing. I guess, even if you're divine, if you sleep for the better part of two days, you still get gunk in your eyes.

"Good to see you up and about," I said. "How you feeling?"

"Somewhat akin to my former self," she said with a small smile. "I thank you for the bed. It has been some time since sleep was required of me, and I am grateful to you for allowing me to do so in relative comfort."

"I could've made it more comfortable, but I wasn't really up to carrying you downstairs to my guest room."

Egungun-Oya gave a musical laugh at that and jumped down off the exam bed. I noticed that, even though she didn't touch anything, her clothes just suddenly were perfectly in place, not askew in the least.

"I can feel that my spell is in place," she said. "Malsum remains bound."

I nodded. "And we found the person responsible." I quickly filled her in on what happened after she fell into her coma.

She put a hand on my shoulder, and I felt instantly at ease. "I am truly sorry for that experience, Bram Gold. It is never easy to learn that family is not what you think—harder still to be the one forced to condemn them for their crimes."

That sounded like it came from personal experience, but I didn't pry. I've been in the middle of godly spats before—that was how I wound up with the Dozarian, just for starters—and they were always ugly. "Technically, Miriam condemned her, but yeah. If you want, I can check you over, and—"

"That is not necessary, though I appreciate your ministrations. I simply need to spend some time among my people."

"Your fellow loa or your worshippers?"

Another of her bright smiles. "They are not truly worshippers, but they are whom I mean."

"So you just go among them?"

"On occasion."

"In that case, why didn't you stop Madame Vérité?"

"As I said to you previously, Bram Gold, I was engaged elsewhere. Even if I were, the binding spell was directed at us, and it would have been difficult to stop it." She favored me with another of her musical laughs that made me feel like I was at a Vivaldi concerto. "Besides, I do not reveal myself as divine to my people."

"Didn't seem to have any problem telling me and Velez."

"You and José Velez are conversant in the world that exists off to the side of the everyday universe. What was your response to your learning of my divinity?"

I grinned. "Relief that there was an explanation for you appearing and disappearing that didn't involve me being nuts."

"Just so. Were I to reveal myself similarly to, for example, the people in Seton Park the day that Bonita Soriano attempted to cast her spell, their response would be to deem me a madwoman."

"Yeah, probably." I snapped my fingers as I realized something. "Oh, by the way, Mrs. Truth actually succeeded in casting her spell. My cousin's first attempt to free Malsum was to cast Babb-Jobson to try to disrupt the binding holding Malsum. It didn't work, and the spell reflected outward and disrupted binding spells all over town. That's why Madame Vérité's spell didn't work—I actually got there too late to stop her finishing it."

"Then some good has come of your cousin's foolishness, Bram Gold. You may rest assured that Bonita Soriano having control of the loa would have been as disastrous in its own way as Malsum's freedom would have been."

"Hadn't thought of that." I scratched my nose and stared off into space for a second, thinking about Rebekah.

That way lay madness, so I shook my head and said, "You need anything?"

"As I said, only to be among my people. I will take my leave."

And then she was gone. One nanosecond she was standing in front of me, the next, she wasn't. There wasn't even a displacement of air, which made no sense at all. Magick—at least when human beings wield it—still has to obey the laws of physics.

Maybe she didn't actually have a real physical presence.

Whatever, I needed to visit Katie.

◄—THE BRONX—►

The next several days were a blur.

I spent most of Thursday at the hospital visiting Katie. She was still in a coma, and nobody had the first clue why. The surgeons had taken care of the gunshot wound to her abdomen—her small bowel was perforated, and there was damage to both her liver and colon—and the ER doctor who'd treated her and the one who was in charge of her case now that she'd been admitted would keep an eye on her GI tract and prescribe meds to make sure the damage didn't have other effects. She'd had a psych consult, which was pretty much *pro forma*, given that she was comatose, but there was no physical medical reason for the coma—it was just a GSW to the abdomen, after all.

I spoke to all six doctors who'd looked at her—yay, professional courtesy—but of course I couldn't tell them my own theory as to why she was still unconscious. I just hoped she woke up some time in the next three weeks...

Thursday night, I met up with Esther, and the two of us pretended to Isaac and Judy that Rebekah had gone missing. We went with them to fill out missing-person paperwork. That was a damn nightmare. I felt like the worst kind of heel lying to them, but the truth would've been way worse. At least this way there was hope, even if it was false hope, but they'd remember Rebekah fondly, not as the murderer she actually was. And having a rabbi there eased my conscience a bit. If she was willing to lie to her in-laws, I could do it, too.

Besides, Isaac and Judy didn't believe the truth about how *their* in-laws were killed, I doubt they'd believe that their daughter dabbled in magick and murder.

Friday, I spent with one of my regular customers, Mrs. Gilson, an octogenarian who had a house sprite that always went missing. The sprite had been part of the house on La Salle Avenue in Pelham Bay since it was built a hundred years ago. As Mrs. Gilson had been getting older, she'd been losing track of it, and the sprite liked to take advantage. I never had much trouble finding the thing, and once I brought it home, the sprite and I both wound up listening to Mrs. Gilson's stories about life as a woman in the Marine Corps, which was where she met her late husband, and also about all the places she and Mr. Gilson visited after they both retired (with her outranking him, something she never tired of mentioning). She'd outlived not only her husband but both her kids, and her grandchildren weren't local. I honestly believed that the sprite deliberately got loose so Mrs. Gilson would call me and have someone to talk to. That day in particular, I needed it.

Saturday, I had lunch with Hugues and his wife and their newly graduated daughter at the Baptiste apartment in Co-op City. Toni went on at great length about the new job she was starting next week.

My attempt to extract advice on whether or not to go to McAnally's wake was met with exactly the response I expected: "Go or don't go. Jesus shit, child, what makes you think it matters to anyone but you? If you wish to go, then go. If you do not wish to go, then do not, okay? Why do you pester me with stupidity, child?"

"Because Bernie said it was my fault, and I'm not sure he's wrong."

"It's a wake, child. It isn't about you or Bernie, it's about Johnny. Point is to remember a life, not lay blame for a death."

I couldn't argue with that. And even if I could, Hugues didn't particularly want to hear it.

Someone called in sick at Montefiore on Sunday for a 1 to 9 PM ER shift, so when Park called and asked me if I could fill in, I said yes. I needed the distraction, so I took the Bx10 bus over there. By nine, McAnally's wake would have been starting, so I'd just take another bus over to Woodlawn and then cab it home.

It was a slow day, of course, so I wasn't even a little distracted. Stupid sick people, not cooperating.

Once the shift was over, I hopped on a Bx34 bus, which took me half a block away from the Kingfisher's Tail. I walked that last half block still not sure if I should go in or not.

I stood in front of the blue door for — um, a bit. I couldn't really hear anything inside, but that was by design. Sheehan had kept the thick blue door because it muted sound. As he'd said once, "Don't want to disturb the drunks walkin' down the street with the drunks in here."

"Bram?"

I turned around to see Dahlia getting out of a green cab. Her brown hair was tied back in a ponytail, which highlighted the angles in her face. She was also wearing a suit, and it occurred to me that my usual turtleneck-denim-jacket-and-jeans ensemble might've been a bit too dressed down. "Hey, Dahlia. Uh, nice suit."

She rolled her eyes. "Please. I had to meet with a client who insists on a dress code whenever I meet with him, even on a Sunday evening. The very wealthy are extremely strange." Then she smiled, and the angles left her face. "And very generous with their fees, so I put up with it. Anyhow, I didn't have time to change."

Good, that meant it wasn't dressy. I forgot to check. Then again, if it was formal, Hugues would've had to wear his suit again, and I knew for damned sure he hadn't gotten around to cleaning it since he wore it last weekend. Either way, that was the sort of thing that would've come up at lunch yesterday.

I shoved my shoulder into the door and went in, Dahlia right behind me.

The place was quieter than usual, and then Antonelli started talking. "Then me and John start workin' our way through this guy's attic."

He was obviously in the middle of a story, so Dahlia and I landsharked to the bar in silence while he spoke. Sheehan was already pouring my beer and grabbing a bottle of rum so he could put together Dahlia's mojito. I nodded to Abby and Hugues and Eddie, and a few others.

Iturralde was standing way in the back, clutching a tequila.

"We get up there," Antonelli was saying, "and we can hear all kindsa noises behind the boxes. Ain't hardly no room to move—it's all storage, y'know? Anyhow, we figure it's one big-ass poltergeist, and we're set. I'm wearin' my Hasan amulet and John's got the Maduro charm ready to go. John activates the charm, I grab the amulet."

Antonelli paused a second, and you could hear a pin drop in the room. I sipped my beer while Sheehan finished up Dahlia's mojito and handed it to her.

"And this big fuckin' *dog* leaps out from behind the boxes!"

I almost snarfed my beer, barely managing to swallow it before laughing. In that, I was not alone. Eddie actually did spew his Coke all over the table.

Rolling his eyes, Sheehan limped out from behind the bar with several napkins.

"What breed of dog?" Abby asked.

"How the fuck should I know? It was a *dog*. Anyhow, me and John take the mutt downstairs—which ain't no easy task, 'cause the fucking pooch is *filthy*, just all *covered* in dust and shit—and we show it to the guy. Guy turns to his wife and says, 'You said that Farley ran away!'"

We all laughed some more. I had to say, "They named the dog Farley?"

"Yeah."

"On purpose?"

"Looks like it, yeah. Fuckin' nuts."

Hugues said, "You still charged the full fee, though, yeah?"

"Damn right. And John made sure they paid for a new Maduro."

Dahlia swallowed her mojito, blew out a quick breath—looked like Sheehan was more generous with the rum than usual—and then said, "C'mon, Maduros are a dime a dozen."

"Yeah, but John was all about the principle, y'know? It's what was fair. Hell, if it was me, I woulda charged 'em double the MSRP on one'a them charms. Fact is, I told him to, but he said no way."

Eddie said, "John was always very fair-minded."

"That's how I trained him," Sheehan said. He was back behind the bar, and he had a pint of dark beer in his left hand. Sheehan never drank when he tended bar, but tonight was an obvious exception. I had forgotten that McAnally had apprenticed under Sheehan back in the day, but it made sense. Their families were both from County Wicklow, after all. "To always be fair and to always be considerate. There's enough evil in this world, and God knows, we have to fight a lot of it. If we're to be tasked with hunting the evil, best that we try to be as good as we can."

"Amen to that." Abby took a big gulp of her own Sancerre.

Antonelli regarded Sheehan with a cheeky grin. "C'mon, Brendan, we been tellin' stories about John for an hour. Your turn—you trained the motherfucker, you gotta have some good ones."

"Not from training." Sheehan smiled. "I don't wish to speak ill of the dead."

We all chuckled.

"But there was that time that those students at Fordham University summoned that Chinese horse creature."

Dahlia nodded. "The Tikbalang, and it's from the Philippines, not China."

Sheehan pointed at her. "Right, that."

"Jesus shit, I remember that." Hugues shuddered.

That was before my time, though I remembered Mike Zerelli bitching about it when I was a teenager.

"It was John's first paid case," Sheehan said. "The dumb kids were supposed to hold onto one of the thing's spines from its mane in order to bind it to their will, and they lost it. The thing got loose, and so the university paid me, John, Hugues, and Pedro Milán to wrangle it."

"What ever happened to Pedro?" Eddie asked.

I knew that one. I'd worked with him on a few cases. "He moved back home to Puerto Rico three years ago. He got killed by a nixie."

"Damn," Eddie muttered.

Dahlia frowned. "You can only stop a Tikbalang with a leather cord that's got the right sigils on it."

"And we had one," Sheehan said. "Specifically, Pedro had one. While the rest of us herded the creature onto the parade ground at the center of Fordham's campus, Pedro got ready to jump it." Sheehan took a quick sip of his beer. "The monster threw Pedro into a tree, and the cord fell onto the grass. Hugues and I then tried to subdue it the more traditional way while John grabbed the cord. It threw *us* into a tree, and that just left John holding the cord. He just stood there, me and Hugues and Pedro groaning on the ground, him holding the only means to stop the thing.

"So he turned and ran away."

"Sonofabitch." Antonelli shook his head.

Abby stared at him. "I thought you didn't want to speak ill of the dead?"

"I'm not!" Sheehan took another sip from his pint. "The creature chased after John halfway across campus, and he lured it into the courtyard between two of the dormitories. He climbed one of the trees and jumped down onto the thing, wrapping the cord around it."

"Tikbalangs," Dahlia added, "are sucky climbers."

We all laughed, and then almost everyone took their turn telling John McAnally stories. Eddie talked about how John was the first person he thought to talk to when he got into trouble for killing a vampire last week. Abby talked about the time she and John had to clear out an entire nest of tengu, Dahlia regaled us with the story of the Mayup Mamman that was menacing the fishing boats on City Island, and how John—who couldn't swim—went after them anyhow, and I talked about the time John and I were called in to St. Nicholas of Tolentine on University Avenue to salvage an exorcism that had been botched.

After a few hours, and a lot more stories—and a lot more beer—Iturralde finally stepped forward. He'd been completely quiet the whole time, staying in the background, which was about a hundred percent out of character. It scared me, and just led to me drinking more beer.

Finally, though, he decided to say something. "I just wanna say that John was my friend. He was a good man, and he shoulda lived longer. But we don't always get to do that." He raised his tequila. "To John!"

We all cried out, "To John!"

Iturralde slammed down the rest of his drink, put the glass on the bar, then continued forward and walked right up to me. "Gold, I need to talk to you outside."

I just kinda stared at him for a second.

"It ain't a request." He grabbed my arm and pulled me toward the blue door.

Nobody else moved or said anything; the place got real quiet.

The late-night breeze cut right through my turtleneck as we stepped onto the Katonah Avenue sidewalk. Iturralde hadn't given me the chance to grab my jacket, and I'm not sure it would've helped.

"Look, I got somethin' important to say, Gold, and I want you to shut the fuck up and don't say anything till I'm done, okay?"

"Um, okay." As long as he was talking, he wasn't beating me up, so that was good.

"I've always thought you were kind of an asshole, Gold. It ain't your fault—Baptiste is a shit-ass trainer, and honestly, if you didn't have your head so far up the wardein's ass, you'd've been dead inside a year. But she protects you, so what-the-fuck-ever. Point is, you suck at this job."

I was starting to think that getting beat up would be preferable. But I didn't say anything, in case I was wrong.

"But it ain't your fault that John's dead. Look, I had a perfect shot on that werewolf, and I barely grazed her. Even if I didn't hesitate, it woulda been just as shitty a shot, maybe worse, and she might still've ripped John's throat out. Point is, job's dangerous. Sometimes you're lucky, like Brendan, and get to retire and open a bar. But mostly? It's like John, and like Pedro, for that matter—you end up on the ass end of some monster you're gettin' paid to stop. John knew that, I know that—I bet even you know that."

"It came up in training, yeah." I couldn't help myself.

"Yeah. Anyhow, we're good. Just wanted you to know that. I heard you might not come tonight, and I'm glad you did. John liked you for some stupid reason."

"Thanks, Bernie."

The blue door got yanked open, and the heads of both Sal Antonelli and Abby Cornwell jutted out. "You guys, okay?" Abby asked.

"Yeah, just getting some air." I turned to Iturralde. "Wanna go back in? I'll buy you your next tequila."

"Thanks, but nah. I'm gonna go home and sleep this fucker off. G'night."

He strode away, his dirt-stained coat flapping behind him like a low-rent Batman.

Abby walked outside and put a hand on my shoulder. "You okay, Bram?"

I watched Iturralde saunter down Katonah for another second, then turned to face the blonde Courser. "Yeah, I'm good. C'mon, Sheehan still has some beer we haven't drunk yet."

And we spent the night toasting our friend. John McAnally may have been dead, and Katie Gonzalez may have been in a coma, and Rebekah may have been exiled to a nether realm, but at least Malsum was still imprisoned and the Bronx was safe.

That was definitely worth a drink. Or seven.

About The Author

KEITH R.A. DECANDIDO WAS BORN IN WHAT IS NOW THE WAKEFIELD campus of Montefiore Hospital in the Bronx. He attended Cardinal Spellman High School and Fordham University, both also in the Bronx, and has lived in the Boogie Down for all but one decade of his life. In 2009 and 2010, he worked for the U.S. Census Bureau, involved in dozens of different operations throughout the Bronx. So writing an urban fantasy series taking place in the northernmost of the five boroughs is a particular thrill.

He introduced Bram Gold in the short story "Under the King's Bridge" in the 2011 anthology *Liar Liar*, and the next book in Bram's series, *Feat of Clay*, will also be released by eSpec Books. He's told tales of other Coursers in the *Systema Paradoxa* novella *All-the-Way House* and in short stories in *Bad Ass Moms* and *Devilish and Divine*.

His other work includes a long-running series of fantasy police procedurals published by eSpec Books, the latest of which is *Phoenix Precinct*; a cycle of urban fantasy stories set in Key West, Florida, collected in *Ragnarok and Roll* and *Ragnarok and a Hard Place*, both published by Plus One Press; and the new *Supernatural Crimes Unit* urban fantasy series, forthcoming from Weird Tales Presents. He's also got an extensive résumé of media tie-in fiction, having written novels, short fiction, and comic books in more than thirty licensed universes, from *Alien* to *Zorro*, the latest of which includes the *Resident Evil* comic book *Infinite Darkness: The Beginning* and short stories in *Star Trek Explorer*. In 2009, he was given a Lifetime Achievement Award from the International Association of Media Tie-in Writers, which means he never needs to achieve anything ever again.

When he's not writing, Keith is an editor (for clients both personal and corporate), a martial artist (he achieved his fourth-degree black belt in karate in 2021, and he regularly teaches karate to kids), an avid New York Yankees fan, and probably some other stuff he can't remember due to the lack of sleep. Find out less at his inadequate website at www.DeCandido.net.

COMING SOON!

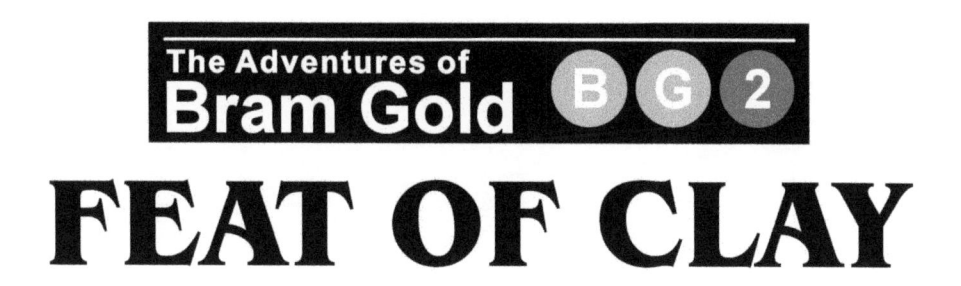

The Adventures of Bram Gold BG2

FEAT OF CLAY

No One Wields Guilt Like a Jewish Mother…
Unless it's a Jewish Aunt…

Bram Gold became a Courser—a supernatural hunter-for-hire—after his parents were killed twelve years ago by a golem run amuck. Now the person responsible wants to hire Bram.

It's happening again. This time a golem has been sighted at the synagogue where Bram's Aunt Esther serves as rabbi—and which has been targeted by thieves and vandals. And just like a dozen years ago, the powerful golem is out of control.

Can Bram corner the creature and put a stop to its spree before someone else's family is torn asunder?

←THE BRONX→

The next book in a new series of urban fantasy thrillers taking place in the Boogie-Down Bronx from best-selling, award-winning author Keith R.A. DeCandido.

SPRING 2025